MOONBLINK

The Zoo Crew Series, Book 5

DUSTIN STEVENS

"Montana should come with a surgeon general warning that it's addictive. The sky is big and blue, and the air is always fresh and crisp and scented with pine. There's a frontier spirit, but also ... a beauty in the landscape that slows your pulse."
Robin Bielman

PROLOGUE

Smelt.

A verb derived from Middle Dutch in the 16th century, used to describe the process of extracting metal from its ore through heating and melting. A form of extractive metallurgy, its primary function is to produce a base substance from a larger ore.

Silver. Iron. Lead.

Copper.

The process starts with a large quantity of unrefined ore. Heat and a chemical reducing agent are added. Together they decompose the rock, stripping away impurities, reducing them to nothing more than gas and worthless slag.

Leaving only the metal base behind.

In a perfect world, none of this would be necessary. The needed mineral would be found naturally, like gold. The entire process would be little more than digging it from the earth.

Because the planet is far from perfect in any way, most ores are instead found as compounds.

Oxides. Sulfides. Carbonates. Forms that must undergo a chemical reaction to become anything useful.

Or at least, desirable.

For sulfides and carbonates, a roasting process is required. Used to expel sulfur or carbon. Force the unwanted elements out into the atmosphere. Leave behind a substance that can be directly workable.

Placed into a secondary transition, known as reduction. A final, high-temperature step that pulls away the last lingering oxygen atoms from the base.

Leaves behind the raw metal.

In total, a start to finish known as smelting.

A process that can take anywhere from hours to weeks. Require untold chemicals and heat sources. Produce massive quantities of waste, in both chemical and thermal states.

Early forms of the process have been dated back more than 8,000 years. Back to the Stone Age, when useful metals such as copper were first discovered.

Found to be suitable for armor. Weaponry. Cooking utensils.

Through time, the process evolved, as did the end goal. No longer were these metals needed to make knives or arrowheads. Instead they became bullet casings. Collectable tankards for ale. Jewelry.

Again, in a perfect world, that which was so desired would have been easily attained. It would have been found in a natural state, able to be dug from the ground with minimal effort.

As history has shown time and again though, there is no perfect world. Natural state elements rarely exist.

Even more rarely are they found.

In their absence though, it does beg the question as to why nobody ever questioned why that was. Or, at the very least, if they should be concerned with everything that went into turning ore into something they found more desirable.

Perhaps even more importantly, if they should be worried about everything that could come out of those very same processes.

Smelting.

The act of turning one thing into something more useful, whether it be chemically or thermally.

After effects be damned.

CHAPTER ONE

Dusk.

Twilight.

Those last few moments before night descended, plunging the world into darkness.

Perched behind the wheel of her faded '94 Honda Accord, Kyla Wegman leaned forward to stare out through the windshield. Squinted her eyes, narrowing them to little more than slits. Tried to focus.

Received little to no improvement for her efforts.

"What the hell?" she muttered, easing her foot down onto the brake. Pulled up to the light blazing red above her. Pressed both palms into her eye sockets and left them there until pops of light appeared behind her eyelids.

At 31-years-old, she was far too young for her vision to already be failing her. She didn't smoke. Ran at least three times a week. Ate fruits and salads as often as her budget could afford.

Her most recent physical had displayed excellent blood pressure. Cholesterol levels. Lung capacity.

Still, for whatever reason, she found herself in this same position with increasing frequency. Rubbing her eyes vigorously, trying to wipe away the gray fog that would pass through like smoke during summer fire season.

Behind her a single blast on a horn erupted, pulling Kyla's hands from her face, bringing a twinge of embarrassment. Feeling the palpitations rise from her stomach and up through her chest, she raised a hand in apology between the front seats.

Raised her foot from the brake and started forward anew.

Three months had passed since her move to Missoula. With the closing of her divorce, she had left her lifetime home of Anaconda and moved west.

Decided to - as her mother put it every time they spoke - give *big city life* a try.

The phrase still brought a smile to Kyla's face each time she heard it. The town was no doubt larger than what she was used to, but still a far cry from being considered a big city.

At just over 100,000 people in the whole county, she wasn't entirely certain it could even be called a city.

Despite the lack of stature the town possessed, there was a certain undeniable charm that Kyla found infectious. She had been looking for a new start after things went sideways with her childhood sweetheart, someplace free of accusatory looks and prying questions.

Missoula had already proven itself to be that and then some.

Unlike most of the other bergs and metropolis's dotting the Gem State, Missoula was a college town. Attracted people from across the country. Even a handful from much further than that.

Created a melting pot of ideas and energies. The kind of environment Kyla had never known. Found herself growing more curious about with each passing day.

Recently, a coworker had even pointed out that the company they worked for offered a pretty solid tuition assistance program should she want to consider enrolling at UMontana in the fall.

Just as it had the first time it was mentioned, the notion brought a smile to Kyla's face. It allowed thoughts, ideas, visions to fill her mind. All that was and would never have to be again.

Like becoming her own person, free from the dreaded label of just being someone else's wife.

The smile remained in place as Kyla rolled west along Brooks Avenue, the southernmost thoroughfare of town. At just after 6:00, most of the evening rush hour had already thinned considerably.

If such a thing even existed in Missoula.

Coming home to find her cupboards empty and the fridge containing only a few items that looked to be well on their way to becoming penicillin, the plan was to make a quick Albertson's run. Grab whatever she needed. Be back home in time for *Grey's Anatomy*, one of the few guilty pleasures she couldn't help but indulge.

With those thoughts in mind she rolled forward, watching as the last of the sun disappeared before her, taking the final sliver of orange light below the horizon.

Along with it went any semblance of vision, the world plunging straight to black.

Feeling her heart rate spike, her breathing grow rapid in her chest, Kyla squeezed the wheel tight with both hands. Continued to feel the car move forward. Heard the sounds of traffic around her.

Prying her right hand away from the wheel, she jammed the thumb and forefinger of her right hand into her eye sockets. Rubbed vigorously. Again saw the dots of red and yellow erupt before her.

Opened her eyes to nothing but black.

"No," she whispered, feeling sweat form on her lip. "No, no, no."

Once more she rubbed at her eyes, digging her fingers in past the point of painful. Opened them as wide as she could. Saw just the faintest orbs of streetlights flitting by on the edges of her vision.

Nothing more.

"Okay, okay," she whispered, her heart hammering in her ears. She searched through her memory, trying in vain to register the most recent landmark she passed. Matched it against her limited knowledge of the area.

"Three blocks," she muttered, "three blocks from Albertson's means I should be coming up on the old shopping plaza. I can pull in there and call for help."

Easing her foot off the gas, she felt the car slow. Again heard the angry wail of a car horn behind her, this one lasting many times longer than the previous blast.

Moving on pure reflex, she pressed her foot down, the Honda lurching forward, throwing her body back against the seat.

Felt her head slam against the chair behind her.

Heard the clatter of metal-on-metal as the front end connected with something semi-solid before her.

Never once saw a single thing as it happened.

CHAPTER TWO

Susan Moritz pulled the pot roast from the oven at half past 6:00. Wrapped in aluminum foil, it resembled an enormous misshapen silver football.

Smelled infinitely better.

The scent permeated the kitchen as she placed it on the rack atop the counter. Pressed her right knee tight against her left. Raised her heel to push the oven door shut.

Felt the heat fall away from her calves just a moment before hearing the door slam into place.

Around her, stacks of dishes were piled high. Most had been there long before this evening. Stood at least a decent chance that they would still be there come morning.

Seemed to almost be mocking her as they balanced precariously in the sink, spilling over onto the counter.

Pushing out a lengthy sigh, Susan ran a finger down the side of the stack. Selected a trio of plates that seemed to need the least amount of cleaning and pulled them out. Ran a stream of warm water over them before using a dish towel to wipe away whatever remained.

It would have to do.

Thursday night dinners were something Susan had instituted months prior. A single evening each week where she left work early – or rather, on time – and came home to cook. The kids both pushed aside whatever items were on their bustling social agenda.

Everybody sat at the table.

No television. No iPads. Not even a cell phone.

For any of them.

Finding the time to sit down wasn't always easy. Enforcing the rules even less so, but through sheer willpower and stubbornness, all three were making it work.

Just as they always had.

If given her way, Susan would rather the dinners fall on Friday nights. It would be infinitely easier for her to cut out early. There would be less stress heading into the weekend.

She might even have time to clean the dishes afterward.

With her son now in 6th grade, an official junior high student, the odds of getting him to forfeit his Friday nights were slim at best.

Non-existent for her daughter, a newly minted freshman in high school.

If family dinner was what Susan wanted, it was Thursday night or nothing.

Depositing the three plates onto the table, she stepped down the narrow hallway leading away from the kitchen. Stopped halfway down it and raised her face toward the top of the staircase running parallel to her.

Wiped her hands on the dish towel still clutched before her. Felt bits of dried food rub against the pads of her fingers.

"Ben, Mandy, dinner!" Susan called. Heard the music that had been playing fall away. The sound of footsteps walking across a hardwood floor.

Returned back in the direction she had come from. Took up a plate of bread and a bowl of potatoes from the counter. Carried them over and placed them around the outside of the table.

Left a hole in the center for the main attraction of the evening. Folded the same dirty dishtowel and placed it in the space, using it as a potholder for the steaming pan sitting nearby.

Less than 10 feet away, Susan heard the thunderous sound of a young one spilling down the stairs. Shook her head at the amount of noise a single teenager could create.

Fought a losing battle to keep a smile from her face.

"Hey," her son Ben said, swinging out from the hallway and into the room. Without waiting for a response, he went straight to the table and snatched up a piece of bread, shoving it into his mouth.

A month past his 13th birthday, he was already several inches taller than she was, his frame long and lanky from the most recent growth spurt. Shaggy brown hair fell over his ears and eyebrows, a point of contention that Susan had long since given up trying to coax out of him.

Dressed in baggy jeans and a sweatshirt two sizes too large for him, he was the epitome of most teenage stereotypes she'd ever heard.

"Hey," she replied. "Where's your sister?"

Continuing to work on the bread, Ben shrugged a single shoulder. "I dunno. Haven't seen her."

Reflexively, a frown tugged at the corner of Susan's mouth. Thus far neither of the kids had complained about the dinners. A few times they had even seemed to genuinely enjoy themselves.

Still, it had been easy then. It was winter. There wasn't much else to do.

If this was how it was going to be now with spring approaching, there could be problems.

Pushing away from the table, Susan walked over to the breakfast bar extended from the wall. Pressed her thighs flush against it.

Picked up her phone and held it to her lips.

"Dial Mandy."

On cue, the device did as commanded, a ringtone sounding out in the kitchen. Six times it buzzed through the air, Susan gripping the phone before her, Ben continuing to work on the bread, this time swiping it through the potatoes sitting close at hand.

"Hey, this is Mandy. I can't come to the phone cause I'm out living my life. I suggest you leave a message and go do the same!"

Susan rolled her eyes at the voicemail message, both at the words selected and the singsong voice used to deliver them. She waited for the beep before telling her daughter she had five minutes to get home before they started without her.

Attempted to use her official legal voice, hoping it would add a bit of gravitas.

Knew it probably didn't work, despite her efforts.

Dropping the phone into place, Susan circled back around toward the roast. Peeled the layer of aluminum foil away from it. Felt a spray of warm steam wash over her face.

Instantly regretted the decision, knowing she would have to wash the work blouse she was still wearing, that the scent of beef would cling to it until she did.

Grabbing a silver serving spoon from the sink, she thrust it down into the dish. Used the edge of it to break the meat into manageable chunks.

Jammed a pinkie down into the gravy and tasted it for seasoning.

Involuntarily gave a small groan of approval as the flavor spread across her tongue.

The dinners had been instituted as an excuse to spend more time with the kids, though in truth they had served a secondary function as well. They had forced her out of the office at a reasonable hour, back to doing something she thoroughly enjoyed and was surprisingly good at.

Most nights, take-out or frozen dinners were fine.

Not every night, though.

Grabbing up a pair of potholders, Susan carried the roast to the table. Positioned it just so. Swatted at Ben as he attempted to go for a third slice of homemade bread.

"Slow down on that. Everybody knows you don't fill up on bread when there's beef to eat."

"Hey, you said dinner was ready," Ben countered. "I ate what was here."

The moment Susan was beyond range he took up more bread, this time plunging it into the dark brown gravy filling the baking dish.

Once, twice, Susan opened her mouth to fire back before giving up on it, resigning herself to nothing more than a smile.

"Okay, well, try to save at least a couple pieces for your sister."

Behind her, the phone on the bar began to buzz, the sound drawing her toward it.

"Speaking of which," she said, drifting off to the side. Without glancing at the screen she took it up, pressing it to her face.

"Hey there, we were just about to go looking for you. Dinner's getting cold."

For a moment, there was no response. Nothing but the sound of traffic, the idle chatter of voices in the background.

When at last the caller spoke, it was not her daughter.

It wasn't even a female.

"Hello," said a deep voice. Older. Harried. "Is this the mother of a young woman? Mid-teens, long brown hair? Rides a powder blue beach-comber bike?"

CHAPTER THREE

"Of all the restaurants in all the towns in all of Montana, you had to pick this one?!"

Ajax made no effort to lower his voice to a volume acceptable for public consumption. Even less to hide the derision hanging from every word.

As the statement floated out through the dining room of St. Michael's Hospital, a few heads turned toward the corner. Saw the quartet of people clustered tight around a table. Dismissed them with little more than a smile and a shake of the head.

"I don't think that's how the quote goes," Drake Bell countered. Made a point to keep his voice lowered. Hoped the insinuation would be picked up on.

Wasn't about to hold his breath.

"Yeah, yeah, yeah," Ajax said, bobbing his head in rhythm to the words. "I know the quote, I'm just making a point. This is not the type of place one goes for a celebration."

Drake leaned back in his chair. Assessed his friend and roommate seated across from him. Could see both Sage and Kade Kuehl in his periphery to either side. Knew that neither one would say a word, letting this play out between Drake and Ajax however it may.

"Who says this is a celebration?" Drake offered. "Why can't this just be the Zoo Crew getting together for dinner? We don't only have to do outdoor activities, you know."

A sour expression passed over Ajax's face. "No, don't do that."

"Do what?" Drake inserted quickly.

"Try to make me be a bad guy here," Ajax snapped, voice back up to the original volume. "You found out today you passed the bar exam. Score high enough to waive into any other state, if Montana wasn't so damn archaic with their reciprocity rules."

"And if I had any interest in practicing in another state," Drake said.

"And therefore, we are celebrating," Ajax said, not to be deterred. "At least we were supposed to, until you said to meet here, of all places."

Drake opened his mouth to respond. Closed it just as fast. Folded his arms across his chest and drew in a deep breath.

The Zoo Crew.

A self-dubbed moniker given seven years before to one of the more random groupings Montana had ever known.

As individuals, none of the four quite fit in. Had spent a week or so attempting to do so. At the first sign of pushback, abandoned the notion altogether.

Instead found each other. Took a quick and easy liking to one another, had been inseparable ever since.

The true origin of the Crew could be traced to the recruiting patterns of the University of Montana football team. The linebackers coach at the time had somehow found his way to West Tennessee. The secondary coach stayed much closer to home, covering the schools on the Flathead reservation 60 miles north of town.

Both saw something they liked. Extended scholarship offers.

Ten months later, Drake and Kade – the recipients of said offers - met.

Two weeks after, Drake moved from the temporary dorm assigned during summer football camp. Discovered he was paired with Adam Jackson from Boston, Massachusetts. Showed up expecting to find a lily-white guy with Irish ancestry and buttoned-down collars.

Instead found Ajax, the man currently giving him a hard time from across the table.

Serving as the three originators of the Crew, the trio made a pact at the end of their freshmen year. Winter had been slow in relenting. Finals were bearing down on them quickly.

In response, the group made the agreement to not let either stand in their way.

With the exception of away football games, holidays, or the rare emergency event, nothing else would stop them either.

A few years later, Kade's sister Sage rounded out the roster. Quickly assimilated to the point none of the others could even remember a time before her arrival.

The goal of the group was simple and straight forward. Get up early, get outside, do something life affirming at least three mornings a week.

Otherwise, there didn't seem to be much point in living in the grandeur that was Montana.

Time of year didn't matter, ditto for the particular activity. Just seek out someplace where nobody would notice their differences and put real life in the rearview mirror. Release every bit of jubilation, trepidation, or angst that might be lingering.

In the summer, that usually consisted of hitting the abundant streams and rivers nearby, fly rods in hand. On the opposite end of the calendar, they could be found frequenting the ski slopes.

During the very narrow windows in between, hiking, golfing, kayaking, and a host of other things filled the void. With the exception of maybe cross-country skiing, no activity was off-limits. Every person had an equal say in deciding the schedule.

"Okay," Drake said. "If this a celebration-"

"Which it is," Ajax countered.

Bowing his head slightly, Drake pushed on. "First, you know what a celebration to me consists of."

"Yeah, we know," Ajax said. Gave another flippant wave of his hand. "Order in from half a dozen places in town, sit on the couch and watch Maggie Grace movies."

A smile crossed Drake's face. It was, word for word, exactly how he would describe his perfect celebration.

Again, was not about to let on as much.

"And second," he said. "How could it be a celebration if we weren't all together? You know as well as I that Sage is on shift tonight until 11:00."

Beside him Sage started to object, Drake already knowing what she would say. Earlier she had twice offered to call off from her post as RN for the evening.

Before she could say a word, he extended a hand in her direction.

"Please, allow Mr. Jackson here to answer for himself."

The comment brought a smile to Sage's face, a flash of white teeth from her brother across the table.

An instant look of disgust to Ajax.

Several moments passed in silence, Ajax's mouth twisted up. At the conclusion of whatever internal debate he was having, he offered a simple head bob.

"That's just mean spirited, you know that?"

A nod was Drake's only response as he shifted his attention to the man in a red polo and matching ball cap that entered on the far end of the cafeteria.

To the black thermal bag balanced across his hands.

Rising from his seat, Drake extended a hand overhead. Used it to motion the man toward the corner. Watched all three of his friends turn as the man drew closer.

Proved himself to actually be a boy as he came near, with red hair and a pimpled chin to prove it.

"Are you Mister..." he said, pausing to check his receipt, "Bell?"

"I am," Drake replied.

Without another word, the young man peeled back the flap on the bag. Pulled three large pizzas from it, the words Firetower Pizza stamped across the top.

"Already paid in full, so we're all set," the young man said, retreating just as fast as he had arrived.

For a moment, nobody in the group said a word. Exchanged quick glances. Tried to pretend there wasn't a mouthwatering aroma wafting up from the middle of the table in front of them.

"Okay," Ajax finally relented. Kept the disdainful look locked in place just the same. "Now *this* is starting to feel like a celebration."

CHAPTER FOUR

"Is she going to die?"

The question was asked innocently enough, without an inflection of any sort. The kind of thing most every person that has ever seen a loved one in a hospital bed has thought.

Only someone a month into being a teenager would lack the inhibition to actually voice.

"No," Susan snapped. Forced the word out quickly. Allowed more hostility to creep in than she actually intended.

It wasn't her son's fault that he still lacked a proper mind-to-mouth filter. Just a few years before, Mandy had gone through the same phase.

Looking down at her now, Susan almost wished she were back there again.

Seated in a red cloth chair, Susan leaned forward. Rested both elbows on her knees. Clutched her daughter's hand between her own.

During the half hour since arriving, her gaze had not stopped sweeping over the room, her mind praying that this was all nothing more than a bad dream. Something she could force herself awake from. Discover she was actually home safe in bed.

That Mandy was fine, tucked in upstairs, as she should be.

Try as she might, though, Susan could not push the images away. Was instead forced to stare down at the broken image of her young daughter before her.

The last time Susan had seen her was 12 hours before, leaving the house for school. Dressed in jeans, a t-shirt, and a zip-up hooded jacket, her long brown hair was swept up in a ponytail. She still had not yet fallen prey to makeup, her long eyelashes and blue eyes free of any enhancement.

A healthy splash of freckles covered her nose and cheeks.

Thankfully, one of the very few things she had inherited from her father.

Juxtaposed against the person now lying before her, Susan could not help but wince.

The freckles were completely obscured from view, an oxygen tube running across the middle of her face, pushing air into her nostrils. Beside her, a breathing apparatus rose and fell in time with her breaths, the sound inescapable in the tiny room.

Clear fluid glistened beneath the tube, running down from her nostril and over her top lip, pushing its way toward her jawline. An angry red gash was visible on her forehead. A chunk of hair had been shaved away above her right ear.

Susan knew that somewhere beneath the heavy bedding enveloping the rest of her daughter, gauze bandages covered much of her forearms. Road rash, as the doctor called it, had scraped away most of the skin on either one.

At the bottom of the bed, a thick plastic boot extended from the white blankets piled high.

Broken tibia.

The list had been lengthy, the doctor exhaustive as he detailed each of the injuries. Once he was done, he told Susan that the road ahead would not be easy, that surgery to insert a rod into Mandy's leg would likely be necessary.

Stressed that for the time being, their focus was on the hairline fracture to her skull. That the brain was built to withstand front-to-back impact, but that unfortunately Mandy had been struck broadside. That her position atop her bicycle had prohibited her from breaking her fall as she hit the asphalt.

There was enormous concern that heavy swelling could occur internally. Do far more damage than any of the cosmetic wounds dotting the outside of her body.

"Hey there," Susan whispered. Voice thick with worry, bearing just a trace of the tears that had been falling in a steady pattern since getting the call two hours earlier. "It's mom. Ben's here, too."

Glancing up, she could see his reflection on the heart rate monitor across from her. See his arms folded across his body as he leaned against the wall. Kept his gaze aimed down, his mouth drawn in tight.

"Sure am sorry you missed dinner tonight," she said. Drew in a deep breath through her nose. Heard phlegm catching as she did so. "I made pot roast. We didn't get to try any yet, but the gravy was good."

"Mom, I don't think she cares about the dinner she missed," Ben whispered, concern plain in his tone as well.

Without responding, Susan let her eyes drift shut.

Of course, Mandy didn't care about dinner. She didn't want to hear it any more than Susan wanted to say it. The doctor had told her that in brain trauma cases, hearing was often the first sense that would return.

That one or both of them should talk to her. No matter the topic. No matter how monotonous. Just keep speaking. She would be able to hear them. The cognition of computing it would keep her mind active, would bring her through the fog that much faster.

With her eyes still shut tight, Susan pulled in another breath. Allowed it to expand her chest, to lift her shoulders a few inches. Searched the recesses of her mind for something else to prattle on about.

Came up with nothing. Instead kept returning to the fact that her daughter was hurt, broken, almost shattered, on the bed before her. That she felt helpless, like a failure as a mother.

Two feelings she hated more than any other in the world.

Eventually she made her way back to the scene in the house just a few hours before, the only thing she felt reasonably certain she could talk about without breaking down.

"The only reason your brother doesn't want me mentioning dinner is because he was going to eat it all without waiting for you..."

CHAPTER FIVE

Zero.

Absolutely nothing.

That was the blood alcohol level Kyla had blown at the scene of the crime. The same exact number she had scored again 40 minutes later at the Missoula Police Department.

Completed the trio with a clean score on a third go-round an hour and a half after that.

Each test was performed on a different breathalyzer machine. Observed by at least two officers. Submitted to voluntarily by Kyla.

Between each bout, she sat quietly in the interview room of the police department. Kept her shoulders rolled forward, her hands hanging between her knees.

Her focus, which seemed to be much better under the bright lights of the room, was aimed at the slate gray table before her.

Never before had Kyla been arrested. Not for a drug or alcohol related offense. Not for trespassing or vagrancy. Never for even a moving violation.

Certainly not for hitting a cyclist.

The thought of what she had done, the fact that she hadn't actually seen much of anything, that nobody had yet told her how bad the girl was, made it so much worse.

Lifting her gaze from the table, Kyla put her attention on the mirrored glass across from her. She knew that somewhere behind it at least a handful of officers were watching her every move. Probably speculating as to how she managed to beat the blow test three times. Commenting about how she didn't look like someone that would willingly mow a young girl on a bicycle down in the middle of the street.

Sitting and staring back at herself, Kyla had to admit, they weren't wrong.

Despite being just north of 30, gravity had not yet started to pull. No lines outlined her mouth or eyes, no skin sagged along the bottom of her neck. Standing 5'10", her form still strongly hinted at the high school athlete she had once been.

Just an hour removed from work when the accident occurred, she was still dressed in charcoal slacks and a white blouse. Her dishwater blonde hair was down, framing an angular face with high cheekbones and watery blue eyes.

The only thing at all that even hinted at what had happened were the smears of the young girl's blood across her lap and stomach. Residue collected after she called 911 and sat holding the girl's head, crying her eyes out.

Asking her repeatedly to wake up, to please be okay.

The entire sequence had taken less than 20 minutes, aid responding to her call almost instantly. The first to arrive had been the paramedics, pulling Kyla back and securing the scene.

The girl was already strapped in and almost loaded by the time police arrived. Took a few minutes to examine the scene. Pulled Kyla aside to talk to her.

Clearly didn't believe a word she said.

Asked her to submit to a blood alcohol test. Told her they were going to impound her car. Brought her downtown without cuffing her.

The entire ordeal flashed through Kyla's mind in a mismatched series of images, none of them quite aligning. Interspersed between each was chunks of gray, her vision blocking things out, keeping fine details at bay.

Kyla was still deep in thought, replaying the night, as the sole door into the room opened beside her. Through it walked a man in his early-to-mid 40s. Pale white skin and light brown hair fast receding toward the crown of his head. A height that would be hard pressed to match hers.

Wore jeans and hiking shoes. A bad sports coat with an even worse tie.

"Good evening," the man said, his voice a touch higher than expected.

Pulled out the chair across from her and lowered himself into it, blocking her reflection from view.

"Evening," Kyla managed. Sniffed hard. More than an hour had passed since the last bout of tears, though she knew they weren't far away.

"My name is Detective Bear McGrady. I understand you've had quite an evening."

Kyla nodded without responding.

"I know you've made a statement," he continued. "My guys say you've been very cooperative, but would you mind going through it with me again?"

"How is she?" Kyla asked, cutting off the line of inquiry.

At the moment, all she cared about was the girl. Whatever became of her, whatever punishment was leveled, she would accept. She just needed to know that the girl was alright. That she hadn't done something that could never be corrected.

Across from her, McGrady remained silent for several moments. Seemed to be studying her. Stayed that way until she lifted her gaze and stared back at him.

"Please," she whispered. "Is she going to be okay?"

Another moment passed before McGrady slowly nodded, the over-head lights flashing against his elongated forehead.

"She will be, though she's pretty banged up. Broken leg, fractured skull, ton of bumps and bruises."

There was no malice in the delivery, though it did nothing to ease the guilt as Kyla accepted the list. Felt her face crinkle.

Willed herself not to break down again.

Failed miserably.

Lowering her face toward the table, Kyla pinched her eyes tight. Felt warm tears pool in the corners, clinging to her eyelashes before dripping down onto the smooth surface before her.

Her entire body shuddered as she folded her arms over her stomach and tried to force air into her lungs.

Once every bit of remaining moisture was gone from her body, she maintained the pose for several moments. Did not bother to wipe her face. Allowed the film of mucus in her nostrils to stay where it was.

"Tell you what," McGrady said across from her, the sound of his voice surprising her, causing her to flinch slightly. "I can tell you're still pretty shaken up right now, so why don't I give you a few minutes?"

It took a few beats for the question to register with Kyla, for the words to work their way into her psyche.

Once they did, she nodded slightly. Said nothing.

"But before I go, though, I do have one question," McGrady said. "My guys tell me you mentioned several times that you couldn't see. Would you mind explaining to me what exactly you meant by that?"

CHAPTER SIX

The top of the ground was still painted white with frost as Drake and Ajax exited Drake's truck. Peeled back from their respective doors and reached into the bed to extract two sets of golf clubs.

A pristine set of Callaway's for Ajax, an aging collection of Ping's for Drake.

Around them, a handful of cars already dotted the parking lot. Unlike some of the more high-end courses in the area, there were no Lexus's. No Rolls-Royce's. Not even a single BMW.

Instead, there were three other pickup trucks. A pair of sedans. An El Camino that looked like it had last been driven sometime in the late '70s.

"You realize just because it is spring doesn't mean it is actually warm yet, right?" Ajax asked. Used the twin straps on his bag to heft his clubs onto his back. Wiggled once so it could settle between his shoulder blades.

"Hey, you were the one pushing for some sort of celebration," Drake countered. Slung his single strap over a shoulder. Shifted his body angle a bit to the side to account for it and walked straight toward the clubhouse.

"Again, I don't think you fully grasp the definition of the word *celebration*," Ajax replied.

Leaving his response at nothing more than a wry smile, Drake fell in beside his friend. Heard the frozen pavement crunch beneath his feet. Smelled pine needles and ice crystals in the air.

Side by side they passed through the front gate and came to a stop outside the single building that comprised the pro shop, clubhouse, and grille for the university course. Little more than 20 yards long, it was formed from concrete block painted brown, had a pair of windows framing the front door.

Together they each dropped their bags to the ground and stepped inside, Drake going to the counter and getting a large bucket of balls for the group to share. Ajax lingering along the back wall under the heater, sucking up as much warmth as possible.

To see the way he handled the cold, one would think him a native of Hawaii. Or Florida. Or even Jamaica.

In reality, he was a trust fund kid from Boston, someone that should have been intimately familiar with the cold. Standing 6'4" and weighing slightly north of 165, though, his body was just not equipped for it.

Or anything south of 70 degrees, for that matter.

To the untrained eye, it would be assumed that he had been recruited out to campus to a fill a spot on one of the varsity athletic teams. Between his caramel skin tone, braided dreads that hung to his shoulders in a perpetual tangle, and his even gait, the assumption would be a fair one to make.

The handful that knew him, though, knew that to be far from the truth. He had been the one to seek out Montana, choosing it because it was far removed from a family that seemed intent on suffocating him with their privilege. For years they had attempted to use their wealth to force him to cut his hair, to act as they deemed worthy.

In response, he had picked a spot almost as far away as possible. Added an extra layer of insulation by ensuring it was the whitest place he could think of.

The plan had worked.

Free to his own devices, he had become one of the most sought-after video game designers in the country. Now owned the house he shared with Drake. Could own the rest of the block if he so chose.

At the front counter, a bleary-eyed undergrad accepted Drake's ID and handed him an enormous green bucket. Pointed to the bin outside that they could fill it from.

Responded to Drake's thanks with little more than a grunt.

Nodding over at Ajax, Drake stepped back outside, the morning air swirling around him. He felt the warmth from the clubhouse fall away as he took a step forward, a smile forming on his face.

"Well, if it isn't the Keuhl kids."

Across from him stood Kade and Sage, both seeming to have appeared from nowhere. Both were already dressed for the weather, appearing ready to go, their clubs propped up beside them.

On the left was Kade, wearing jeans and a fleece pullover. The offspring of a German father and a Native American mother, he wore the genetic material of both plainly.

Long dark hair that hung straight, reaching just past his shoulders. High cheekbones. An angular face.

Light blue eyes. Pale skin.

Growing up with mixed ancestry on the Flathead Reservation, he had spent his life as a bit of an oddity. The Native American community was wary of him, being half-white. Same for the Caucasian crowd, his Native heritage also obvious.

As could be expected, a healthy amount of feistiness was ingrained at an early age, never to be relinquished. Made for an excellent athlete, an even better friend to the few people that made it into his circle.

Standing two inches below 6', he had not aged one bit in the seven years Drake had known him. The Native American genes kept his skin clear, free of lines. A career as a fire jumper did the same for his physique.

Six months of the year, he ranged over the western half of the country. Fought fires with a zeal that bordered on lustful. The other six months he was in Missoula, chasing ladies at the local establishments with a lust that bordered on zealous.

Three feet away stood his sister. Two years younger than the other three, she bore an obvious semblance to her sibling, her features the same muted amalgamation of European and Native American.

After finishing her time on the reservation, she had pushed a bit further east, landing in Bozeman for nursing school. Completed her degree and came back to Missoula, where she began working at St. Michael's.

"Morning, Sunshine," she said as way of a greeting.

"Morning," Drake replied. "Everybody bright eyed and bushy tailed today?"

"You know it," Sage replied, flashing a smile. "We have a fourth today, or we playing a man down?"

Matching the smile, Drake twisted at the waist. Turned to glance over his shoulder at the front of the clubhouse.

"Oh, he'll be along shortly. Right now he's pretending to be looking at putters, but..."

"He's cold," Kade finished. "We get it."

Based on outward appearance, Drake was easily the most conventional of the Crew.

A resident of Missoula for seven years and counting, he had been brought out originally to play middle linebacker. Later, upon the near-simultaneous passing of his parents and his acceptance into law school, had decided to stay.

As far as he was concerned, had no intention of leaving again.

Splitting the difference between Kade and Ajax, he stood right at 6' tall. Wore his blonde hair short. Had blue eyes and a build that hinted at his former athletic career without maintaining the inflated stature.

The similarities to the rest of Montana stopped there, though. Instead of a Labrador, he preferred to roll with an English bulldog. Had never even owned a flannel shirt or a belt buckle, spoke with a thick southern lilt.

He wasn't local. Didn't try to be.

"Shall we?" Kade asked. Extended a hand toward the driving range nearby, the strip of grass still frosted over, only a pair of golfers clustered together on the far end.

"We shall," Drake agreed. "He'll be along when he's ready."

"Which means once we're done hitting," Sage said, she and Kade both pausing as Drake filled the bucket, the trio stepping from concrete onto grass.

"Pretty much," Drake agreed. "But what he seems to be forgetting is if we weren't here, we'd be riding a ski lift right now."

"And as the guy that has to ride up with him and listen to him complain the whole way, I extend my thanks for going with something different today," Kade said, raising his hand to his brow in a salute.

Nodding in return, Drake set the bucket down. Tipped it on its side. Kicked a handful of balls out in front of him. Selected a pitching wedge from his bag.

"So, Mr. Passed-The-Bar," Sage said as she set her bag down. Removed a pair of golf gloves from the side pocket and began to cinch them into place. "What's the plan now?"

"For?" Drake asked. Stepped out to the side. Used the blade edge of his club to drag over the nearest ball and assumed his stance before it.

"Employment," Sage said. "You been job hunting?"

"Don't need to," Drake replied. Took his first swing. Winced as it sliced badly to the right.

"We saw that," Kade intoned behind him.

"Don't need to?" Sage said, ignoring her brother. "Meaning?"

"Meaning the attorney that was overseeing the clinic has been trying to step down since all that went down in the fall." He didn't elaborate further. Didn't have to.

They'd all been there.

"Now that I'm official, they asked me to stay on through the summer, when they can bring in someone full-time."

A low, shrill whistle slid between Sage's teeth as she stepped up alongside Drake. Kicked a few balls over to the side for herself.

"Damn. Impressive. If you weren't swinging a big metal stick right now, I'd give you a hug."

"Raincheck?" Drake asked, tearing into his second shot, this one much straighter than the first.

"For sure," Sage replied. Addressed her ball. Shot it straight down the middle of the range, bouncing it just short of the 150-yard marker.

"So, wait," Kade said, taking up a post on the far end of the group. "Does that technically mean you're faculty?"

A reflexive smile tugged at Drake's mouth.

"Wondered how long it would take you to figure it out."

The same grin graced Kade's face as he swiveled at the waist and turned to stare at Drake.

"You dog. So that's why you wanted to come play out here today?"

Keeping his gaze aimed downward, Drake said nothing. Pushed another ball into position.

"Oh, Lord," Sage said, turning to look at him as well. "And so it begins, huh?"

"Gotta love those attorney perk packages," Kade added, shifting back to face forward, a driver gripped before him.

At that Drake couldn't help but laugh, coughing the sound out halfway through his backswing, bringing the entire motion to a halt.

"Hey, you guys realize whoever I'm with gets to play for free too, right?"

CHAPTER SEVEN

The request had come in just after 7:00 a.m. An unusual one for sure, it did not originate with the Chief. Not even with the media relations liaison.

Instead, it came from the detective working the case himself.

It was terse, just as State Prosecutor Valerie Stiles expected the moment she saw the name in her inbox. Twice before she had worked with Bear McGrady. Both times found him to be an able law enforcement officer. A bit overzealous at times. At others, quasi-overbearing.

Never were his motives questionable, though.

The e-mail was just two lines in total. The first introduced himself and said hello. The second requested a meeting an hour later at the police department.

No further information. No farewell of any kind.

The timing could not have been worse, Stiles due in court at 10:00 to argue a motion her paralegal had drafted and she had barely read. Still, she knew better than to say no.

Three minutes before the hour, she pulled into one of the visitor stalls lined out in front of the police department. On either side of her were unmarked sedans, no doubt belonging to detectives about to start another day.

Further down she could see a handful of blue-and-whites, the standard local law enforcement vehicle of choice. Light bars across the top, grated windows dividing the front seat from the back.

Leaving her briefcase on the passenger seat, Stiles stepped out. Had a strong gust of wind pass over her. Push her white-blonde hair out behind her. Ruffle the lapels of the business jacket she wore over a silk blouse.

The heels of her Manolo Blahniks clicked against the asphalt as she walked to the front door and stepped inside, the cool morning air replaced by something moist and warm.

A young man in a black uniform looked up from behind the front desk as she entered. With ruddy cheeks and gelled hair, he looked to be no more than 20, though with each passing year Stiles conceded she was getting worse at pegging ages.

At 46, she was a far cry from old, but there was definitely a generation gap that was perpetually widening.

"Good morning, ma'am," the young man said, the nameplate on his chest stating his name as Dianason.

Bristling slightly, Stiles walked up to the counter and tapped a manicured fingernail. "Valeria Stiles from the Prosecutor's Office here to see Bear McGrady."

The smile never once wavered as the young man looked down at his desk. Checked a sheet before him. Found whatever he was looking for and returned his gaze to Stiles.

"Absolutely, he's expecting you. Third door on your left."

Smiling slightly, Stiles nodded her thanks. Listened as the young man buzzed her through the door separating the waiting area from the back offices.

Underfoot, the flooring changed from tile to carpet as she strode forward. The stale air of the front was replaced by something much cleaner, the scent of coffee noticeable.

On either side of her offices filed by, their doors standing open, most with their lights off at such an early hour. Just as Dianason had said, Stiles found McGrady in the third one down. Hunched over his desk, it looked like he had already been at it a while.

Jacket off. Tie loosened. Sleeves rolled to mid-forearm. The ceiling lights shined down off the bald spot he was trying in vain to pretend wasn't happening.

Curling her index finger tight, Stiles tapped a single knuckle against the frame of the door. Heard the hollow metal send out a distinctive sound through the room.

Watched as McGrady jerked his head up toward her. Surprise, followed by annoyance, and finally recognition, all flooded past his features.

"Is it really 8:00 already?" he asked, no small amount of exhaustion in his voice.

"Rough night?" Stiles asked. Ignored his opening statement. Walked into the room and took a seat in one of two visitor chairs across from him.

It was the first time she had ever been in his office, though the place ran pretty true to all others she'd encountered. Standard government issue desk. A rolling chair for him. Two basic armchairs for any visitors. A bookcase along one wall. Metal filing cabinet along the other. A plastic tray piled high with paper, the proverbial inbox for those from an earlier generation that preferred doing things the old-fashioned way.

The only real difference Stiles could see between this room and most others was a complete lack of personal touch. No family photos. No commendations, medals, or awards for McGrady himself.

All business, just as she remembered.

"Long one," McGrady corrected. "Thanks for coming in."

"Your email made it sound like I didn't have much of a choice."

At that, McGrady arched an eyebrow. Leaned back in his chair. Laced his fingers across his stomach.

"Potentially."

If the response was meant to evoke something, to pique her curiosity, to entice further questioning, it fell woefully short. All it did was raise the ire within her, making her think back to the draft filing still tucked away in her briefcase on the passenger seat.

"I'm listening," Stiles replied.

Sensing the hint of an edge in her voice, McGrady nodded. Drew his mouth into a tight line.

"What's something you've wanted to go after for a long time now?"

Her eyes narrowing slightly, Stiles stared at the man across from her a moment. The question seemed to have floated in from somewhere far beyond what she expected.

And she was someone that was paid to seek out the most random and prepare for it.

"Meaning?"

"Just what I asked," McGrady replied. "What's an issue you've wanted to tackle for a long time, but never had the right case present itself?"

Finally picking up on what the man was trying to say, Stiles nodded. "Abolishing the death penalty."

"No, not you the prosecutor, you the individual."

Again, Stiles fell silent. She didn't appreciate the game of hide-the-ball the detective seemed to be playing. Couldn't deny that for the first time though, her curiosity was beginning to spike.

"Rights for cyclists."

A thin smile spread across McGrady's face. He formed the thumb and index finger on his right hand into a pistol and pointed it at her. "Bingo."

Feeling a tiny flare somewhere deep within, Stiles sat a little higher in her seat.

Three years before, her husband had been sideswiped by a speeding pickup truck. Evidence had proven that he was well within the bicycle lane along the side of the road, that the truck had swerved while taking a corner too fast.

It didn't matter.

The laws in Montana – and most of the country – were so archaic when it came to cyclist rights that the driver got off with a simple assault charge. Couple months of probation. Didn't even lose his license.

Her husband's arm was in a cast for eight weeks.

McGrady had handled the case. Apologized to both Stiles and her husband after the fact that there wasn't more that could be done.

"What happened?" Stiles asked. Ran her palms down the front of her thighs. Could feel warmth traveling through her body.

"Accident on Brooks last night," McGrady said. "Right after sundown, woman hit a young girl on a bike."

"How bad?" Stiles asked.

"Pretty damn. Broken leg and a fractured skull. Far as I know, she still hasn't woken up."

A small sound slid from Stiles as she winced, sucking air in between her teeth.

"Pretty much," McGrady agreed. "Fourteen-years-old."

"Damn. Hit and run?"

"No," McGrady said. Swiveled his chair a few inches to the side and hooked a thumb back over his shoulder. "Woman stopped her car and called 911. Was found cradling the girl's head when EMT's showed up.

"Spent most of the night here crying her eyes out."

Several emotions passed through Stiles in quick order. When her husband had been hit, the bastards didn't even slow down, let alone stop. Had denied any involvement until a pair of witnesses ID'd them.

At least this perpetrator had the good sense to stop and help, even if she was a terrible driver.

"Foul play?"

McGrady opened his mouth to respond before pulling up short. The right side of his face scrunched slightly as he looked at her. Held a hand up and wagged it on edge.

"Well, maybe. I'm not sure yet."

To that Stiles wasn't sure how to respond, waiting for him to continue.

"Three different breathalyzers all came back clean," McGrady said. "And I don't mean below limit, I mean nothing at all."

"Hmm," Stiles replied. "Drugs? Marijuana?"

"No," McGrady said. Again shook his head. "But she's claiming she couldn't *see*."

CHAPTER EIGHT

Familiar.

Vaguely, as if from another time and place, maybe even another life.

The sound of the voice caused Susan Moritz to raise her chin from her arms folded along the side of her daughter's bed.

Did nothing to relax the two-handed grip she had on her hand.

Slowly, she turned to see her boss, Public Defender Barb Rosenthal, standing in the doorway behind her. Whatever words Rosenthal had actually said upon arrival, Susan couldn't be certain.

Instead, she narrowed her gaze slightly and offered a perfunctory, "Hmm?"

Rosenthal remained silhouetted in the doorway a moment before stepping forward. Moving slowly, she made it to the foot of the bed, allowing herself to be illuminated by the overhead lights, before pulling to a stop.

"How's she doing?"

If that was a copy of the first comment, Susan had no way of knowing. Didn't much care. For 12 hours, she had been seated in the same position. Her back ached. Her neck throbbed.

For more than 24 hours she had been wearing the same clothes.

Could still smell the results of the pot roast facial she'd gotten the night before.

Sleep had been impossible. She had said everything she could think of twice to Mandy. When she was completely tapped, she had Ben pull up random Wikipedia articles on his phone and read those.

Postings from Mandy's favorite books. Lyrics from her favorite songs. Even the latest in celebrity gossip.

When his battery finally died, she sent him home for the charger. Told him to take a shower, to try and sleep some if he could.

They both knew school was out of the question, so she didn't even bother mentioning it.

She was just glad Missoula was small enough she could have him catch the bus without having to worry about him too.

"No change," Susan said, her voice bearing no small amount of weariness, resignation.

"I'm so sorry," Rosenthal replied. "I just found out a few minutes ago."

Susan nodded, taking in the woman standing across from her. The charcoal gray pant suit. Plain white tank top beneath it. Shorts curls framing her head.

No jewelry. No makeup.

An exact copy of the uniform she wore every day. Whether it was an actual style choice or a self-imposed mandate given her position, Susan had never been able to determine.

Had zero interest in trying now.

"Thanks for coming," Susan whispered.

"Of course," Rosenthal replied. Motioned with her chin toward Mandy. "What's the prognosis?"

Another sigh passed from Susan. "I could give you the full litany, but the big one right now is a fractured skull. She seeped brain fluid from every opening all night."

She could hear a sharp intake of air beside her. Envision the wince on Rosenthal's features.

Didn't bother looking over to see it.

"The doctors tell me that means there's swelling internally, that the body is trying to ease the pressure."

"Responsive at all?" Rosenthal asked.

Coming from some, the question would have seemed harsh. A tad indelicate, at the very least.

Susan knew she didn't mean a single thing by it. She was a lawyer, had been for nearly two decades.

Asking questions was what she did.

As far as bosses went, Susan couldn't rightly complain. Working in the public sector meant they were all overtaxed and underpaid. Stress and deadlines were part of the deal. Never once, though, had Rosenthal imparted hers onto Susan and at the end of the day, that's all that could be asked for.

Everybody having their own cross to bear, and all that.

"She is," Susan replied. "She can't squeeze my hand on her own, but there is brain function. Reflexes all work, respond to stimulus."

A day before, there was no way Susan would have even known what all that meant. She would have been able to speculate, but not deliver with certainty.

The fact that she had heard it so many times in the preceding hours it was now second nature both frightened and angered her, managing to cause her stomach and fist to clench simultaneously.

"Please know, you are welcome to take as much time as you need with this," Rosenthal said. "I'll see to it you are paid for it as well."

A handful of responses came to Susan's mind, extending the spectrum from thankfulness to opposition.

Ultimately, none of them were voiced.

Instead, something that was mentioned a few moments earlier sprang to her mind.

"If I may, how *did* you hear about this?"

Standing at the foot of the bed, Rosenthal paused for a moment. Seemed to study Susan. Eventually nodded, a short gesture that barely moved her chin at all.

A look Susan knew to be one of approval.

"We got a call at the office. Seems the police department has advised the woman that hit your daughter she should obtain legal counsel."

Instantly, things began to line up in Susan's mind. Her eyes slid shut as she drew air in through her nose.

Over most of the past day, her focus had been singular. Be by her daughter's side. Hold her hand. Be the first thing she saw when she woke up.

Most days, her attention was consumed with legal matters. Names and dates all floated by her consciousness, but never truly entered her psyche. As a paralegal, her job was research. Drafting. Tracking things down.

She saw the charges. Read the testimonies. Had even occasionally sat in on depositions.

Rarely, if ever, had she stopped to consider the full backstory. The families that were affected. The people just like her that had spent nights at the hospital by a loved one's side, worried sick.

"What are they saying?" Susan asked.

"I don't know," Rosenthal replied. "I got as far as hearing your daughter's name and cut them off. Told them there was a conflict of interest and our office wouldn't be touching the case."

"If they needed anything, they'd have to call down to Missoula Legal Services."

CHAPTER NINE

Eighty-nine.

Not the best score Drake had ever carded, but for the first round of the year, breaking 90 was good enough to buoy his spirits. Put a smile on his face as he passed through the front door of the Missoula Legal Services office. Found his friends Greg Mooney and Wyatt Teague seated at their respective desks, both staring at him, matching half smiles in place.

The clinic program was something that every student passing through the Montana School of Law had to take part in. Deemed as practical, hands-on legal application, it was really an enormous amount of pro bono work heaped onto a town that already didn't have enough to keep its cadre of lawyers busy.

And an enormous pain in the rear to the students forced to take part.

Each year the offerings were different, based on what offices or organizations around town needed help.

Non-profits supporting water rights. Animal rights. Rancher rights.

Longer established organizations that needed help with a particular project. The Rocky Mountain Elk Foundation. Stockgrower's Association.

Serving as the backbone of the program were the more stable positions. The ones that could be counted on year after year in perpetuity.

The district court. The public defender's office. The prosecutor's office.

Montana Legal Services.

Designed to provide legal advice and services to the indigent in the community, Drake had signed up for it the previous spring for three distinct purposes.

First, he believed in the mission. If he was going to be forced to work for free, he wanted it to matter, having no desire to spend the equivalent of a full-time job in a basement somewhere writing briefs. He had done that the previous summer, working for the Innocence Project in Nashville.

Hated every minute of it.

Second, of all the clinic offerings, it called for the least amount of oversight. Nobody looking over his shoulder at every turn. No proverbial hand holding.

Sink or swim. Baptism by fire. Whatever overwrought cliché one wanted to attach to it.

Finally, it allowed Drake to work with Teague and Mooney, his two closest friends in town that weren't in some way affiliated with the Crew.

"All hail the King," Teague said. Dropped his pencil down on his desk and laced his fingers behind his head.

"Or do you prefer Grand Poobah?" Mooney offered. Tried to offer his best serious face. Ended up with something radically different.

Barely three feet inside the door, Drake couldn't help but smile. He had yet to even tell his friends of the official job offer, though somehow, they already knew and were giving him a hard time about it.

Nothing in the legal world moved as fast as gossip.

"Morning, boys."

"Ha!" Mooney spat. "Look at him trying to play it nonchalant over here, like he's not our new boss."

Across from him, Teague unlaced his hands. Extended his index finger toward Drake. "Just don't think this means we're going to start kissing your ass or anything."

If not for their complete lack of anything resembling athletic ability, or interest in sports in general, Drake couldn't help but think the pair would make great additions to the Crew. For the most part, they were always in good spirits. Engaged in witty banter the way other masters might pedal in literature or the arts. Had a complete and utter lack of self-awareness.

Easily the biggest reasons Drake got along with them so well.

Unfortunately, neither stood taller than 5'7". Teague had thinning brown hair and a set of knock knees that rendered him barely able to jog, let alone ski or hike.

Mooney was graced with a shock of bright red hair that was visible on the darkest of nights. A paunch that was growing by the day, aided considerably by beer and chips and an addiction to reality television.

"Well, before I'd even consider it, I'd have to ask that you shave first," Drake said. Lifted the strap of his shoulder bag up over his head. Held it by the top handle alongside his thigh.

Raising a hand to his chin, Mooney ran his fingers over the bare skin. "Shave what?"

"My ass," Drake said. Smiled. Slapped Mooney on the shoulder as he walked past.

Ignored the laughter pouring from Teague as he made his way to his office along the back wall. Entered and dropped his bag onto one of two visitor chairs, both with cracked black leather seats and polished metal frames. Moved around the battered desk extended straight out from the wall and fell into his own chair, the third item matching the other two.

Shook the mouse on his desk to pull his computer to life. Looked down at the slip of yellow paper resting atop his keyboard, at the blue ink scribbles he recognized as Mooney's handwriting across it.

Bear McGrady. 406-555-1222.

Rising just as fast from his seat, Drake walked back around the desk. Rested his shoulder against the frame of his door. Shoved his hands into the front pockets of his jeans.

"Hey, Wyatt."

On cue, both his friends turned to look at him.

"Who's Bear McGrady, and why am I supposed to call him?"

Whatever mirth that may have lingered from their earlier conversation fell from Mooney's face, replaced by a solemn look.

"He's a detective down at MPD. Says they have someone in holding that you should talk to."

Upon first seeing the message, Drake had thought it was a potential client. Never had he heard of a man named Bear McGrady. Assumed it was a rancher. A logger, perhaps.

This, he was not expecting.

"And he asked for us? Not the public defender's office?"

"What the man said," Mooney replied, raising his palms toward the ceiling. "All things considered, I figured it was something the new boss should handle himself."

CHAPTER TEN

Bear McGrady.

Drake had allowed the name to paint a mental image for him.

The first half was pretty straight forward. *Bear* tended to denote size. A massive man. Thick neck. Enormous hands. Chest and stomach that all extended in one unending arch.

The last name was also pretty clear. Irish in origin, Drake envisioned dark red hair. A grizzled beard.

Found out in an instant just how wrong his preconceived notions were.

With the exception of the thin hair with a possible reddish tint on the man's head, nothing he had put together ahead of time seemed to fit.

The overall appearance of the man had taken Drake back for just a moment. Caused him to pause, to take stock of what actually sat across from him.

A man in his mid-40s. Blotchy forehead flashing beneath overhead lights. Terrible tie loosened at the neck. Bags under his eyes that denoted he hadn't seen a bed in days.

"Good afternoon, Detective," Drake said. Lowered himself into the seat directly across the desk from McGrady.

"Mr. Bell," McGrady said. Sat with his back flat against his chair.

Laced his fingers before him. Seemed to be measuring Drake, making no effort to hide it. "Thanks for coming so soon."

"Absolutely," Drake replied. Nodded once for emphasis.

After getting the message from Wyatt, he had called back directly. Attempted to have a conversation with McGrady. Hoped to hash out whatever the nature of the first call was about.

Had it cut short by the detective. Was told it would be best if he came over to meet with him in person.

Thus far in the seven months Drake had worked with Legal Services, he had not had a single encounter with MPD.

In his seven years as a resident, he had not had one either.

What the nature of the meeting was, he couldn't be certain, running home to change into slacks and a dress shirt just the same. Found himself sitting in McGrady's office less than an hour after getting the message.

Another moment passed, nudging just shy of becoming awkward, before McGrady broke the silence. Sighed heavily and leaned forward. Keeping his fingers laced, he rested his forearms on the desk.

"I know this is a little unusual," he opened. "In fact, it's the only time I've ever known it to happen, and I've been here the better part of 20 years."

Drake kept his face impassive. Said nothing.

"But we had an incident occur last night," he said. Tone that hinted he would rather be discussing just about anything else in the world. "The perpetrator is a young woman, doesn't have much money."

Again, Drake nodded. Nothing more.

"And there is a clear conflict of interest that prohibits the public defender's office from taking her case."

Without realizing it, Drake felt his eyebrows rise. In an instant, things began to line up for him.

The reason he was called. The foreboding looks from McGrady. The begrudging tone.

There was someone, most likely seated in the same building they were now in, that required legal counsel. The law required it. Arresting officers were mandated to state it as part of the *Miranda* warning.

You have the right to counsel. If you cannot afford one, one will be appointed for you.

Drake was the backup plan, someone that nobody had wanted to call, but had done so only because there wasn't another choice.

"I know I don't have to explain the letter of the law here," McGrady said. "Even to someone as young as you. If you don't take the case, then we will have to find someone that will."

The dig was uncalled for, wholly off-sides, but Drake let it slide. Instead, he focused on the second part of the statement.

Montana Legal Services was charged with providing services to the poor in the community, but they weren't the public defender's office. They were in no way required to take every case that walked through the door.

More than once Drake had turned someone away.

Now, more than ever as the acting supervisor, he had that right.

And while McGrady seemed to be aware of that, he was still managing to do a terrible job of pitching the case to him.

"What happened?" Drake asked.

Another moment passed. The earlier look of appraisal returned. Drake couldn't tell if McGrady was seriously still trying to size him up or was attempting to issue some sort of silent challenge to goad him into taking the case.

Didn't much care either way.

"Automobile accident," McGrady said. "Last night, on Brooks. The driver was a young girl, new to Missoula. She ran through a red light and hit a bicyclist moving through the intersection."

Drake felt the skin around his eyes tighten just slightly.

Said nothing.

"A 14-year-old girl on her way home for dinner," McGrady said. "Broke her leg and fractured her skull. As of 15 minutes ago, she still hasn't woken up."

The last part McGrady seemed to derive just a bit too much enjoyment from, letting it be known that the case was open-and-shut, that regardless who the attorney was who took it on, he already had it nailed down.

And maybe he did. There was no doubt that he had just given a scrubbed down version of events. That there were enormous chunks of information that were being withheld. Things that would make prosecuting that much easier.

Still, something about the entire thing seemed to rub Drake the wrong way.

"County Memorial?" Drake asked.

"St. Michael's."

Drake nodded. Grunted softly. "Charges?"

"None yet," McGrady replied. Maintained his stance behind the desk. "Still investigating."

Even in his limited time in the legal world, Drake knew what the statement meant. Opposing counsel was never privy to the full litany of charges until the moment they were filed.

"You holding her now?"

"We are," McGrady said. "Waiting to see if the girl wakes up. Obviously if she doesn't, that will escalate things dramatically."

Something bordering on hope seemed to permeate the statement, raising the growing ire within Drake.

Nobody, in any profession, liked to be handed a losing bet. Nowhere was that more pronounced than in the legal field, where a string of ugly cases could torpedo a career right out of the gate.

On the flip side, nobody could make a career out of nothing but softballs either.

"Can I speak with her?" Drake asked.

"By all means," McGrady said. Relaxed his features just slightly. Unlaced his fingers and waved a hand toward Drake.

"Does that mean your office will take the case?"

Drake's face remained rigid.

"Depends. What's the conflict of interest?"

CHAPTER ELEVEN

DUI.

The third in less than six months, enough to constitute criminal charges under Montana law, the kind of thing Valerie Stiles could prosecute in her sleep.

Practically had, on more than one occasion.

She was just putting the finishing touches on such a hearing when the call came in. A proceeding so boring it almost offended her that she had to be present. Yet another country rube attempting to represent himself.

Once it was over and her judgment awarded, she saw the number on her caller ID. Collected her things. Went through the required number of handshakes and thank you's with those around her.

Retreated from the state courthouse in the middle of town. Took the front stairwell out through the main entrance. Cut across the front lawn of the three-story white brick building.

Climbed into her Acura and slid behind the wheel. Returned the call without turning on the engine.

It was snatched up on the third ring.

"McGrady."

"Stiles."

There was a pause. The sound of chair wheels rolling over a plastic mat. A door closing.

Once there was no concern of prying ears, McGrady said, "Thought you'd like to know, PD turned down the cyclist case."

Stiles's eyes bulged slightly at the information. In her time as a prosecutor, she couldn't remember a single instance of such a thing occurring.

"Reason being?"

"Conflict of interest," McGrady said. "The girl that got hit? Her mother is a paralegal there."

As macabre as it felt, Stiles couldn't bite back the smile that formed on her lips.

More than once, she and Barb Rosenthal had gone to battle not 100 yards from where she currently sat. The thought of not having to do so again was a welcome one indeed.

As if sensing her reaction, McGrady said, "Yeah, I thought you might like that."

The smile grew a touch larger, this time tinged with embarrassment, though Stiles remained silent.

Earlier when they spoke, she had forced herself not to get too excited. It certainly seemed like the kind of opening for policy change she had been hoping for. All too often, though, she had seen similar shots evaporate on much more pressing topics.

And to be sure, bicyclist rights in Montana were far from a hot button issue.

"So who'd you call?"

"Ever heard of a guy named Drake Bell?" McGrady asked.

Twice Stiles whispered the name to herself. Tried to place it. Drew a blank and nothing else.

"No. Should I?"

"Not especially," McGrady replied. "He runs the shop over at Missoula Legal Services. Rosenthal told me to give them a call when she turned it down."

Somehow, the news managed to do the impossible.

It doubled the size of the smile stretched across Stiles's face.

Missoula Legal Services was a clinic offering when she attended Montana Law back in the '90s. It wasn't a bad office, provided a necessary function for sure, but there was no way it was capable of competing with her in court.

Not only was she no longer having to deal with Barb Rosenthal, she would likely be pitted against a neophyte that was more attuned to handling landlord disputes or minor-in-possession claims.

"Let me guess," Stiles said. "Young guy? New to the profession?"

"Practically still has his spots," McGrady confirmed, the same amount of relish she was now feeling creeping through his voice.

"And he took it?"

"He hasn't yet," McGrady replied, "but after I all but dared him to, I really don't see him turning it down."

CHAPTER TWELVE

For the second time, Drake fell victim to preconceived notions.

The first was about Bear McGrady. The second was about the case he had been called in to discuss.

When the detective had referred to her as a girl, Drake allowed himself to picture a teenager. Someone newly licensed, possibly borrowing their parent's car.

At most, a freshman in college.

The person sitting across from him was certainly not that.

If forced to guess, Drake would peg her as somewhere around half a decade older than his 25 years. Almost certainly she had been around a bit longer than he had, but the heavy puffiness around her eyes and cheeks made it impossible to determine by how much.

At first glance, those things were her most prominent features. Seated behind the plain metal table in the middle of the interview room, there was no way to know how tall she was. The prison-issue jumpsuit she wore reduced her entire form to one amoebic shape.

"Hi," Drake said by way of an opening.

The girl nodded. Tried to swallow. She wasn't crying, but it appeared the tears weren't far off.

"Hi," she whispered.

"My name is Drake Bell. I'm an attorney with Missoula Legal Services."

Again, she nodded. Said nothing.

Drake had been given a file to read through while she was brought from her holding cell to the interview room. Painfully thin on details, he suspected it had been scrubbed of anything resembling useful information.

Part of him wanted to believe it was done as a precaution until he accepted the case. The less naïve side figured it was more of the previous hubris he had witnessed in McGrady.

"Normally in these situations, someone from the public defender's office would be down to see you," Drake said. Kept his gaze fixed on the girl.

Watched as she made a point of staring at the table.

"Unfortunately, there was an existing conflict with the other party in the accident last night, so they called on me."

Halfway through the statement, the girl's eyes slid shut and her nostrils flared just slightly. Despite Drake's best efforts to be delicate, there was no way to avoid the obvious.

Still, she said nothing.

Adjusting his tact a bit, Drake lowered his head. Used the new angle to look up at her.

"Kyla? May I call you Kyla?"

Using first names, especially for people being held, was something his boss at the Innocence Project had been adamant about. Told Drake that if he learned nothing else in his time there, it should be that.

Always make it personal. Humanize them. No matter what they've been accused of. Force them to see their counselor as an ally.

"Mhmm," she mumbled.

"Okay, Kyla," Drake said. Reached out and pushed the folder before him to the side. "I've read the case incident from last night, but why don't you tell me what happened?"

Across from him, the girl's shoulders slumped. Her eyes flicked from him to the one-way glass hanging on the wall behind him.

Leaning forward, Drake lowered his voice. Brought the tip of his nose almost halfway across the table.

"We both know they're there, but they can't hear a thing," Drake said. "This is a confidential meeting between an attorney and his client. If they even try, we can get the whole thing thrown out."

Again, her gaze went from him to the glass.

"For real?"

"For real," Drake echoed. "Just start at the beginning. Take your time. Leave nothing out."

In response, Kyla drew her mouth into a tight line and studied his face for a moment.

"How is she?"

It wasn't made clear exactly who *she* was, though Drake didn't bother asking. He already knew precisely who she was referring to.

"I don't know," Drake said. Leaned back a few inches. "I was just brought in a half hour ago myself."

The girl seemed to shudder slightly at the news.

Said nothing.

"But I do know she isn't awake yet," Drake added, having no intention of hiding anything from her, whether he ultimately took the case or not. "Which is why you're still being held."

In one slow, smooth movement, Kyla's eyelids slid down. Remained that way for several seconds. When finally they opened again, a red spider web pattern of veins crossed over the whites of her eyes.

"I didn't even see her," she whispered. "I could go back to the very beginning and tell you the whole thing, but there isn't much else to it."

"I didn't even see her."

The second time she made the statement, the words were so faint Drake could barely hear them. She shook her head softly as she did so, pushing her long blonde hair across the top of her shoulders.

For a moment, Drake sat and tried to compute what she was telling him.

"Meaning..." he began. "She darted out into traffic? Tried to get a jump on the light?"

"No," Kyla replied. "I don't mean she came out of nowhere, I mean I literally couldn't see her. One minute the sun was up, I was driving along just fine. The next it was gone, and my whole world went black."

This time it was Drake's turn to try and formulate a response he just didn't have. He felt his jaw work up and down as he leaned back in his seat, attempting to assess what was before him.

As best he could tell, Kyla Wegman was being straight with him.

At least, what she believed to be straight.

There appeared to be no malice on her features. No attempts to shirk responsibility for what she had done.

"I know it sounds crazy," she said. Watched him. Seemed to sense what he was thinking. "For some time now, I've been having trouble seeing in the dark. This was the first time, though, that the lights have gone completely out.

"I couldn't see a thing."

Unsure exactly how to respond, Drake waited. Knew the silence would get to her. That she would need to make herself understood.

It took less than a minute.

"At first, it just scared the hell out of me. I mean, imagine if the lights just cut to black in here right now. We'd both freeze up for a second, right?"

It was clear the girl had had some time to sit and stew on things, to put together how she best wanted to state her case.

After the earlier persona that looked to be bordering on catatonic, it was a welcome change, even if nothing she said was quite making sense.

"Right," Drake agreed.

"So that's what happened. I had a car behind me that kept honking. My hands clenched tight, my whole body locked up."

Somewhere inside, Drake wondered if he should be writing notes. Just as fast he dismissed the notion, wanting to stay with the story. To hear it out, if nothing else.

"Okay," he said. "And then what?"

Again, she paused. Looked at him. Drilled her gaze into him, determining if he was leading her on, getting an internal laugh at her expense.

Drake met the gaze. Refused to look away.

"I eased off the gas, started to drift to the side of the road. I had a rough idea of where I was, thought maybe I could get into the parking lot of the old shopping plaza."

Drake knew the area well, had driven it many times before. Could picture things playing out in his mind.

"But before you got there?"

"Right," Kyla replied, her eyes glassed over. "All I heard was the sound of metal hitting metal. The airbag didn't deploy and my car didn't slow, so I knew it wasn't something big, but I slammed on the brakes just the same."

On either cheek, a single line of moisture appeared. Traveled straight down from the underside of her eyes to her chin, dripping onto the faded orange front of her jumpsuit.

"I jumped out of the car and ran around front. Had to stop and wait a second by the corner, trying to figure out where I was."

"So you still couldn't see?" Drake asked.

His question seemed to surprise her as she flicked her gaze up to him.

"Not at first, but after a few seconds staring into the headlights, I could make out shapes. Saw the twisted metal of the bicycle. The girl..."

At that she let her voice trail off as a second pair of tears headed south down her cheeks.

"What happened after that?" Drake whispered.

"I called 911," Kyla replied. "Went over, cradled her head in my lap and cried like a baby. Told her how sorry I was over and over again."

She sniffed loudly, drawing phlegm up into her nose. A renewed flush of blood covered her cheeks and lined the rims of her nostrils.

"Look, you seem like a nice guy, and I'm sure you're a good lawyer, but I don't deserve your help. I did this. I hit that poor girl, and I'll take whatever punishment they give me for it."

CHAPTER THIRTEEN

"Three nights in a row? Careful, people are going to start talking."

Slouched down in a chair at his spot in the corner, Drake hadn't seen her enter. Had purposely sat with his back to the rest of the cafeteria and was deep in thought, eyes pressed shut, thumb and forefinger covering them, when Sage arrived.

A smile crossed his face at the sound of her voice.

"Yeah, I guess I should have given more advance notice," he said. Stood and turned to find her a few feet away, closing the gap quickly. "Hate to interrupt whatever hot Friday night plans you had on tap."

Dressed in running shoes, scrubs, and a long-sleeve thermal, Sage twisted her head. Sent her ponytail flopping behind her.

"Let me just say it involved a 90-year-old man and a bed pan. *Hawt!*"

A reflexive laugh spat from Drake as he spread his arms. Enveloped her in a hug. Squeezed twice before releasing the embrace.

"Sounds dreamy. Should I come back later? Just talk to you tomorrow?"

"Ooh, I don't know if I'd leave it to chance," Sage said, shoving her hands into her pockets. "Things go well tonight, we could be catching the red-eye to Vegas."

"Yeah?" Drake said. Tilted his head toward the ceiling and waved a hand before him. "I can see it already. Now introducing, Mr. and Mrs. Bed Pan."

Beside him, Sage balled her hand into a fist and punched him right at the base of his shoulder. Soft enough to be playful. Hard enough that he felt it.

"No, seriously, what's the occasion?" she asked.

Leaving the question hang, Drake snatched up a pair of trays from the bin. Extended one toward Sage. Peeled off toward the hot food as she descended on the salad bar.

Five minutes later, they met by the registers. Plate of beef stroganoff for Drake. Salad with some overcooked chicken for Sage.

Sweet tea for the former. Mineral water for the latter.

Paying cash for both, Drake followed Sage back to their spot in the corner. Waited for her to get everything where she wanted it and begin eating before starting himself.

"Don't make me ask a third time," Sage said, kicking off the conversation anew.

Smiling as he chewed, Drake wiped his mouth. Twirled his fork idly through the brown gravy and noodles.

"Two things. One, I was right down the street at the police station anyway. Made sense to swing by, being in the neighborhood and all."

"And second?" Sage asked. Stabbed at a chunk of baby corn. Inspected it before taking it down in one bite.

"Had a couple of questions," Drake said. "This being Friday night, it could have waited, but..."

"Nothing better to do, huh?" Sage asked. Smiled.

"Nowhere else I'd rather be," Drake corrected. Matched the smile.

For a moment neither said anything. Sat in silence.

Drake broke first.

"How's your salad?"

Pausing just long enough to let him know she recognized what had happened, Sage shook her head slightly. Returned her attention to her food.

"It's a salad. The beef?"

"From a can," Drake replied. Forked away another mouthful. "Damn sure not the Firetower."

"Few things are," Sage agreed. Set down her fork and took up the water. "So, questions. Shoot."

Finishing his bite, Drake again wiped his mouth and glanced over his shoulder. Made sure they were still far removed from anybody else in the cafeteria. Found the crowd to be especially light, even for a Friday night.

"Last night a patient was brought here," Drake said. "Named Mandy Moritz. Bicyclist, hit by a car, fractured her skull. Last I heard, she hasn't woken up yet."

Sage's eyebrows rose as she drank. Nodded her head. Returned the bottle to the tray and screwed the cap down tight.

"Oh, yeah. Place has been talking about it most of the day. Word is she was on her bike and somebody ran through the crosswalk. Broadsided her."

The facts fell directly in line with what Drake had heard that afternoon. A small miracle, considering how much things could get twisted, both in hospitals and police reports.

"Why?" Sage asked. Paused. Raised her eyebrows again as dawning set in. "You spent the afternoon at the police department."

Drake matched her stare. Let her see the look on his face that said he wasn't especially happy with the way things had played out.

"Yep. I guess the girl's mom works at the public defender's office, so they called me."

"Eesh," Sage said. Glanced down at her salad. Thought better of it. "You have to take it?"

"No. I have until Monday to decide."

"Which way you leaning?"

"I have until Monday to decide," Drake echoed. "That's part of why I'm here."

Again, a wry look settled over Sage's face. "So you're here asking for insider information."

"No," Drake said, shaking his head for emphasis. "Actually, I'm here for a bit of medical expertise."

Shooting him a look that said she didn't quite believe him, Sage raised her fork. Went back to work on the mixed greens.

"Let me guess, temporary amnesia?"

"Not at all," Drake said. "She takes full responsibility, so much so that I'm not even sure she wants my help."

"But your hero complex won't let you say no?" Sage asked. Arched an eyebrow. Tried to stifle a grin to let him know she was kidding.

"Yep, that's it," Drake said, employing his best mocking tone. "Mrs. Bed Pan figured me out."

At that, the smile grew to full wattage across Sage's face. "Nice."

"Thank you," Drake said. "It's funny you mention temporary amnesia, though. She's actually claiming temporary *blindness*."

Across from him, Sage chewed a mouthful of lettuce. Said nothing.

"She swears the minute the sun went down, her whole world went black. Couldn't see another thing until after the accident, when she climbed out and saw the poor girl lit up by the front headlights. You ever hear of anything like that before?"

Swallowing heavily, Sage let her focus drift above Drake's head. Her eyes glassed as she stared, searching back through her memory bank.

"No," she finally said. "But we don't really do optometry here. I can ask around, though. Maybe set you up with somebody local to talk to."

"Please do," Drake said. "I'd appreciate it."

Sage waved off the comment. "I'm guessing it needs to be soon?"

"If possible," Drake replied. "Like I said, I have until Monday to decide."

CHAPTER FOURTEEN

Forty-two hours had passed since Susan Moritz got the call. Dropped everything, even left dinner sitting on the table and rushed to St. Michael's.

In the time since, her world had been reduced to the tiny patient room in the critical care unit. A few times she had made her way down to the cafeteria for food or coffee. Twice she had stepped outside for some air.

Nothing more.

In the preceding days, Ben had made a couple of trips home. Brought her clean clothes. A toothbrush. Some paperback novels to read to Mandy.

Dutifully, he had spent almost as much time as she had in the room. With his headphones in and his gaze glued to the latest electronic device, he was content to sit for days. Would glance up every so often to see there was no response from his sister and go back to whatever he was doing before.

It was a stance Susan desperately found herself wishing she could take.

Instead, each passing hour only ratcheted the worry inside her. Made her fear the worst. Sent her digging deeper into WebMD, trying to find out what this could all mean for her daughter. Found big, caustic, bold-faced phrases like **brain damage** and **loss of motor function** staring back at her.

Made frequent trips to the restroom. Tried to hide the obvious signs of crying from Ben when she returned.

In the two days since the accident, scads of Mandy's friends had sent gifts. Called. Texted.

The rules of the critical care unit prohibited them from coming back, but the fruits of their effort were beginning to pile up around the edge of the room. The smell of flowers permeated the air. Boxes of candy were stacked against the wall.

Seeing it all brought about a split reaction within Susan.

On one hand, it was nice to see how beloved her daughter was. That people genuinely cared and were thinking about her.

At the same time, it only punctuated how cruel it would be if she never woke up. If all this was stripped away from her before she at least got to see it.

The thoughts were swimming through Susan's mind as the alarm on her phone went off. Sounding like a set of bongo drums on a beach some-where, it prattled on for a full 30 seconds. Long enough for Ben to hear it, to lower the headphones to his neck.

"Mom."

Susan could hear it, but didn't think much of it. Assumed it was some random monitor going off in a neighboring room.

"Mom," Ben repeated, pulling her attention toward him. "I think that's you."

It took just a split second for Susan to register the words. Another for her to place why the alarm had been set.

Just as fast, she dropped the battered copy of *The Maze Runner* from her lap to the floor beside her. Ran her hands down the front of her jeans. Stood.

"I have to go meet with some people in the cafeteria for a few minutes. You be alright here?"

"I got this," Ben replied. Slid his headphones back into place.

A flicker of a smile pulled at the corner of Susan's mouth as she ran a hand over the top of his head. Exited the room and made her way toward the cafeteria.

The 10th such trip in the last few days, she made the walk from pure muscle memory. Didn't bother to so much as glance at the signs along the way. Arrived at exactly noon to find Barb Rosenthal seated at a table in the back, a woman with white-blonde hair sitting across from her.

The request to meet had come in late the previous afternoon. Barb had called and asked for 15 minutes of Susan's time. Promised it was important, and that it wouldn't take long.

Every part of Susan had wanted to say no. To tell Barb she appreciated the concern, but really just needed to focus on her family for the time being.

No part of her actually felt like she could tell her boss that.

At the sight of her Barb stood, she too wearing jeans. A bulky red sweater. Across from her, the other woman took her feet as well. Turned to display she was in her mid-to-late 40s. Donning jeans, a blouse, and a blazer.

Full makeup. Extensive jewelry.

Something about her seemed familiar as she openly stared, though Susan couldn't quite place it.

Remaining on the far side of the table, Barb drew her mouth into a straight line as Susan approached. Made no effort to walk around or offer a hug of support.

"Good morning," she said. All business.

"Good morning," Susan said. Let out an involuntary sigh, her body's natural reaction to everything that had occurred.

Was occurring at the moment.

"Thank you for coming," Barb said. "I know this is a hard time right now."

Scads of retorts sprang to Susan's mind. She bit them all back.

Said nothing.

Instead took a seat. Watched as the other two did the same.

"Knowing how much you must want to get back upstairs, we'll be brief," Barb said. Extended a hand across the table. "This is Valerie Stiles, from the prosecutor's office."

Susan made a note of the fact that not once had Barb asked how

Mandy was doing. Let her gaze linger for a moment. Turned it to Stiles and nodded.

"Hello."

The face, now that she had a name, clicked into place. She had seen it on dozens of case files and assorted paperwork through the years. Watched her preen before cameras on local television whenever she got the chance.

Heard Barb deride her at least 100 times because of it.

"Hi," Stiles said. Put on her best concerned tone, letting it drip from her voice. "Thank you so much for finding the time this morning."

Both women had now made similar comments. Neither had actually said what it was they wanted. Without even realizing it, Susan could feel animosity starting to rise.

"Yesterday, I got a call from MPD telling me what happened," Stiles said. "Obviously I was concerned, but when I heard the girl that had been injured was one of our own, I immediately reached out to Barb."

More than once, Susan had gotten the distinct impression that most lawyers looked at paralegals as hired hands. For Stiles to now be saying that the daughter of one –who worked at the public defender's office, no less – was one of her own, was a stretch.

At best.

A small bit of distrust crept up within Susan. Mixed with the animosity. Began to clench in the pit of her stomach.

"Thank you," Susan mumbled. Managed to keep her voice free from inflection. "We appreciate it."

"Well," Stiles said, allowing a small smile. "We appreciate you, and people like you. The legal community couldn't function without you."

Susan felt the same feelings spike within her. Swallowed them down. Said nothing.

"Which is why we would like to help."

Though not an attorney, Susan had been in the legal field for decades. Knew how the system worked. Who could bring suit and for what.

"Help?" Susan asked. Flicked her gaze to Barb. "Meaning what exactly?"

As a prosecutor, Stiles would certainly be the one bringing charges for whatever the police found. Susan had not yet heard what those might be. Could speculate anywhere from operating under the influence to a host of other things she didn't dare even consider.

None of them required Stiles to be meeting with her. That's just not how things went.

Across from her, Stiles rose up a bit higher in her seat. Looked across to Barb. Once more offered a stiff smile.

"Well, as you may or may not know, something similar to this happened to my husband a while back. A driver sideswiped him while he was cycling. Broke his arm and didn't even have the courtesy to stop and check on him."

Somewhere inside, ingrained behavior told Susan she should offer her condolences. Already sensing where things might be going, though, she said nothing.

"And, as you also may or may not know, under Montana law - and most states in the country I might add - there isn't a whole lot that can be done to help victims in cases such as these."

A wince tightened the skin around Susan's eyes, both from the use of the word *victim*, and the fact that Stiles was already packaging her daughter with whatever had happened previously.

"Meaning?" Susan asked. Looked to Barb, who seemed to have zero interest in joining the conversation.

"Meaning, there might be an opportunity here," Stiles said. "A chance for some real good to come from something so tragic."

Again, Susan simply sat and stared. Said nothing.

"A shot to make some real positive political change in this state," Stiles said. Added a bit of bravado to her voice, making it clear that this was her big finish.

The bait that Susan was supposed to jump at.

Several moments passed as Susan sat and stared back at her. Saw the flicker of excitement on Stiles's face slowly recede, taking on a look approaching surprise as Susan stood from her seat at the end of the table.

"If you'll excuse me, I promised 15 minutes, and those are now up. I really should get back to my daughter."

CHAPTER FIFTEEN

Solitude.

An almost eerie level of quiet.

Unlike just a day before, there was shockingly little activity at the Missoula Police Department as Drake pulled up. No other cars in the visitors spots out front. No foot traffic coming and going through the main entrance.

Not until he rang the bell on the front desk did he even see another soul, another young officer appearing from the back. With hair disheveled and a pastry clamped between his teeth, he looked like every bad cliché Drake had ever heard.

Seemed to be suffering from the kind of night Kade was famous for.

"Help you?" the young man asked.

"Here to meet with Kyla Wegman," Drake replied.

A look of confusion passed over the young man's face as he tried to place the name.

"The young woman being held for the traffic accident two nights ago," Drake offered. Smiled so it appeared he was helping.

In truth was just speeding along the process.

The previous meeting had not gone well. It hadn't gone poorly, but Kyla had been pretty clear in that she didn't want or need his services.

It was also clear that she was operating under a tremendous amount of stress when she asked him to leave. Perhaps now, a day later, with a bit more perspective, it would be an easier sell.

Or at least an actual conversation.

"Oh, right," the young man said. Dropped the pastry down onto the desk before him, not bothering with a napkin, or even a piece of paper. "You know where you're going?"

"Same interview room as yesterday?" Drake asked.

"Must be," the young man replied. "We just have the one. Go on back, I'll bring her in."

The young man paused only long enough to buzz Drake through before disappearing, leaving Drake to navigate the empty hallways alone. Unlike the day before, there was none of the usual inner-office bustle. Every last doorway was closed. Every office interior dark.

Even Detective McGrady, who the day before wore the appearance of a lifer that never left, was nowhere to be seen.

Gripping the strap of his shoulder bag before him, Drake wound his way to the interview room. Stepped inside and flipped on the lights. Heard a low buzz as they warmed up overhead, casting a pale pallor over the room.

The faint scent of pine cleaning solution tickled his nostrils as he went for the same seat as the day before and dropped his bag onto the floor beside him. In it were a handful of printouts he had made earlier that morning. Preliminary research he had done trying to determine if what Kyla Wegman had alluded to was even possible.

Things he would not dare mention to her, not wanting to get her hopes up. Would wait until he spoke with an optometrist before even spending too much time pondering.

In total, his wait was just over five minutes. The sound of slippers against a tile floor was the first thing to find his ears, drawing him to his feet. A moment later Kyla Wegman entered, the same young guard behind her. He followed as far as the threshold of the room. Stopped and leaned in, one hand on the frame of the door.

"Take all the time you need. Slow day."

Drake nodded his thanks. Bit back a retort about the comment being an understatement. Watched as the young man disappeared from view, the door swinging shut.

Remaining standing, Drake watched as Kyla circled around the table. Continued to shuffle along without lifting her feet. Pulled out the chair across from him and slumped down into it.

"Hey," she said, looking up to meet his gaze.

"Good afternoon," Drake said. "Thanks for meeting with me again."

"Thanks for coming back," she said. "I know I wasn't exactly very appreciative yesterday."

Drake gave no outward reaction as he returned to his seat. Matched her pose, leaning back as far as he could and resting his hands on his thighs.

Just like the day before, the thought of pulling out his legal pad and pen crossed his mind, but was just as fast dismissed. Again, this needed to be a conversation. He had to get a feel for the person sitting across from him.

First determine if she was worth helping.

Second, if she even wanted it.

"Understandable," Drake said. "Yesterday was crazy. You were under a lot of strain, had a lot coming at you. Would rattle anybody."

Shifting her weight a few inches to the side, Kyla looked past him. Checked her reflection in the mirror and raised her eyebrows slightly.

"Yeah. Takes some getting used to."

"Like being in a fishbowl, I'm sure," Drake replied.

At that, Kyla shifted back to upright. Unlike the day before, her eyes seemed clear, with no puffiness on her cheeks to indicate recent crying.

"Okay," Drake said, "so what say we try this again?"

Raising a hand from her lap, Kyla curled her fingers back toward herself for him to continue. Said nothing.

"Like I mentioned, my name is Drake Bell and I work for Missoula Legal Services. There was a conflict with the public defender's office, so they called and asked me to meet with you."

"I can't pay you," Kyla replied.

Drake gave no outward response. It wasn't an unexpected comment, something most people he met with mentioned at least twice.

"You don't have to. I'm employed through the law school, they pay my salary."

"You're a student?" Kyla asked.

"No," Drake said. Realized it was the first time he had ever gotten to say as much. "Faculty."

Kyla raised her chin a few inches in understanding.

"But let's start with you," Drake said. Pushed the conversation closer to where he wanted it to go. "Can you give me a bit about your background?"

"First," Kyla said, "is she okay? Has there been any change?"

The night before, Sage had called him after her shift ended. Given him the most recent update, which was to say there wasn't one.

"Not as of 15 hours ago," Drake said. "Since I'm not technically counsel yet, I wasn't able to call and ask this morning."

The information was accepted in silence. It was clear there was more she wanted to ask, though to her credit, she didn't voice anything.

"Kyla Wegman, 31-years-old, divorced. Lifelong resident of Anaconda, moved here a few months ago."

Out of pure reflex, Drake raised his right hand to take notes. Realized he had neither pen nor paper and returned it to his lap.

There would be plenty of time for all that later, if need be.

"What brought you to Missoula?"

Cocking her head a bit to the side, Kyla scrunched one eye. "A new start? Seemed like a good idea at the time."

"And probably right up until 6:00 on Thursday, right?" Drake said, putting it out there carefully, as an attempt at levity.

Somehow, it found the mark.

"Yeah," Kyla said. Allowed a small smile.

Removed it just as fast.

"Okay," Drake said. "From Anaconda to Missoula. Are you a student here?"

"No," Kyla said. "Was thinking maybe this fall, though. Right now, I'm just working at The Depot, paying the bills and all that."

Drake knew The Depot to be one of the more high-end restaurants in town. If Kyla was working there, she was likely doing better than just paying the bills.

Not living high on the hog, but making ends meet for sure.

"Is there someone in Anaconda that you've worked with before you would like me to call?" Drake asked. "The attorney that handled your divorce?"

"No," Kyla snapped, easily the sharpest reaction she'd had in their two meetings together. "Until six months ago, I'd never even met an attorney. The one that handled the divorce was my ex-husband's uncle. Completely hung me out to dry."

She paused there a moment, the look on her face making it clear that a lot of animosity still lingered over the subject.

"I'd prefer they not even know this happened, if it's all the same to you."

"Of course," Drake said. "I just thought I'd ask, based on our previous conversation..."

He let his voice trail off there, watching as some of the vitriol bled from her features.

"Right." She paused a moment before adding, "And while I do appreciate you coming back, I guess I don't see the point. Like I said yesterday, I hit her. I admit it, and I deserve whatever punishment comes my way."

All morning Drake had known she would offer the same defense, had prepped himself for the best way to respond.

"And I get that, but that's not exactly how the system works. Even if you are accepting guilt, you still need someone to help guide you through the process. Stand with you at any proceedings, file necessary paperwork on your behalf."

At the mention of possible court dates and filings, Kyla's mouth dropped into a small circle. She openly stared at Drake.

Said nothing.

Gave him the opening he was looking forward.

"And in this particular instance, provide a fresh perspective. Maybe poke at something you haven't even thought of."

He waited a moment after the last line. Hoped she might smell the bait. Be curious enough to come forward a bit.

"Meaning?"

"Meaning," Drake said, "I've been thinking about what you were talking about, saying that everything went to black. That's not normal, you know."

A moment of silence passed before Kyla raised her hand. Again motioned for him to continue.

"I've asked to speak to an optometrist here in town about what might cause that. Determine if you have a medical condition that might have contributed to what happened."

It was obvious from the look on Kyla's face she had not considered the notion. Had never once even thought that there was any medical basis for her inability to see the moment the sun went down.

"It doesn't matter," she whispered. "I still hit her."

"Yes," Drake agreed, "you did. And I will never try to get you to state otherwise. But if it can be proven that something was physically wrong, it might go a long way in determining what punishment is leveled against you."

The look of surprise remained on Kyla's features, giving her the appearance of being temporarily paralyzed. The only things to move at all were her eyes as they focused above Drake's head.

Shifted back and forth, deep in thought.

"Well," she finally conceded, "I guess that wouldn't be so bad."

Drake remained quiet another moment. Allowed her to continue working through things in her mind. Waited until her gaze shifted back to him before speaking.

"Does that mean you'll agree to have representation?"

Drawing her mouth in tight, Kyla nodded stiffly three times in succession.

"Sure," she finally whispered, "so long as you answer one thing for me first."

This time, it was Drake's turn to motion for her to continue.

"Why would you even want to?"

CHAPTER SIXTEEN

"So what did you tell her?"

Kade had been the one to ask the question. Both Sage and Ajax were standing beside him, though, all three intent on hearing the answer.

"Remember back before I started law school?" Drake countered. "When we used to talk about stuff outside of whatever case I was working on at the time?"

"Pssh," Ajax intoned, pushing the sound out several seconds in length. "Revisionist history right there. This time of year has always been tough."

"Right," Kade echoed. "NCAA tournament just wrapped. Baseball hasn't started. NBA and NHL are still months from actually mattering."

"They have a point," Sage added. "We're scraping the barrel here. Help us out."

"*Et tu?!*" Drake said, his eyes bulging a bit, attempting to make it look like he was in some way offended. Knew instantly they wouldn't buy it, that they would know he was only trying to deflect.

Saw the expression on Sage's face letting him know just that.

"Does it matter?" he asked. "It worked, and later today I am driving to Anaconda to meet with the optometrist she's had since she was a kid."

"Never let it be said you don't know how to live," Kade said.

"I'm almost sad I can't join you," Ajax said, making a faux pained face. "Deadlines looming and all that."

The last half of the sentence was an obvious opening. Something Drake normally would seize on, been sure to make a pointed crack about. Given the circumstances though, he thought better of it.

Knew it would only continue the three-on-one onslaught he was currently under.

Instead, he slammed home the door of his truck. Pushed his running gloves down over his fingers and adjusted the fleece ski cap over his ears. Bounced on the balls of his feet a few times, forcing some blood into his legs.

"Alright, boys and girl, as much fun as this is, what's the plan for the day?"

Monday morning. The start of a new week. A great many things all of them needed to get to in the coming days.

None more important than the first Zoo Crew outing. After taking the weekend off, all were rested up and ready for some movement. Anxious to continue taking care of the first tendrils of spring creeping in around them.

Across from him, all three people gave him pointed looks. Let their body language relay they knew what he was up to.

For a full 30 seconds, he tried to pretend it wasn't happening. Looked everywhere he could but at them.

Finally relented.

"Okay, fine!"

Watched a trio of thin smiles appear before him, slashes of white teeth against a dark backdrop.

"I told her the reasoning was two-fold. One, she was smoking hot and two, it had been a long time. Happy?"

On either end of the line, Kade and Ajax both threw their faces toward the skies. Let out hearty laughs. Didn't care if anybody was nearby, allowing their voices to echo through the parking lot of the Rattlesnake Forest.

Between them, Sage rested her hands on her hips. Arched an eyebrow.

Said nothing.

"Seriously? Like, for real, serious?" Ajax asked.

"And why *haven't* we heard what this girl looks like yet?" Kade added. More laughter from both.

Shaking his head slightly, Drake focused in on Sage. "They're incorrigible, you know that?"

The arched eyebrow rose a bit higher. "Hey, you're the one that said it."

Pulling chilled air in through his nose, Drake allowed the breath to roll his face toward the sky. Felt his eyes slide shut. Maintained the pose a moment.

"I told her it was two things," he said. Raised his voice to be heard over the laughter. Kept his head aimed upward.

"First, it was the stated mission of the organization I work for. We are designed to help those in need, especially those with nowhere else to go."

Across from him, the laughter died away. He expected to hear some crack about how corny the line was, but to their credit, none came.

"And second," he said, dropping his gaze to look at them, "I told her the detective pissed me off."

All smiles fell away. Kade glanced to his left, back to Drake. "How so?"

"Basically insinuated I was too young to have any business being at the police department. Should go away and stop bothering him."

Two days prior, Drake had felt ire rising like bile in the back of his throat just thinking about the encounter with McGrady. The man had not done anything overt, had not insulted Drake directly, but the feeling was there.

And he had no problem letting it be known.

That same reaction began anew as he thought back on the encounter Friday afternoon.

"Aw, hell," Kade whispered. "Man done messed up now."

"And what did she say?" Sage asked.

For the first time all morning, it was Drake's turn to smile.

"She ate it up. Said she'd gotten the same reaction from him. Agreed to let me help on the spot."

There was no response from the other three. All stood with hands on hips or folded across their chests. Bodies covered in caps and gloves. Fleece and Gore-Tex.

Said nothing.

"Now then," Drake said, slapping his hands together in front of him. "Since the entertainment portion of the morning is out of the way, what say we go hiking?"

CHAPTER SEVENTEEN

Thomas.

Albie.

Newt.

Susan Moritz had figured out what the various names of the characters were referring to long before the author got around to explaining it. Could still appreciate how deftly it was handled and the fact that it was done just about perfectly, considering the young adult audience it was aimed at.

As a whole, *The Maze Runner* wasn't that bad. Not quite as good as *Harry Potter*, but infinitely better than *Twilight*.

If she was going to be forced to spend hours folded up in a stiff chair, there were certainly worse ways she could pass the time.

Starting that morning, she had insisted that Ben return to school. Had politely listened to every last one of his objections as he covered all aspects of wanting to be on hand in case Mandy woke up.

Knew, more than anything, that he just wanted to sidestep having to answer copious amounts of awkward questions.

Once he was done, she had compromised. Written him a note asking that the school let him keep his phone in hand all day. Be accessible should a change in status occur that needed his immediate presence.

It wasn't quite the win he was looking for, but still better than nothing.

He had left just in time to catch the 8:00 bus that morning, leaving Susan alone with Mandy. Twice nurses had come by to check on them, to ask if she needed anything.

In a few hours, the attending physician would return for afternoon rounds. Otherwise, it was just her and Thomas, Albie, and Newt. One woman trying in vain to keep her thoughts at bay. To dive into a book that was created for someone 25 years her junior.

The thought rested at the forefront of her mind as a knock sounded out behind her. The thin, singular sound of a knuckle hitting wood.

Shifting in her seat, Susan turned. Felt her stomach clench at the sight of Barb Rosenthal standing there.

"Hey," Rosenthal said. Made no attempt to enter. "Mind if I come in?"

Allowing her face to recede from neutral to cool, Susan said, "Depends. You alone this time?"

Taking the response as an invitation, Rosenthal took a few steps in. Let a look vaguely resembling a smile cross her face.

"Yeah, was that not a crock of shit, or what?"

Tracking her movement, Susan kept her gaze locked on her boss. Said nothing.

"And I do apologize," Rosenthal added. "I hope you could tell by my reaction the other day, I had nothing to do with that. I was just as shocked as you that she took it there."

For a moment, Susan gave away nothing as she recalled the interaction from a few days before. Pushed past her anger long enough to focus on Rosenthal seated across the table.

Realized the woman was telling the truth.

"Yeah, it was a touch indelicate."

"To say the least," Rosenthal agreed. "When she called and asked to meet, she played it like she wanted to bring us up to speed on the case they were compiling. Made it sound like it was a professional courtesy thing between her office and ours."

Again, feeling the same resentment rise within her, Susan said, "Well, it is *one of our own* here and all."

At that, Rosenthal couldn't help but smirk. Let it rock her head back just slightly.

"Right."

"I mean, come on," Susan said, feeling no need to hold back what she'd been thinking for the previous couple days. "She's really trying to equivocate her husband having a broken arm with this?"

As she said the final word, she shifted from Rosenthal to Mandy. Looked at the breathing tube still hooked through her nostrils, saw the freshly shorn hair above her ear.

Felt a sheen of moisture surface over her eyes.

"And that's what I came to tell you," Rosenthal whispered. "I could tell after the meeting that you needed some time to cool down. Believe me, I was just as hostile as you at that point."

Susan nodded, doubting it very seriously.

"After you left, we stayed down there a little longer and had a discussion."

At that, Susan shifted back to look at Rosenthal. Still remained silent.

"It sounds like Stiles has designs of going to the legislature. There's still a month left in the session, and she can get something thrown together pretty quick."

Feeling her brow come together, Susan asked, "Something for?"

"A new law," Rosenthal said. "Something to raise the stakes on accidents involving cyclists in this state."

"Oh, Jesus," Susan said. Raised her hands to her forehead. Allowed them to cover most of her face.

Already she could imagine the amount of press something like that would call for. The number of interviews that would be requested of Mandy when she woke up.

Of her, if her daughter never did.

"Yeah," Rosenthal said. "Complete self-interest masked to look like the public good."

For a moment, Susan gave no response at all. Kept her hands where they were.

Eventually dropped them back into place.

"And she needs us − me - to make it happen?"

Rosenthal gave a non-committal shake of her head, allowing the top to dip from side to side.

"Not entirely, but it would help for sure. Going to be an awful lot of awkward questions if people ask why she's doing this now and you're not there to join her."

For a moment, the mere thought of it almost made Susan laugh. Just as fast it passed, replaced by the same lingering clench in the pit of her stomach.

"What do you think?"

This time, the face Rosenthal made was anything but uncertain. She stared directly at Susan, making sure her intentions were known.

"I almost told her to go to Hell right then. Could tell by your reaction you'd never go for it."

Susan held the gaze a moment. Measured her boss. Tried to determine if she was being straight with her or putting on a show. As a seasoned courtroom attorney, Lord knew she was learned in how to milk an audience.

After several seconds, Susan shifted back to Mandy. Reached out and squeezed her daughter's hand.

Cold, but not icy.

The doctor had said that was a good thing. So long as there was some blood flow to the extremities, it meant everything wasn't rushing to her organs. There wasn't any immediate fear of shutdown.

She appreciated that Rosenthal had taken the time to forewarn her. Still couldn't believe they were even being forced to have such a conversation, given the circumstances.

"I'm not saying never," Susan said. "But damn sure not right now."

CHAPTER EIGHTEEN

Barren.

Stripped clean.

Bleached white.

From Interstate-90, it was very apparent when the town of Anaconda was growing close. All foliage fell away. No trees. No forestation. Nothing more than scrub grass stained blonde.

A stark contrast to everything else visible for the preceding 70 miles from Missoula.

Standing directly in the center of the bald spot was a tower. An aged smokestack that had gone out of service decades before, could never be moved for fear of what it might release.

"Anaconda," Kade said from the passenger seat. Lowered himself a few inches to get a better view. "If Butte is the hole of Montana, then this place..."

He let his voice trail off. Didn't bother to finish.

Didn't have to.

Even for those that weren't already familiar with the conjoined history of the two towns, the enormous phallic symbol standing before them made it obvious where Kade was going with the statement.

"They do have a hellacious golf course over here, though," Kade said.

"Yeah?" Drake asked. Alternated glances between the road and the scene just outside.

"Yeah," Kade said. "Hard as hell, but pristine. Black sand bunkers, the whole deal."

He paused a moment, almost giving the impression of paying proper respect. "Too bad you aren't faculty there, too."

Seated behind the wheel, Drake offered a grin, his lips still pressed together. He had known the comment was coming.

Just as surely knew there was nothing he could do to stop it.

A playful swat hit his arm as he pushed the truck off the side of the highway. Covered the last two miles into town in short order, following the simple directions he had copied from the internet and pulled up to the curb outside a small building inside city limits at five minutes before the agreed-to time.

Short and squat, it was no more than 20 feet square. Painted light yellow, it had a scraggly line of box hedges across the front and a small sign affixed next to the door.

Alexander Breslin, MD. Hours of operation.

Nothing more.

"Huh," Kade said, assessing the building. "I guess being a doc isn't quite what it's cracked up to be."

Drake snorted in response. Took up his bag from the seat between them.

"Apparently not in a town like Anaconda."

Both doors squeaked slightly as they pushed out. Felt a puff of chilled air cross their bodies. Detected the slight smell of chemicals in the air.

Reaching the front door first, Drake held it open. Waited for Kade to enter. Followed him in.

The interior of the building was just as small as the outside had indicated. A thick gray rug lay inside the door, covering a small chunk of plain white tile floor. Facing the door was a single desk, a computer atop it, nobody behind it.

Around the outside of the room were vertical racks of spectacles and sunglasses. On the walls were mirrors and posters hawking various optical products.

A single door for a restroom was off to the side. A second one was centered on the back wall, the makings of an examination room visible through the opening.

Coming to a stop side by side on the carpet, Drake and Kade paused. Waited until a man emerged from the examination room. Saw that he was drying his hands with a paper towel as he came closer.

Dressed in khaki slacks and a pale yellow Oxford shirt, he strode straight for them. Finished drying his right hand and thrust it out.

"Alex Breslin. You must be Drake."

"Yes," Drake said. Stepped forward and accepted the moist handshake. "My partner, Kade Keuhl."

Drake waited as the two shook hands. Took in the ring of light brown hair around the man's head. His pale blue eyes. His skin that was white to the point of translucence.

"Thank you for meeting with us."

"Not a problem at all," Breslin said. Motioned to a pair of plastic chairs along the wall. Walked behind the desk and rolled a third chair out for himself.

"Please, have a seat. I do apologize, this is probably the most people I've had in here at once in quite a while."

Smiling at the attempted humor, Drake took a seat. Looped the strap of his bag over his head and sat it on the floor.

"So, you mentioned on the phone, this was something about an optic malady?"

"Sort of," Drake said. Recalled that he had been particularly vague when requesting the meeting. "It's actually about a patient of yours."

The corners of Breslin's mouth turned down just slightly. "Okay."

"Kyla Wegman," Drake said. "Are you familiar with her?"

The frown grew a bit more pronounced. "I am. Been seeing her since, well, she was old enough to see."

It was apparent that the man wasn't quite old enough to have had Kyla as a patient for that long.

The point was made just the same, though.

"Is she okay?"

"She is, in a manner of speaking," Drake said. "But I was hoping you could tell me, in all the time you were treating her, did she ever have any problems with her vision?"

Crossing his right leg over his left, Breslin locked his fingers and hooked them around his knee. "I'm sorry, you said you were her..."

"Attorney," Drake said. "So obviously everything we discuss is in complete confidence. We were just hoping to get a bit of background on her is all."

"Which would be pertinent how?" Breslin asked.

It was apparent the doctor was uncomfortable. If placed in his position, Drake couldn't help but believe he might react much the same.

An attorney showing up, asking a lot of pointed questions, had to be unnerving. Not having the foggiest idea why, even more so.

"I'm sorry," Drake said. "She was in a car accident the other day. There were some injuries, and an investigation is under way."

"Oh, my," Breslin replied, offering just the right amount of concern. "And you say she's okay?"

"She is," Drake said. "Others weren't so fortunate."

He let the words sink in a moment. Watched Breslin unhook his hands and switch legs.

"In the course of speaking with her, she mentioned that she was having some trouble seeing after dark. We were just wondering if you might be able to explain that sort of thing, especially as it pertains to Kyla."

For a moment, Breslin was completely motionless, staring back at them. After that, he released his knee. Raised a fist to his chin. Twisted his features as he thought on it.

"You know, after you called, I pulled Kyla's records. I'm sorry to say, there was nothing in there at all. She's never worn glasses or contacts.

"You know how young people are, the only reason I even have a file on her is a couple of near misses over the years. A nasty swipe from a pet when she was a child, a scratched retina while skiing a half dozen years ago. Nothing lingering."

"Hmm," Drake said. Nodded.

Already he had noticed that Kyla didn't need glasses. Knew she couldn't have been wearing contacts, given the amount of crying that had taken place.

Still, he had hoped something might turn up.

"What about the other part?" Drake asked. "The sensitivity to darkness, might there be something to that?"

"Well, certainly," Breslin replied. "I mean, that's actually pretty common. Think of how many people are forced to stop driving after dark.

"That sort of thing usually comes much later in life though, and almost always with somebody that already has a history of deteriorating vision."

"Right," Drake said, "not someone that's 31 and in good health."

"Exactly," Breslin said. "I mean, I haven't seen Kyla in several years or so, but I can't imagine that since then..."

He paused there. Shifted his attention out through the front window. Pondered. "Anything would have come along that would cause something like you're describing."

CHAPTER NINETEEN

Red.

Blood red.

The kind that could only be caused by one of two sources and maintained its color a lot longer than the real thing.

Alex Breslin had not wanted to take the money. Hated himself every single time he saw the deposit enter his bank account.

Hated even more the thought of losing his practice. Of having to go home and tell his wife that it was all a sham.

The Lexus in the driveway. The membership at the club. The Prada bags she couldn't seem to use more than a few times before having to acquire a new one.

He was a doctor. In other places, big cities like Seattle or Denver, people understood. They got that optometrists didn't make what plastic surgeons did. That his income was directly tied to the clientele he served.

People like Kyla Wegman, or worse. Folks that came in once or twice a year. Got a quickie eye exam. Went home and ordered their contacts or frames from the newest discount website.

Gave him a total of $50 for his troubles.

No, people in places like Anaconda got as far as the MD by the door and assumed that he was raking in money hand over fist. That he was supposed to drive a certain car, dress a certain way.

The purge had begun years before. Started around the time that the state voted to eliminate optometry from the Medicaid program, forcing him to start turning away patients.

Or, worse yet, see them at cost, or even for free.

Once that happened, the bottom rose quickly. He was forced to change locations. Take a place with half the square footage and none of the previous amenities.

Next up was the merciful retirement of his longtime assistant. The fact that no effort was ever made to replace her.

How they had known when he was just an eyelash from shutting his doors, there was no way for him to know. Probably never would. Of course, he had asked a time or two through the years, but had been told each time not to worry about it.

Was finally informed never to ask again.

That was as far as the threat had gotten. He knew better than to press it.

All he knew was that when the offer was extended, there was no way he could turn it down. In fact, he had practically jumped at the chance. Stood in the very spot he now occupied and threw his head toward the ceiling.

Howled with pleasure. Danced a jig. Made a complete ass of himself to anybody that might have happened to walk by.

The arrangement was pretty straight forward. Keep a close watch on every person that walked through the door. Observe for any maladies that could be potential trouble.

Downplay them tremendously to the patients. Make sure they knew that whatever it was they had was completely normal, perhaps even their own fault.

Report it up the line immediately.

Considering the amount of compensation Breslin had raked in over the years, it seemed almost an unfair arrangement. No more than a handful of times had he ever had to call to report something.

None of them amounted to much.

Once the pair of young men left, Breslin had remained in the front of the office. Pretended to straighten up the racks of glasses lining the front window, using the vantage to discreetly watch them leave.

Once they were stowed away in their oversized pickup, their tail-lights disappearing down the street, he retreated back to the desk. Extracted his cell phone from the top drawer. Hit speed dial #666, a number deliberately chosen both because of the obvious irony and because there was no way he would ever dial it by mistake.

It rang just twice before being snatched up, the same voice as each time before waiting for him on the other end.

"Dr. Breslin."

Deep voice. Rich baritone. Male. If Breslin had to guess, he would peg it somewhere close to middle-aged, not that he could know for certain.

Never had he met the man on the other end in person.

"Yeah," Breslin replied, stopping just short of introducing himself to someone that clearly already knew who he was. "I just had one come in. Might not be anything, but I thought you should know."

"I'm listening."

No pause. No inhalation of air. Straight to business.

"Just had an attorney and his partner stop by," Breslin said. Ran his tongue out over his bottom lip. "Asking questions about a patient of mine."

"An attorney," the man repeated, his voice half an octave lower. "From here in Anaconda?"

Something about the way the question was framed, the tone with which it was delivered, made Breslin think that the man was indirectly telling him that nobody in town would be foolish enough to even consider such a thing. That they too were enjoying the same financial rewards he was.

"No, Missoula."

"Who's the patient?" the man asked.

"Kyla Wegman," Breslin replied. "31-years-old, been seeing her more than half of that."

A short grunt was the only discernible response.

"And the attorney?"

Leaning back in the chair, Breslin pinched his thumb and forefinger across the bridge of his nose. Already this conversation was much longer than their previous ones combined.

Either he had struck a nerve, or the people on the other end were feeling squeezed, starting to step up their game.

"Kid named Drake Bell. The other guy with him said his name, but I didn't quite catch it." He paused there, thinking for a moment. "Indian guy, or at least part Indian."

Another grunt on the opposite end gave Breslin the impression that notes were being taken.

"They have a case?"

"Maybe," Breslin said. "I couldn't tell you without actually seeing the girl again, but what they're describing is certainly possible."

"Possible," the man replied, "as in, connected?"

Breslin had known the question was coming since the moment he made the call. Had tried to think of some way to sidestep it. At the very least sugarcoat it a bit.

Knew there was no chance at doing either.

"Very well could be."

CHAPTER TWENTY

Two phone calls was all it took, both placed by Sage.

The first was made at 10 minutes before 8:00. Right before the day shift came on, bringing the supervisors to the floor. Placed directly to the head nurse's station, she got the complete update on Mandy Moritz's condition.

Which was to say, there was no update.

Everything was stable. Vitals looked good. She was responsive, but not yet awake.

The second call was to pass along the information to Drake.

He hadn't asked her to make the first call. As counsel of record, he himself could have easily gotten the information. Tread through a lot more red tape to eventually end up in the same place.

As with most things involving the Crew, there was no need to ask. Sage was aware he would need the update and got it for him of her own volition.

If they were the kind to ever keep score on favors owed, she certainly would have garnered one.

Armed with the most up-to-date prognosis, Drake made his third trip to the Missoula Police Department in the past week. Was greeted by a third different officer at the front desk, another young pup no more than a few months out of the academy.

Couldn't help but smirk at the number of people even younger than him running around the department, given the way McGrady had insinuated he was too junior to be doing what he was doing.

At exactly half past 8:00, Drake entered to find McGrady sitting behind his desk. Just a few minutes into his day, the lid was not yet off his coffee and he still wore his jacket.

As Drake knocked and paused at the threshold of the door, the detective looked up. Gave a look that could melt glass. Let it be known this was a visitor he had not planned on, did not particularly care to be dealing with.

"Good morning," Drake said. Pretended not to notice the glare.

"Mr. Bell," McGrady said. "What brings you by this morning?"

Without being invited, Drake stepped inside the office. Stopped behind the visitor's chairs.

If all went as planned, he wouldn't be staying long.

"My client," Drake said. Paused. Watched the glower grow a bit more pronounced.

Almost relished what was about to happen.

"I'm here to see about her release."

The comment landed just as Drake thought it might. Instantly, McGrady's jaw dropped open. A flush of color passed over his forehead, seeming to bring a veneer of sweat along with it. Twice his mouth worked up and down, no sounds escaping.

"Her what now?"

"Her release," Drake repeated. Kept his tone even, his face serene.

Every part of him wanted to be a little smug. To come right back over the top at the detective and treat him the same way he'd been treating Drake since they first met.

Opted against it, knowing it would do nothing to help Kyla.

"Well now," McGrady said. Leaned back in his chair. Let a bit of that very same smugness creep into his features. "As we discussed on Friday, that simply isn't possible. She's being held as a person of interest."

"No, actually *that's* impossible," Drake countered. "Because none of the infractions she could be liable for rise anywhere near the level of jail time."

Again, McGrady started to speak before stopping short, turning his head a few inches to the side.

"Come again?"

Tapping his left hand against the bag hanging along his hip, Drake said, "I admit that when we first spoke, I wasn't terribly familiar with the laws regarding cyclists in this state, but over the weekend I had a chance to brush up on them.

"Turns out, a driver that strikes a cyclist on the roadway can't be charged with anything higher than assault. An offense, as I'm sure you well know, that can't hold a person for more than 48 hours."

The look on McGrady's face - a mask that was equal parts embarrassment and outrage - told Drake that he was very much aware of this.

Why he had gone to such trouble to hide such a thing, knowing Drake would check, there was no way of knowing.

"She claims she couldn't even see at the time of the accident," McGrady countered.

"And again, unsafe operation of a motor vehicle gets at most another 48 hours," Drake said. "By my watch, Kyla Wegman's combined jail sentences ended about 12 hours ago. At this point, you either have to charge her, or release her."

The look intensified on McGrady's face, relaying how disgusted he was with the situation and with Drake. With the fact that his day was less than an hour old and already off to a miserable start.

Across from him, Drake forced himself not to react in any way.

Said nothing.

CHAPTER TWENTY-ONE

Concerning.

Mildly, at least.

Michael Pittman had handled the call from Dr. Alex Breslin person-ally, just as he did every one that came in for that particular phone number.

There was a time, years before, when it wasn't uncommon for the line to erupt every day. Sometimes, multiple times a day. All from various persons planted in the central Montana region. All with some vested interest in matters that could be connected, such as Breslin.

Those times had steadily tapered over the years, falling away to little more than a trickle, never more than an instance or two a month.

This was the first one to have originated with Breslin in a long time. So long, in fact, that Pittman had openly asked the other advisors if it was worth the expense of keeping his services on retainer.

After receiving this call, he had to admit he was glad that they had invested the extra money.

As close to glad as he ever got, anyway.

There was no doubt in Pittman's mind how he wanted to handle matters after the call was received. Forced himself to slow down, to conduct things in the predetermined manner that had been established.

Make a few phone calls and bring the team together. Hash things out, the same way they had for years.

There was no trace of the concern Pittman felt visible as he sat at the head of the conference room table and waited for the others to arrive. Dressed in matching black slacks and dress shirt, he reclined with his elbows resting on the arms of his chair. Laced his fingers in front of him. Stared as Cam Larkin arrived and took a seat to his right.

More than a decade younger in age, Larkin had taken over the position from his father when he passed unexpectedly a few years before. With thin hair and pasty skin, he was dressed in a plaid shirt and khakis. Met Pittman's gaze only long enough to nod before settling into his seat and making a point of staring anywhere but at the older man beside him.

Years before, Pittman had found the interaction amusing. Would allow a smirk to cross his features as he watched the younger man trying to play things off.

Now, preoccupied with the call from Breslin, it barely even registered with him.

Three minutes later, the final member of the trio arrived, stepping through the lone door into the room and letting it slam shut behind him. Donning a striped shirt and tie, a long black trench coat swung open by either hip as he walked forward and took the chair to Pittman's left.

Darren Welker was the only remaining person in the organization that had been around as long as Pittman. Serving as a counterpart of sorts, he ran what remained of the place, leaving tasks such as surveillance and coverage to Pittman. A few years older in age, his hair was unnaturally dark and parted to the side, a pair of thick spectacles resting on the bridge of his nose.

"No coffee?" he asked, leaving his coat on, falling into his seat.

Using his toe, Pittman rotated a few inches so as to face straight ahead. Forced himself not to display any small amount of annoyance at the question.

Had Larkin asked, his response would be different. Given that Welker was for all intents and purposes his unwanted partner, he was forced to play the part.

"No," he said. "We won't be here long enough to have bothered with it."

Welker met his gaze for just a moment. Seemed to understand what he was being told. Rocked his head back a couple of inches.

"This is the first one in a while."

Pittman grunted in response. Nothing more.

"Who called it in?"

"Breslin."

Again, Welker allowed his head to swivel backwards slightly. "Been a long while since we heard from him."

"Mhm," Pittman replied.

On the opposite side of the table, a film of sweat appeared on Larkin's skin. Refracted the overhead lights shining straight down on him as he watched the two interact.

The only reason he was there was because WEPCO bylaws demanded that there be a third voting member present in the event of a tie vote. Everybody in the room knew he would never say a word unless he absolutely had to.

Even then, it would be with great reluctance.

"Serious?" Welker asked.

"Enough for him to call it in," Pittman said. "Young woman was in a car accident in Missoula. Injured someone, kept telling the police that she couldn't see."

Welker's eyes narrowed slightly as he processed the information. "And somehow that got back to Breslin?"

"No," Pittman replied. Had been waiting for the question so he could set the hook. "It was relayed directly to him by her attorney, who later showed up asking questions."

"Oh. Shit," Welker replied. Each word delivered in a halting manner.

"Pretty much," Pittman agreed. "Hence, this meeting."

On the last line he unlaced his fingers, gesturing toward the table between them.

A moment passed as Welker chewed on the information. Looked to the wall above Pittman, his face twisted up in thought.

"Serious?" he asked again.

"No way of knowing," Pittman said, wondering the same thing all morning.

"Hmm," Welker replied. Nodded and flicked his gaze to Larkin. "What's our guy up to these days?"

Once more, Pittman was forced to hide any outward reaction. He had known since hanging up with Breslin that eventually things would be turned over to Lon Telesco, the *our guy* Welker was alluding to.

"He's around," Pittman said. Knew perfectly well exactly where their goon-for-hire was. Had no intention of divulging as such, of letting it be known that he was already thinking the same.

Doing so would probably only bring about animosity.

"Available?" Welker asked.

"For what he pay him?" Pittman replied. "Better be."

One final time Welker nodded. Stood, his trench coat rustling loudly as he did so and glanced to each of the men in turn.

"Make the call. Let's get this moving. Agreed?"

There was no sound from Larkin as he bobbed his head in accord.

"Agreed," Pittman replied.

CHAPTER TWENTY-TWO

Two scents seemed to emanate from Kyla Wegman, both in equal parts, filling the interior of the truck.

Staleness and body odor.

The first part of that was no doubt attributable to the attire she was wearing. Back in her own clothes, she was dressed in slacks and a dress shirt, both liberally speckled with dirt and grease.

Droplets of blood that had crusted black.

The outfit she had been wearing when the accident occurred, it also bore to reason there was quite a bit of sweat staining it as well.

Not that Drake could blame her. In a similar situation, he would have reacted the exact same way. Any person with even a scintilla of humanity would have.

The second part of the smell was most likely derived from the four-plus days she had spent at MPD. While they would have given her access to a shower, any cleaning products they had were generic, the very minimum to perform the task for which they were designed.

Completely unscented.

Beyond that, 23 hours a day of lying around in an oversized jumpsuit would most likely undo whatever good a shower had done anyway.

"Thank you for driving me home," Kyla said. Kept her body pressed against the far window. Hands folded in her lap. Attention aimed outside.

"No problem," Drake said. Saw her posture. Knew she was probably just keeping some distance from him.

Decided to attempt to bridge the gap just the same. Reached out and adjusted the thermostat.

"You warm enough? Too warm?"

"Oh, no, I'm fine," Kyla said. Shook her head softly. Turned to look at him, offering the faintest hint of a smile.

Outside, the morning sun was already several inches above the horizon. Casting a yellow glow through Hellgate Canyon, it sparkled off the surface of the Clark Fork River knifing through the center of town.

As he drove south away from the police department, Drake could see a healthy smattering of people using the trail along the banks of the river. Mothers pushing strollers. College students out for a jog between classes. Even a couple of fishermen standing knee deep in the water, waders strapped over their shoulders.

"Thank you for getting me out of there, too," Kyla said. Drew Drake's attention back toward her. "I was kind of starting to go crazy sitting around staring at the walls."

Drake winced slightly at the thought, at the realization that he should have brought her some books or magazines to keep her occupied.

It was his first case working with a client that was newly incarcerated. Probably wouldn't be his last.

He would know better moving forward.

"You know what I can't figure out?" Drake said, moving right past her thank you. "McGrady already knew everything I was telling him. So why even try? What good did he stand to gain by holding you?"

Pulling up to a red light, Drake glanced over. Saw Kyla meet his glance for a moment, her lips parting to respond, but no sound escaping them.

"Anyway," Drake said. Knew the questions were more rhetorical than anything, didn't want her to feel obligated to respond. "They did say you weren't to leave town for a while, at least not until they see what happens with the girl."

At the mention of her, Kyla's head fell. She stared down at her lap.

Drake could almost imagine her focusing on the dried blood smeared across her thighs.

"How is she?"

"No change," Drake said. Turned south onto Higgins Avenue and made it only a couple dozen yards before having to stop at yet another light, the closest thing Missoula ever came to actual traffic.

"You're sure?" Kyla asked.

"Positive," Drake replied. "One of my best friends is a nurse there. She'll keep us updated if anything changes."

"Hmm," Kyla said. Raised her gaze out through the front windshield. Watched a gaggle of students from Hellgate High School cross the street, taking off for an early lunch.

"Can I go see her?"

The question wasn't one Reed was expecting, but he probably should have. Kyla's entire focus in every meeting he'd had with her was about the girl.

It made sense that that would continue.

"No," Drake said. "At least not right now."

In his periphery, he could see her nod just slightly.

"Why's that?"

There were a host of reasons Drake could give her. That it looked bad, appearing to be an admission of guilt. That it could easily escalate into something that neither one particularly wanted to deal with.

Ultimately, he decided to go with a slight alteration of the truth.

"My friend at the hospital told me the family isn't seeing any visitors. Right now they're just focused on the girl, hoping she wakes up."

Clenching slightly, Drake waited. Hoped that the words found their mark.

A slight sniffle a moment later told him that they did.

The remainder of the drive passed in silence. Following the directions Kyla had given him when they first piled inside, Drake pushed the truck down toward the end of Higgins. Past the university athletic complex, past the golf course he had been on a few days ago, back before he had ever heard the name Kyla Wegman or knew the first thing about traffic laws concerning bicyclists in the state.

Ten minutes after leaving the station, he pulled up to a low-slung duplex at the foot of the South Hills. Painted mud brown, it was void of any landscaping, had limp curtains hanging in the windows.

"This you?" Drake asked. Left the engine in gear, his foot on the brake.

"Yeah," Kyla said. Looked from the house to Drake. Shrugged slightly. "Just a rental for right now, until I get settled here."

Raising the gear shift into park, Drake made a show of leaning forward over the steering wheel.

"Good location for it. Pattee Canyon right there, just a few blocks from Brooks Street."

"Yeah," Kyla said again. "And thank you again for getting me out, for driving me home."

"No problem," Drake said. "If you need any help getting your car from the impound, just let me know."

"You think it's a good idea to do that?"

"Well," Drake said, "I wouldn't be out after dark for a while, but yeah, I think it's okay. Besides, every day that it sits there is another one they can charge you."

Opening the flap of his bag, Drake took out a business card for MLS. Scrawled across the back of it in black ink was his name and number. One of a handful he kept around, just in case.

"This is my cell number," he said, extending it toward her. "You need anything at all, even just to shoot the breeze, let me know."

He almost added that he lived fairly close, could be by quickly if needed, but decided against it.

Kyla accepted the card. Read the front of it. Turned it over and examined Drake's name and number on the back.

"Thank you, I might do that. And you'll keep me posted on the girl, if there are any changes?"

"I will," Drake said.

With that, Kyla nodded. Glanced over at her house. Looked back and slid herself across the front bench seat of the truck in one quick movement. Placed her forehead against Drake's shoulder. Stretched one hand across his stomach.

Held the misshapen hug for just a moment.

Released it just as fast and retreated back to her side of the truck, was out the door less than a second later.

Left a very surprised Drake sitting in her wake.

CHAPTER TWENTY-THREE

Steaming.

Hostile.

Full-on pissed.

Every possible form of the emotion, Valerie Stiles was feeling. Let it fuel her as she stopped by the front desk of the Missoula Police Department for less than a second. Stared daggers through the young buck behind the counter.

"Detective Bear McGrady."

Not a question. Not even a statement.

A challenge.

"Uh," the young man stammered, drawing the guttural sound out several seconds in length. "Is, um, he expecting you?"

"Nope," Stiles said. Tapped the desk once with the tip of her index finger and walked straight for the door leading into the back half of the building.

Knew the young man wouldn't dare object.

Was proven correct a moment later as a dull buzzing sound gave her access.

The heels of her three-inch stilettos beat out a steady cadence as she marched through the hallway. Announced her presence long before her actual arrival. Pulled curious stares out from several offices as she tromped forward.

Not once did she bother to so much as glance into any of them as she went. Instead she kept her chin raised, her eyes narrowed.

Stiles found the office she was looking for less than three minutes after entering the building. Discovered McGrady seated at his desk. A black man with hair beginning to gray stood beside him, both staring down at several sheets spread across the surface.

Each looked up as she stood in the doorway. A full moment passed without reaction before the two glanced at each other. A flush of red passed over McGrady's forehead.

"Chuck, could you give us just a few minutes here?"

Flicking his gaze from McGrady to Stiles and back, Chuck nodded slightly.

"Yeah, sure. I'll get some coffee. You want anything?"

McGrady kept his gaze aimed at Stiles as Chuck drifted around the desk and headed toward the door.

"No, I'm good," he eventually managed.

Stiles waited until Chuck was just a few feet away before shifting herself to the side. Barely returned the nod he gave her upon exiting. Closed the door in his wake.

"I'm guessing this is about Kyla Wegman," McGrady opened.

"You think?" Stiles seethed. Marched toward the desk. Grabbed the back of the visitor chair she had used a few days before and jerked it toward her.

Dropped herself unceremoniously into it.

"How *the hell* did you let this happen?"

McGrady stared at her a moment without responding. Seemed to lose a bit of the shock that had first graced his face.

Replaced it with annoyance, perhaps even a bit of anger.

Which was exactly what Stiles was going for. Something to push him from his comfort zone. To get him moving in the direction she wanted.

"I think the bigger question is, how long did you think we could really hold her with nothing?" McGrady countered.

Stiles narrowed her eyes at the question. Said nothing.

"I mean, come on, even her attorney pointed out this morning we'd kept her four-and-a-half days on basically squat."

Raising her right hand, Stiles extended it directly from her shoulder. Jabbed a finger toward the bare wall beside her.

"Right now, there is a little girl lying in a coma not a mile from where we sit. And you think that is *nothing?*"

"I think we have to follow the law," McGrady challenged. "You know how damn weak things are for bicyclists in this state. Hell, this country. That's why I called you."

"Exactly," Stiles fumed. "So we could do something about it. Make a change. Not let her walk the first chance you got."

"Again," McGrady said. Leaned forward across the desk, an open challenge aimed in her direction. "I didn't have anything to hold her on. What little bit we did have, she'd already served."

At that, he leaned forward a few more inches.

"You're the prosecutor here. If you want any more than that, you're going to have to bring charges."

Somehow, Stiles felt her wrath rise even higher. Pushed herself forward from the seatback behind her. Rested her elbows on her knees.

"If you would do your damn job and get me some evidence, I could do that. I can't just charge someone for being a shitty driver."

"And I can't hold them for it, either."

Both sides held the pose several moments. Stared venom at one another. Took deep, loud breaths. Let the other feed off the body language they made no attempt to hide.

Once it reached a point neither could maintain any longer, they leaned back slightly. Broke eye contact. Retreated into their thoughts for a moment.

This was not the way either was wanting things to play out. Both knew it.

McGrady wanted an easy case. Something shiny that he could take to the papers. A young girl was injured, her attacker was swiftly brought to justice.

Stiles wanted the same thing. To take it even further by creating a law to protect roadways for use beyond just driving.

"What have you got so far?" Stiles asked, keeping her gaze averted to the side.

"Nothing you're going to like," McGrady said.

Stiles shifted her eyes to McGrady. Nothing else moved.

"Meaning?"

"Meaning we pulled traffic cam footage, saw the entire incident. Wegman might not have hit the brakes when it happened, but the girl wasn't supposed to be there anyway."

Her brow coming together slightly, Stiles waited for McGrady to continue.

"She wasn't in a crosswalk or a bicycle lane," McGrady said. "Girl was basically jaywalking. Tried to cut through a gap in traffic."

A low groan rolled out of Stiles as her eyes drifted shut. All the previous vitriol bled from her, replaced by a sudden feeling of dread.

"Yup," McGrady agreed.

CHAPTER TWENTY-FOUR

Drake pulled up to the apartment Sage and Kade shared at a quarter past 3:00. Already Sage's Honda was missing from the driveway, her shift at the hospital starting 15 minutes earlier.

Parked alone along the curb was Kade's truck, the enormous machine supremely out of place on a city street. Easing to a stop behind it, Drake blasted two quick honks. Put the truck in park and leaned back, thinking over what was about to occur.

The meeting the day before had been borderline useless. More or less a long drive and $10 in lost gas. Nothing more.

For the most part, Breslin had seemed like a decent enough guy. The state of the building and the lack of anybody else nearby made it clear that times were tight. He was struggling.

Questioning his chosen profession every day.

Beyond that, Drake couldn't get much of a read on him either way. He had been straight ahead about Kyla Wegman and his history with her. His reasoning about her deteriorating vision at such an age made sense.

No reason to believe anything was amiss.

Before he could parse out the encounter any further, the passenger door wrenched open with a loud squawk of hinges. The front cab rocked just slightly as Kade jumped in and got situated.

"Dude, what the hell is that smell?"

No other greeting of any kind.

One corner of Drake's mouth flipped upward as he dropped the gear shift into drive and departed. Angled them up toward the north end of town.

"That, my friend, is the smell of jail."

"What? Did the damn thing piss on your tires while you were parked out front?"

The smile grew a bit larger as Drake fell in with afternoon traffic. Worked them up toward the railroad tracks lining the north end of Missoula.

"Naw, I gave Kyla a ride home after she was released. What you're smelling is fear and guilt and flop sweat."

Raising his eyebrows, Kade glanced in his direction. Flashed a quick smile. "Oh. I see."

"No, you don't," Drake countered. Matched the glance. Not the smile. "Fear and guilt and flop sweat."

"Right," Kade said. Turned his attention back out through the passenger window.

"What's the word on your PI license?" Drake asked.

"Any day now," Kade replied. "Called last Friday, they said everything had been processed and it would be mailed first of the week."

"From Helena?" Drake asked.

"Yep," Kade replied.

Drake could tell by Kade's tone that he still wasn't entirely sold on the notion. It was no secret he had done it largely at Drake's urging, was allowing himself to be pulled along on excursions such as this out of some form of misplaced duty.

The first couple cases Drake worked upon joining the clinic in the fall had gotten ugly.

Very, very ugly.

At the time, he had only had a female transfer student from Louisiana riding shotgun with him. The first case had left her battered. The second had frightened them both, her enough to return to the Bayou.

In the time since, Kade had proven an able replacement. The state had agreed to accept his years as a fire fighter in lieu of law enforcement, had granted him a PI license.

Something to keep him busy when he wasn't away on blazes.

What Drake would do during those summer months was something he had yet to give much thought on. Preferred not to until it was absolutely necessary.

The late afternoon sun was directly in their face as he hooked a left at the old train depot on the north end of town. Pushed west. Dropped his visor and squinted forward. Checked numbers along businesses as they filed by until he found what he was looking for.

Five minutes before the half hour, he pulled into an angled parking spot facing the railroad tracks. On one side was a battered Dodge Ram pickup, the other a polished BMW.

Only in Missoula.

Climbing out, Drake and Kade jaywalked to the opposite side of the street. Moved toward a building constructed of dark brown brick, everything outlined in wood painted black. A series of windows lined the front, blinds drawn low.

A dark and ominous overall tone for sure.

"You don't think your sister set us up, do you?" Drake asked. Hopped up the three short steps leading to the front door.

"Only one way to find out," Kade said. Reached the door first. Held it open. Motioned with a hand for Drake to enter. "After you."

"Gee, thanks," Drake muttered. Stepped inside to find the space to be a sharp contrast to the exterior in every way.

Floors made of blonde wood polished to a sheen. Mirrors lining the walls. High ceilings. Bright lights.

Off to the right was a waiting area with a half-dozen padded leather chairs. Magazines for adults. Toys for children.

To the left was an updated version of the spread in Breslin's office, the newest in sunglasses and eyewear.

Placed in the middle of the room was a girl that looked to be a day or two out of high school. Red hair pulled back. Braces on her teeth.

She smiled brightly, sat up straighter, as they approached. "Hell-o."

"Hi there," Drake said. Pulled up just short of the desk. "Drake Bell and Kade Keuhl here to meet with Dr. Westerman."

"Sure," the girl replied. Raised a black plastic phone from the desk before her. Spoke into it for a moment. Returned it just as fast. "She'll be out in just one minute."

Drake nodded his thanks. Took a step back from the desk.

Had barely stopped moving when a carbon copy one generation removed of the girl seated before them appeared from a back room. Dressed in a green dress and white lab coat, she had the same thick red hair and oversized smile.

The only difference was a pair of tortoise shell glasses encircling her eyes.

"Hell-o," she said, echoing the cadence of her daughter. "Apologies if I kept you waiting."

Drake didn't bother to point out they had been standing there just a few seconds.

"Thank you for meeting with us," he said. "We appreciate it."

"Nonsense," Westerman replied. "Anybody that comes so highly recommended from Sage can have all the time they want."

At that, she stepped forward and shook both their hands. Told them to address her as Melanie. Led them past the desk into the room she had just appeared from.

Set up as an office, the space was larger than the entire front half of Breslin's building a day before. Bright and open like the reception area, it had wood floors and white walls. Shelves had been screwed into them on all four sides, lined with family pictures and assorted bric-a-brac. An enormous ficus tree stood in the corner.

"Please, have a seat," she said. Motioned toward a matching set of hardback chairs already pulled out into the center of the room. Dropped herself onto a third one and extended a finger to Kade.

"Let me guess...brother?"

A sheepish grin crossed Kade's face. "That obvious?"

"Little bit," Westerman replied. "You guys both have a..."

"Unique look," Kade finished.

The same sheepish grin crossed Westerman's face. "I was going to say interesting, but yes, that's the idea."

"Yeah, we get that a lot."

With the hand still extended, Westerman pushed it to Drake.

"And you're the best friend?"

Never before had Drake really thought to parse out who in the Crew stood as his best friend. Was surprised a bit by the term, which must have originated with Sage.

Couldn't quite argue that it was wrong.

"Yes, ma'am," Drake said. "And the one that requested she set this meeting up, so again, thank you."

"My pleasure," Westerman said. Cast him a smile that let it be known she noticed what he had done there. "So, how can I help?"

In short order, Drake recapped everything up to that point. He started with the accident, which elicited the expected amount of concern from the doctor, even spawning several follow-up questions about the girl's condition.

From there he mentioned Kyla's statement about having trouble seeing once the sun went down. Watched her face draw itself into thought as she listened.

Finished with the visit to Breslin the day before. At his lack of any reasoning behind what Kyla was describing.

When he was done, the room fell silent for a moment. Kade and Drake both shifted their attention to Westerman. Waited.

Said nothing.

Nearly a full minute passed as she sat and pondered. Ran her teeth out over her bottom lip and chewed softly at it. Brought her brows in tight, a crease appearing between them.

"Okay, so what I think it is you're asking me," she finally said. "Is if what she's discussing is possible?"

"Yes," Drake said. "And do bear in mind, she has admitted guilt. We have no interest in doing wrong by that young woman in the hospital. We're just here collecting information to make sure the prosecution doesn't get any wild ideas."

He didn't bother mentioning that he had asked Sage to set the meeting before he knew about the existing laws regarding striking a cyclist. At this point, he was far enough down the path that he wanted to see it through. Determine what was going on with Kyla Wegman's vision. Get her help if it was needed.

"The short answer is," Westerman said, "yes. What she's talking about does exist. The scientific name for it is nyctalopia, the everyday term being moonblink."

Reflexively, Drake and Kade shared a glance.

The name sounded more like something that would be found in a sci-fi movie or in the pages of a *Game of Thrones* novel than an actual ailment he could ever take before a judge.

"I know, I know," Westerman said. Raised both palms toward them, sending the sleeves of her coat tumbling down her forearms. "But believe me, it's real."

She paused and glanced over her shoulder. Stared at one of the shelves a moment. Appeared as if she might stand and grab a volume to prove what she was saying to them.

Ultimately decided against it. Turned back to face forward.

"Basically, it's a condition that is more likely a symptom."

"Meaning," Drake said.

"Meaning, rarely," Westerman replied, "and I do mean *rarely*, does someone just have moonblink. Normally they have something else going on, and this is a side effect."

"Okay," Drake said, processing the information for a moment. "Something else, such as?"

"Such as a congenital defect, or an acute injury, or even malnutrion."

Drake let his gaze narrow. Tried to force things into place.

Kyla had said the change was getting worse, meaning it could be congenital, though Breslin had stated there was nothing in her record. She had not mentioned any injuries. Certainly didn't look to be malnourished.

"The ocular lens," Westerman said, seeming to sense their confusion, "is comprised of rods and cones. The two work in concert, balancing each other, which enable us to focus on objects near and far.

"When someone is suffering from moonblink, they lose their ability to respond to light. It means not only do they see poorly at dark, but they fail to adjust quickly to large adjustments in light."

For the first time, something clicked into place for Drake.

"Such as right when the sun goes down."

"Right," Westerman said, "or when they first flip on the lights in a dark room. That kind of thing."

Drake fell silent for a moment. Let his mind take this piece of information. Fit it against everything else he already knew about the case.

What the doctor was saying explained why she had such a hard time right at dusk. Why she was able to see Mandy Moritz once she got around to the front of the car. How she was able to function by the time the cops got there.

She wasn't completely blind at night, she just had difficulty adjusting to changes in light.

"Is there anything that can be done for it?" Drake asked. Kept his gaze averted as he continued to parse his way through things.

"In theory, yes," Westerman replied. "There is a corrective surgery for it, but like with most anything past removing a cataract, there are severe risks.

"So severe, in fact, I advise patients against it."

"Even a patient that is 31?" Drake countered.

Westerman opened her mouth to answer - no doubt a conditioned response – but closed it just as fast.

"Yeah, that part is tough. I won't say it's unheard of to see someone so young develop it, but I've never seen one myself. You sure there isn't a family history here?"

"She didn't mention any," Drake replied. "Dr. Breslin gave her a clean bill of health."

"Huh," Westerman said. Seemed genuinely puzzled. Rested an elbow on her knee, her chin on her fist.

"You said in theory a second ago," Kade said, his first contribution to the discussion, pulling the doctor and Drake's attention toward him. "*In theory* it could be treated."

"Oh, right," Westerman said. Shook her head as if trying to clear it, pulling herself back into the present.

"Well, like I said before, most often what we're talking about here isn't a condition, it's a symptom. Meaning, you find whatever the underlying cause is, you can probably figure out how to fix it."

CHAPTER TWENTY-FIVE

Old.

Battered.

Borderline rusted out.

To those that only looked at the outside, the truck was a relic. Something that should have been put out to pasture years before. At the least, given a mercy killing.

To a man in Lon Telesco's particular line of work, it was nothing short of a Godsend.

The outside was a mess. A jumble of mismatched paint splotches. A body design that had first come out in the mid '70s.

Underneath all that, though, was a V-8 engine that had been completely rebuilt and polished to a mirrored shine. An interior that was soft leather with buffed hardwood touches.

A stereo system that could blow a girl's skirt up from 10 yards away.

Built completely on the WEPCO dime, it was one of the few demands Telesco had made when brought on board. Knowing he would be spending an inordinate amount of time staked out, he needed something spacious. Comfortable.

Inconspicuous.

Something that could blend in while parked on any street in Anaconda. Wouldn't be given a second thought in Butte or Dillon.

Anywhere else his business took him.

Parked six spaces down from the small brick office on the north end of Missoula, it was his first time working in the town. Given the proximity to Anaconda and it being one of the larger cities in the state, that fact came as a mild surprise.

That nobody had so much as glanced his way, even considered someone was hiding behind the tinted glass, was not.

The interior of the truck was a tepid 60 degrees as he sat and waited. Dressed in jeans and a canvas jacket, he could remain there for hours. Days if he had to.

On the passenger seat beside him was a quart-sized bottle of water. A pair of Snickers bars.

He'd lasted much longer on much less.

More than once.

It hadn't been hard to track the pair down. Breslin had given them the name of Drake Bell, described he and his cohort to the letter. After that, it was a simple call to his contacts at the DMV.

There was only one Drake Bell in all of Montana. He lived not far from the University of Montana.

Telesco had been posted up down the street an hour and a half later. Had followed at a distance as Bell returned home midday. Appeared a few moments later with a bulldog on a leash, left the house again 20 minutes after that.

If the young man had any inkling at all that he was being followed, he didn't let on. His patterns were direct from one point to another. His head didn't bother to swivel as he moved about.

Just another self-absorbed working man singularly focused on the two inches in front of him.

As an attorney, maybe not even that far.

When first assigned to the case, Telesco had gotten a small charge of excitement. It had been some time since he'd been in the field, his days reduced to manual labor, WEPCO never at a shortage of odd jobs.

Most of the time, they weren't too bad. Paid him a salary that far outweighed the effort he was putting in. It was no secret, though, that the money was more of a retainer, keeping him close by and happy for moments such as this.

Times when things would arise that would require a personal touch.

They had Pittman, that monkey in a tie, to be the face of things. To show up and flash some money, employ that pearly white smile that always made Telesco gag.

But they needed him to be boots on the ground. To be an invisible face. Keep tabs on things and let them know if they were escalating to a point of concern.

Usually, that didn't occur.

Already he could tell this wasn't going to fall in the category of usually.

Twisted behind the steering wheel, Telesco openly stared as the duo left the office building. Seemed to be deep in conversation, both of their faces bent up in concern.

Whatever it was that had been discussed inside had been serious.

Somehow Telesco doubted it had anything to do with the eye health of either one.

Hidden behind his mirrored windows, Telesco shifted to follow them as they crossed the street. Climbed back into Bell's truck. Fired up the engine and drove away.

For a moment, Telesco considered following them. Tracking where their next stop might be. A quick glance at the clock on the dash pushed all such thoughts from his mind. It was already after 4:00, the odds of the duo going anywhere else pretty slim.

Most likely, they had not known how long this appointment would last. Had given themselves plenty of time before the end of the workday. Would now return home with whatever information they had gleaned and regroup.

Checking the time, Telesco decided to give them a few minutes head start. To wait until they were back and swing past Bell's place to make sure his supposition was correct.

He waited until the tailgate of the truck disappeared from sight before turning back to face forward and taking up his cellphone from the middle console. It was answered after just a single ring by the same gruff voice that always picked up.

"Yeah."

"I spotted them earlier this afternoon. You're going to love this."

An unintelligible grunt was the only response.

"They just spent the last hour speaking with an optometrist here in town."

"Christ. They spoke to Breslin yesterday. What the hell were they doing there?"

Telesco knew the question was rhetorical. Had asked himself the very same thing earlier. Didn't bother trying to respond to it.

"Orders?"

"Stay the course."

CHAPTER TWENTY-SIX

Susan Moritz wasn't sure what she was hoping for.

Perhaps something cliché like she'd seen dozens of times in movies. Something where the person lying in bed begins to clench a finger. Draws up the attention of the ragged and forlorn person in the chair beside them.

Slowly opens their eyes.

Almost instantly is coherent. Able to have a conversation. Wears a far-off expression that gives them an ethereal glow.

So many times, she had watched it play out in her mind. Sometimes it was something like *While You Were Sleeping*. Others, it was closer to *Rocky II*.

Every time though, it ended with her and her daughter crying together. Susan raised out of her chair so that her face was just inches from Mandy's, both smiling.

None of that was what actually happened.

The Maze Runner was long since gone, Susan having moved into *The Scorch Trials*. Not quite as intriguing as the original, though it hadn't fallen prey to the sophomore slump, still very much holding her attention.

Ben had stopped by after school. Brought her clean clothes and a sandwich from Arby's. Was going to a friend's house for dinner and would pop by again later.

The attending physician had made his second pass through an hour before. Had checked all the monitors and looked Mandy over. Gave the same standard report Susan had heard now almost a dozen times and counting.

Everything was stable. Mandy could wake up at any time.

Susan had heard the words so many times that she was almost immune to them. Had stopped getting her hopes up. Quit checking every few minutes for signs of a change.

Instead, she allowed herself to just sit and read. They were the first novels she'd gotten to in months. A far cry from the usual Danielle Steele she preferred. Even further from the Janet Evanovich she read when she needed a laugh.

Still, they were entertaining. That's all she could ask for.

Besides, the most important thing was that her daughter heard her voice. Knew she was there and would not leave.

She had just concluded the seventh chapter when she paused for a moment. Took up the water bottle from the floor by her feet. Glanced over to see the hazel eyes of her daughter staring back at her.

Felt her heart lurch in her chest.

The bottle and the book both slid from her hands, slapping the tile on either side of her. The book landed with a flutter of pages. The bottle hit its side, spilling the last inch of water onto the floor beneath the chair.

Susan paid neither one any attention.

"Mandy?" she whispered. Fresh tears belied her eyes. Her voice sounded faint and far away.

The clear tubing still ran beneath her daughter's nostrils. White blankets still covered her body. A bevy of cords and monitors were still attached to her.

Under all of it, there was no movement. No sound. No attempts to speak.

Merely the pair of dark eyes looking up at her, letting it be known that she was awake. That finally her body had gotten a handle on things enough to trust her to function.

"Mandy," Susan whispered again. Launched herself forward to the edge of the bed. Felt hot tears spilling down her cheeks. "Oh, Mandy."

Her first reaction was to grab for her daughter's hand. To clutch it in both of hers, pull it to her face and kiss the back of it over and over.

"Honey, I'm here. You're awake. Oh, thank God, you're awake."

After several seconds of no response, nothing more than the continued stare of her daughter, cognition returned. Told Susan to reach across Mandy's body, to depress the nurse call button.

To push it over and over again until somebody came to help them.

Every part of her wanted to throw herself down atop the bed. To cover her daughter's body with her own. To do anything she could to protect her from something like this ever happening again.

To let them both sob and sob until all the pain, the agony, of the past week was gone. To act out a scene much like the ones she'd witnessed on television so many times before.

She never got the chance.

A single squeak of rubber against tile was the only warning Susan had that a nurse was in the room. She barely had the chance to lift her gaze before the woman was at her side, using her considerable girth to hip Susan out of the way.

She took over with a practiced efficiency that was beyond impressive. Acting in a quick progression of flurried movements, she disconnected a few of the leads, adjusted some of the others.

Had another nurse by her side in moments.

A doctor just an instant after that.

An outsider looking in, Susan allowed herself to drift to the back of the room. There, she met her daughter's stare.

Maintained it as the team worked, despite the steady torrent of tears dripping down her face.

CHAPTER TWENTY-SEVEN

Relief.

Surprise.

The two emotions fought for the upper hand in Drake's mind as he sat and watched Ajax troubleshoot his newest creation. Seated on the far end of the leather sofa in their living room, his left hand was draped over the arm of the couch. Twirling it slowly, he kneaded the folds of excess skin atop the head of his English bulldog, Suzy Q. Heard her make small moans of pleasures with each concentric circle.

In his right was his cell phone, a message from Sage pasted across it.

Mandy Moritz is awake. Lots of commotion here. This is a good thing, right?

The text had come in five minutes earlier. Was still up front and center on the screen as Drake alternated his attention between the device and Ajax's main character wandering through the virtual storyboard of a booming metropolis.

Tried to process exactly what the information meant for him and his client.

On a most basic level, obviously it was a good thing. Being a decent human being dictated that anybody would be glad about it.

Drake's reaction went deeper, though. It gave him some modicum of joy that the very worst of charges - no matter how lacking they might be - couldn't be levied on Kyla. That her enormous guilt wouldn't be too much, wouldn't eventually subsume her.

On the flip side, it meant that whatever momentary lull he and Kade had been afforded to investigate was over. The girl waking up would lessen the charges, but he could imagine McGrady and the prosecutor and whoever else would move quickly now.

Would want to take advantage of any media attention there might be.

May even look to make an example of Kyla.

"Yo, man, you hear me?" Ajax said. Voice raised loud enough to snap Drake from his thoughts.

"Hmm?" Drake asked.

A thin smile cracked across Ajax's face. "I knew you weren't paying attention back there. I asked what you're thinking for dinner."

"Oh," Drake said. Made no attempt to hide that he'd been caught. "I don't care. Whatever you decide is cool."

Turning to face him, Ajax tossed his gaming controller into the armchair sitting perpendicular to them. Left the game he was working on frozen across the screen. Flopped his long body down onto the couch beside Drake, braids swinging free as he went.

"What's up?"

Knowing better than to even attempt brushing it off, Drake kept the screen of his phone facing the ceiling. Extended it so Ajax could read it.

Heard a shrill whistle slide out without looking over.

"And that's the girl..."

"That Kyla hit," Drake finished. "Yeah."

"Damn," Ajax muttered. "She know yet?"

"Not sure," Drake said. "Doubt it."

"Well, don't you think you should tell her?"

A small snort rolled out of Drake, rocking his head back. He drew the phone back to his lap and closed the text message. Exchanged the device to his left hand.

Reached out and swatted Ajax's arm with his right.

"Good call," he said. "And speaking of calls, be sure to grab me some of whatever you decide on for dinner."

"Terrible segue," Ajax said to his back as he departed. Headed for the door in the corner of the living room and passed into his bedroom. "*Terrible!*"

Drake didn't acknowledge the comment as he stepped over the threshold. Closed the door behind him. Padded over and dropped himself back onto his pillow top mattress.

Using his thumb, he scrolled down through his phone. Landed on the string of digits Kyla had entered herself that afternoon.

Pressed send.

The line rang six times, just short of being kicked to voicemail, before being picked up. A few moments of silence passed, the only sound someone breathing on the other end.

"Um, hello?" Drake asked. Held the phone away from his face. Checked to make sure the line was connected.

Just as fast pressed it back to his cheek.

"Who is this?"

Short, terse. A bit hostile.

"Kyla? Is everything alright?"

"Who is this?" she snapped a second time.

Sitting up, Drake kept the phone pressed to his ear. Felt his pulse rise just slightly. "Kyla, it's Drake. Your attorney. What's going on?"

Another few moments passed before a deep sigh signaled what Drake guessed to mean recognition.

"Oh, hey," Kyla said. Noticeable change in tone. "How are you?"

"I think I should be asking you the same thing," Drake said, remaining perched on the edge of the bed.

"No," Kyla replied. "Just been a long night. I guess word got out back home about what happened. Phone has been blowing up all evening."

Drawing his face into a wince, Drake felt the skin around his eyes pinch slightly. "Eesh. Sorry to hear that."

"Yeah," Kyla said. Managed in a single word to let it be known she didn't much feel like discussing it.

"Well," Drake said, pushing on. "Hopefully this will help a bit. I was calling to let you know that Mandy Moritz woke up this evening."

Another loud sigh was audible. A choked sound that resembled a sob cut short. A deep sniffle.

"Oh, thank God," Kyla whispered. "And she's okay?"

"That I don't know," Drake said. "Doubt even they do yet. I just got word, and thought I should pass it on."

This time there was no response on the other end.

Merely the sound of crying. Starting low, it gained intensity. Soon rose into complete sobbing.

Halfway through, Drake disconnected the call. Didn't want to hear her cry anymore. Doubted she wanted him listening.

Said nothing.

CHAPTER TWENTY-EIGHT

"You sure about this?"

The question wasn't meant to rankle. Surely not to inspire the angry look that was returned the moment it left Bear McGrady's lips.

"Why?" Valerie Stiles snapped. "You don't think it's a good idea?"

McGrady leaned back a few inches and raised his eyebrows. Let it be known the reaction was over the top.

Came right back at her a moment later.

"I don't think anything. This is your domain. I just don't see how going up there right now can do any good."

Stiles made no attempt to pull back. To let it even be known that she noticed McGrady invading her personal space.

"Well, like you said, this is my domain."

With that, she left the detective standing in the back corner of the cafeteria. Strode forward to the small throng of reporters that were gathered.

Most of them were from local news. KGRZ. KMSL.

From the corner of her eye, Stiles could spot a couple she recognized from Helena. One she thought might be from Bozeman.

Definitely no network coverage.

Given the amount of time she had to pull things together, that wasn't surprising. Was far from the point. The idea was simply to kick things off. To get the ball rolling so she could start garnering support.

In her experience, the most important thing in any instance such as this was to get out ahead on public sentiment. Turn them how she wanted right up front. Bend the truth if necessary, even do a bit of cajoling where she had to.

As her predecessor had drilled into her, it was far easier to apologize than ask permission.

The location of the impromptu gathering was one Stiles had filed away days before, when she met with Barb Rosenthal and Susan Moritz. It was the first time she had ever been inside the St. Michael's cafeteria, but the murals on the wall were unmistakable. Would make for the perfect backdrop. Add a certain level of gravitas to what she was about to do.

At just half past 8:00, the morning rush was still very much in progress. Scads of people were loading up on their morning caffeine, more still grabbing a late breakfast. Dressed in various shades of scrubs, they ran the gamut of covertly glancing over to turning and openly staring at the throng of interlopers among them.

Seeing the two groups sitting at attention, watching her come forward, almost brought a smile to Stiles's face. Warmed her from within.

This was her moment. The start of something she had been wanting to do for years. It didn't matter that she didn't yet have buy-in from Susan Moritz. That would come soon enough.

"Good morning, thank you all for being here on such short notice," she said. Using her courtroom voice, she walked directly to the head of the loose throng of people. Put her back a few inches away from the mural. Made sure she stood so the arched name of the hospital framed her perfectly.

As she did so, the reporters all leapt to attention and gathered round tight. Behind them, cameramen and interns jockeyed for the optimal viewing positions. Some stood on chairs or tables to get a better vantage. Held cameras or boom mics out before them.

It was just as perfect as Stiles had imagined it, the trepidations of McGrady be damned.

"The reason I asked you all here this morning is to share something that is often quite rare in this line of work – a bit of good news."

She paused there. Gave the obligatory smile, letting the cameras capture such a humanizing moment. Waited for a couple of chuckles from the reporters to pass.

"Six nights ago, a young cyclist was struck by an automobile on Brooks Avenue. The driver of the car had impaired vision and did not even slow as she hit this poor girl, a freshman at Sentinel High School."

Stiles knew that very little had been said about the incident up to this point. For many in the crowd, it was their first time about hearing it.

A few jaws dropped open as they scribbled down notes. Their faces took on the proper amount of solemnity as they waited for her to continue.

"I wish I could say it was only a minor collision," Stiles continued, "but unfortunately, it fractured the young girl's skull and put her into a coma."

Again, Stiles paused. Made sure the mood was just right.

So badly she wanted to say the name Mandy Moritz. Use a trick she often employed in front of juries. Personalize the events as much as possible.

Knew that doing such would be a step too far. Would earn an untold amount of wrath from the family that might undo whatever goodwill she managed to cull together.

"Last night, though, the young girl awoke, and I'm hearing this morn- ing, is expected to make a full and rapid recovery."

Each of the people that had offered faux concern a few moments before now offered the same in relief. Smiled. Nodded their heads. Stared at Stiles as if she herself was a doctor and had miraculously pulled the girl back from the brink.

Perfect.

In truth, she had not spoken to anybody that morning. She knew Mandy Moritz had woken up, but nothing beyond that.

Again, hardly the point.

Never would there be a better moment for her to act. The state legislature was already beginning to wind down. The girl was awake, but too battered to speak. It was all laid out before her. Everything could be connected from one dot to the next like a childhood drawing.

"And it is with that good fortune in mind that I would like to announce that as of today, the Missoula Prosecutor's Office will be taking an unusual step and introducing legislation to hopefully be considered by the state immediately."

Reaching into her bag, Stiles pulled out a sheaf of papers. Clutched them in her hand. Held them high above her head.

"This here is a proposal for a bill that will be the most aggressive step in protecting the rights of cyclists in our country's history."

As she spoke, the looks of joy retreated from the reporters, their expressions returning to those of serious news people as they took down notes, alternating glances between their pads and her.

"We live in Montana, in the vibrant and active city of Missoula, where we encourage residents to get outside, to enjoy nature's abundance, and to preserve it in any way we can.

"One of the clearest and most obvious ways of achieving that, of having a healthy populace and a cleaner environment, is through promoting bicycling. But the only way we can do that is if we can guarantee their safety in doing so."

Around the periphery of the room, Stiles could see that many of the hospital personal had stopped whatever they were doing. Had ceased making an attempt to get to their next destination and were even ignoring their coffee as they stood listening to her.

It was what she liked to call the *Gotcha!* moment. The point in time when she knew she had a jury, a courtroom, even a cafeteria full of people, right where she wanted them.

Everybody was leaning forward, aching to know what else she had to say. It was time to bring it home.

"Under this bill, no longer will a driver that strikes someone in a bike lane be swatted on the wrist, given the equivalent of misdemeanor assault."

She paused one last time. Drew in a deep breath. Prepared for the big finish.

"Last night we were lucky, but it could have been a whole lot worse. If something had gone terribly wrong and that poor girl had not woken up, we need to be able to ensure that justice will be done.

"For her, her family, and for untold others just like them."

CHAPTER TWENTY-NINE

Pittman lounged back in his chair. Welker opted to stand along the wall, coffee cup in one hand, other one shoved deep into the pocket of his slacks.

Just the two of them. No need to bring in Larkin for something he would clearly have no bearing on anyway.

Never before had Pittman seen Valerie Stiles. Didn't need to in order to already know exactly what her end goal was. Enough times over the years he had seen people just like her, practically salivating, their own self-interest on full display.

"Well then, this changes things," Pittman said. Left his voice free of inflection, allowing Welker to interpret as he wanted.

"Yeah," Welker agreed. "How do you see it?"

For a moment, Pittman gave no response. Allowed what little had been reported back from Telesco to fit in with what he had just heard from Stiles.

As far as he could tell, the two entities in Missoula were light years apart. One side was concerned with figuring out Kyla Wegman's visual woes. The other seemed wholly focused on bicyclist's rights, a foolish endeavor in any state, but a downright preposterous one in a place such as Montana.

"I can't imagine anybody going after bicycling rights if they knew we were involved," Pittman answered, leaving his response at that.

"Agreed."

"Makes you wonder what kind of show this woman would put on if she had any idea, though," Pittman added.

"Agreed," Welker said a second time. Glanced over and nodded grimly, driving home the point. "What's Telesco had to say?"

As the press conference on the screen wound down, Pittman pointed the remote at the screen. Left the image in place, but cut away the volume. Slid the implement across the table as Stiles continued to flounce around in silence before them.

"Nothing new," Pittman replied. "Looks like the attorney and his flunkey are making the rounds. Whatever Breslin told them clearly didn't satisfy and they're still out beating the bushes."

"Hmm," Welker replied. Paused for a moment. "Anything else?"

"No," Pittman replied.

He had been through Telesco's reports a dozen times already, had tried everything possible to impute even more into the meager information.

Come up woefully short in doing so.

"What do you think this means?" Welker asked, jutting his chin toward the screen. "Does it provide us enough cover to move on, or just buy us a window to lock down our interests before things really get out of hand?"

It took just an instant for Pittman to track what Welker was alluding to.

"Meaning should we call in our other guy, too?"

There was no audible response from Welker as he rotated his gaze toward Pittman, staring out through the thick lenses of his glasses.

This was how things usually went, at least back when they occurred with enough frequency for there to be a *usually*. Step one was to call in Telesco, have him do some tracking, maybe even employ some scare tactics when necessary.

When the situation didn't seem to call for such strong arming, it was turned over to their legal team. A corporate hotshot from Seattle that nobody could stand, but that served a vital purpose. Collected a hefty percentage of their annual operating costs for his services.

Calling him had been in the back of Pittman's mind for a couple of days. Rarely, if ever, was it something he wanted to do, but years of experience had shown him a certain pragmatism in keeping blood off their hands from time to time.

In Montana, there would always be a certain class of people that responded to nothing short of violence. They lived by a code pockmarked with shotguns and beer cans.

For them, Lon Telesco was a vital necessity.

People like Kyla Wegman, though, belonged to a different breed. They may not be high-end, but they operated within the constructs of the law in a manner that would never fully cooperate with such brutish tactics.

For them, nothing was more sacred than the legal system, nobody wielding more power than an attorney.

"Yeah, I think we've probably reached that point," Pittman said. Met Welker's gaze, both men standing in silence a moment, the enormous conference room that had once held meetings for dozens now reduced to just the two of them. "You?"

"I wouldn't have asked the question if I didn't already think so, too."

CHAPTER THIRTY

Folf.

Otherwise known as disc golf to the purists. A sport that managed to take Frisbee and golf and mash them together.

Could be played virtually anywhere. In city parks. On college campuses. Stretched across the breadth of Blue Mountain, outside of Missoula.

"Alright, who's my spotter here?"

It was a question, but Kade issued it to the Crew as a challenge. Held his arms out wide to either side. Gripped the rim of a bright blue driver disc in his right hand.

"Spotter?" Sage asked. "You mean when you go crashing into that first pine tree again?"

Behind her Drake and Ajax both chuckled. Said nothing.

"Hey, piss on you," Kade said. "Y'all are lucky that tree jumped out on the last hole or that would have been a hole-in-one. Put me so far ahead nobody would ever catch up."

"Catch up? Since when do we keep score in folf?" Sage asked. Twisted her face to match the tone of her question.

"Forget that," Drake said. "Didn't anybody else catch that quip about a tree jumping out at him?"

"Wait, was it the same one that kept getting him on the golf course last Friday?" Ajax asked.

"You know what, I bet it was," Drake said, picking up on the insinuation. Shook a finger at Ajax. "And the very one that occasionally trips him on skis, too."

Not to be outdone, Sage raised a hand. Covered her mouth. "Oh my God, my brother has a stalker."

"And it has nothing to do with some jilted skank he picked up downtown," Ajax added.

Drew more laughter from Drake and Sage.

"Piss on all of you," Kade repeated. Drew his right arm back. Took three shuffle steps and snapped his disc across his body.

From their vantage at the fifth tee box, the Crew could see the bright blue disc take off straight and true. Stand silhouetted perfectly against a slate gray sky, hanging for several long seconds.

Halfway through its flight, the right edge began to dip, pulling the path to the side.

"No," Kade said. Used his body language to try and redirect the trajectory. "No no no."

"Ah, hell," Ajax muttered.

"There it goes," Drake agreed.

Slicing badly, the disc hung for several more seconds. Disappeared into a thick pine grove off to the right of the fairway.

For a moment, nobody said anything, exchanging glances with one another. Waiting for whatever blame Kade was about to cast in their direction.

"One of you had better been spotting me," he finally said. Didn't bother to turn around and look.

Behind his back, Sage's eyes bulged.

Drake looked between her and Ajax. Mouthed the word, "Spotted?"

Saw the same expression on each of his friend's faces.

"Come on," Ajax finally relented. "I'll go help you look. That was too nice a disc to leave behind."

Breathing a sigh of relief that it wasn't his turn in the rotation to go with Kade, Drake dropped the discs he held in either hand to the ground. Folded his arms across his chest. Watched his friends go lumbering down the hillside.

Beside him, Sage dropped her discs as well. Walked over to the roughhewn bench sitting alongside the tee box and took a seat.

"Come on," she said. Patted the wood stripped smooth by the elements. "Might as well get comfortable, this could take a while."

A wry smile tugged at one corner of Drake's mouth as he paused a moment. Thought about the last time Kade sent one into the brush. At the half hour it had taken him to track it down.

Walked over and took a seat.

"Thanks for the head's up last night. Appreciated it."

"No problem," Sage said. Leaned over to the side. Bumped him with her shoulder. "That's what we do, remember?"

"True," Drake conceded. "Though it seems lately you guys are doing a lot more of it for me than the other way around."

For a moment, Sage considered the notion. Made a non-descript noise that relayed she was considering it.

"Meh, maybe, but I'm sure there'll come a point when you get us back. I mean, Lord knows with this group it's only a matter of time before one of us needs a white boy lawyer to help us out."

"Ha!" Drake replied, the response a natural reaction. "Just for the record, I'm not touching that one."

"Smart man," Sage said. Looked at him for a moment before leaning over and dropping her head against his shoulder. "How'd she take the news?"

A sharp intake of breath was Drake's first response. "Cried like a baby."

"Glad tears or sad tears?"

"I don't know," Drake answered. "I didn't stay on the line long enough to ask."

"Probably better that way," Sage agreed. "How'd it go with Melanie?"

The question raised Drake's eyebrows. After the news of Mandy Moritz waking the night before, he had almost forgotten about the conversation the previous afternoon, that Melanie was Dr. Westerman's first name.

"Interesting. Thank you for doing that, by the way."

"Interesting how?" Sage asked. Pretended not to hear the second half of the statement.

"Interesting in how starkly different her opinions seemed to be from the guy we met with in Anaconda."

A sharp snort caused Sage's head to rock an inch or two against Drake's shoulder. Using her shoulder, she pushed herself upright.

"You'll get that. No two doctors ever seem to see things the same way."

More than once, Drake had heard similar comments come from Sage. Knew it was something that drove her crazy, that she dealt with on an almost daily basis.

"Yeah, but on something that basic? Either what Kyla was describing is possible or it isn't. Yes or no. Black or white."

Another snort came from Sage. "Welcome to the world of medicine."

"And people say the law is ridiculous," Drake muttered.

Silence fell between them, the only sound a light morning breeze pushing through. Rattling the bare tree limbs above them. Carrying the scent of pine needles and a thin layer of dust with it.

In just a couple weeks, things would begin budding out. Spring runoff would cause the rivers and streams to swell. The first hatch of the year would bring out the caddis flies, push the trout into a frenzy.

For the time being, the world was at peace. Just beginning a slow and sleepy awakening from a long winter.

"So what now?" Sage asked. Turned to look at Drake's profile beside her.

"Now? Now I pray those two down there are better at finding answers than they are folf discs and we try to figure out which of the doctors was lying."

CHAPTER THIRTY-ONE

The first awakening was short lived. Long enough for the medical staff to go through their checklists. To remove a few of the myriad things attached to her, to connect a few different ones.

Just over an hour after opening her eyes, Mandy closed them again. This time of her own volition. Nothing resembling the comatose state she had been in for the previous several days. Much closer to a fitful sleep, a night punctuated by sharp intakes of breath and occasional muscle spasms.

A short burst of movement every so often.

Perched in her chair beside the bed, Susan watched it all until midnight, well after Ben had fallen asleep beside her.

Free from the duty of reading, of allowing her daughter to hear her voice, she finally allowed herself to sleep as well. Slouching down in the chair, she let her chin hit her chest.

Fell straight to black.

Such slumber was shattered several hours later, the morning rounds under way again. In one fell swoop, the doctor managed to wake all three members of the Moritz family at once. All smiles and optimism, he went through a few perfunctory exercises in checking over Mandy. Asked her a couple of questions, eliciting the first words from her in six days.

Vanished just as fast as he had arrived.

In his wake, the family was back together. Had their first chance to speak.

"Hey there," Susan opened. Still clutched her daughter's hand. Made no effort to hide the sheen of moisture covering her eyes.

"Hey," Mandy replied, her voice thick from going unused, fainter than usual. "Hey, Brother Bear."

A sheepish smile crossed Ben's face. "Hi."

"What happened?" Mandy asked. Seemed to recognize where they were, that she was the one lying in the bed.

"What do you remember?" Susan asked. Didn't want to force anything extra on her daughter that she didn't have to. Even less wanted to relive any of it herself.

Rolling her head back against her pillow, Mandy looked to the ceiling. Thought for a moment.

"I remember the softball game went into extra innings and I was rushing home, trying to make it back in time for dinner."

Susan felt her eyes slide closed. She had made such a big deal about the dinners, of having the kids be home in time to join her, that she had potentially caused all of this.

If she hadn't pressed so hard, maybe...

"Instead of going down to the corner of Arthur and taking the long way, I tried cutting across there by the Walgreen's," Mandy continued. "Almost made it, too."

Tears pooled at the bottom of Susan's eyes. She hadn't actually bore witness to the scene on Brooks a few nights before, but had pictured it a thousand times a day in her mind since.

The car stopped in the middle of the road, lights throwing out a bright cone. The broken body of her daughter sprawled in the middle of it.

"There weren't many cars out, and I thought maybe it would slow down once it saw me..."

She let her voice trail off there for a moment. Tears appeared to underscore her eyes as well.

Susan and Ben exchanged a glance. Neither dared speak.

"After we collided," Mandy said, "my leg felt like it was on fire. Like someone had jabbed a hot poker into my calf and left it there."

For an instant, Susan considered telling her that it was from a broken bone. That there was a walking cast covering the lower half of her leg.

Opted against it. There would be plenty of time for that later.

"The last thing I remember is hanging in the air. The sensation of being weightless, before everything cut to black."

Pinching her eyes shut tight, Susan felt the residual tears slide down her cheeks. Try as she might, she couldn't push away the image of her daughter hanging suspended in the air.

Landing in a crumpled heap.

"From then on, all I remember is the sound of your voice," Mandy said. Squeezed Susan's hand lightly.

"Yeah?" Susan asked.

"Yeah," Mandy replied. "At first it was light and faint. Far away, like I was underwater or something. After a while, it started to come into focus."

She paused there, returning her attention to the side of the bed.

"Were you reading *The Maze Runner* books to me?"

Unable to stop herself, Susan gasped out a laugh. Caused Ben to laugh beside her as well.

"Yeah," she admitted. "They told me to talk to you, and well, turns out I just didn't have all that much to say."

"Yeah, right," Ben chimed in, speaking for the first time, forcing all three to laugh again.

Without any of them realizing it, a shadow had passed into the doorway behind them. Stood watching the last few moments of their interaction. Raised a hand and tapped lightly against the wooden door, drawing their attention away from each other.

"Hey there," Barb Rosenthal said. Kept her voice low, wore her best maternal smile.

Touched Ben on the shoulder as she walked to the foot of the bed to stare down at Mandy. "Good to see you up and awake."

"Thank you," Mandy said. Offered nothing more. Seemed a bit confused by the woman she barely knew standing there.

How Rosenthal continued to gain access to the Critical Care Unit, Susan could only guess at.

"I'm so sorry to interrupt," Rosenthal said, "especially at a time like this, but I wanted you to know I had nothing to do with it."

Instinctively, the smile bled from Susan's face. Her stomach roiled into a knot as she stared at Rosenthal. Tried to recall what she might be alluding to.

Came back with nothing.

"Nothing to do with what?"

For a moment there was no response as Rosenthal stared at her, letting her gaze trace over Susan's features. Seemed to be measuring if Susan was being straight with her or trying to save face in front of the kids.

"The press conference this morning," Rosenthal said. "Valerie Stiles. Again, it wasn't me. I would have said something if I'd known."

The roiling in Susan's stomach intensified as she stared at her boss. Felt a healthy dose of dread well up inside as well.

"You didn't know," Rosenthal said.

"No," Susan said. Shook her head and motioned to Mandy. "Been a little busy here."

Placed just a tiny bit of scorn in her voice.

"Right," Rosenthal said, "but with it being right down the hall, I thought word might have gotten up here to you."

It took a moment for things to compute. For what Rosenthal was saying to connect in Susan's mind.

"*What?*" she asked, the edge in her voice rising a bit higher.

"Yeah," Rosenthal replied. "She held it right in the cafeteria. Stood in front of the St. Michael's mural, drew in quite a crowd, too. Cameras ate it up."

In a matter of seconds, the dread within Susan vanished, replaced by unbridled vitriol. An unparalleled desire to protect her own.

"Did she..." Susan asked. Flicked her gaze to Mandy. Let her question be known without stating as much.

"No," Rosenthal said. "Not by name, anyway."

Left it there. Let Susan infer the remainder.

Valerie Stiles had not mentioned them specifically. Had still used the incident to incite sympathy, to attempt to motivate public action.

"There's no way," Susan said. Was careful to mince her words, no matter how badly she wanted to let the anger come spilling out.

Her daughter would not be a billboard for some self-motivated crusade.

"Not now. Not ever."

CHAPTER THIRTY-TWO

Dripping.

Sopping.

Kyla Wegman was soaking wet, just a few seconds removed from the shower when the first round of knocking sounded at the front door. Made her jump several inches. Almost sent her toppling over on the wet porcelain of her tub.

On instinct, Kyla felt heart palpitations begin. Felt for certain that the fear she had been with all night was being confirmed. That a mistake had been made and she would have to return to jail.

Grabbing a towel from the rack on the wall, Kyla wrapped it around herself. Let her long hair lay wet against her back. Stood completely silent in the shower.

Hoped the visitor would figure her gone and leave.

Had that thought dashed a moment later by a second round of knocking. No more forceful than the time before, but no less, either.

Whoever it was had no intention of leaving any time soon.

"Just a minute!" Kyla called. Stepped from the shower. Grabbed her robe from the back of the bathroom door and covered herself, cinching it shut across her stomach. Wrapped the towel around her head and left it piled high.

Not the way she would have preferred to meet someone - especially an officer of the law - but it still seemed better than leaving them standing outside all morning.

The previous night had been hard. Long. After Drake had called, she had spent more than an hour crying. Eventually attempted to eat, but found she didn't have the stomach for it.

Tried watching television. Couldn't find the required attention span to pull it off.

Shortly before midnight, she had tried retiring to bed. Found her mattress a welcome change from the brick she'd been sleeping on the last few nights, but still couldn't find rest.

Not until a swallow of the cheap wine she had bought to celebrate her divorce but never actually drank went down was she able to sleep in the slightest. A choppy, fitful rest that barely replenished anything followed by a rough morning, the alcohol having far more effect than any bits of sleep.

By the time the first few streaks of light appeared through her bedroom window, she gave up on it for good. Laced on her running shoes. Took an extra-long run, pushing past the lactic acid, past the icy burn along the back of her throat.

Managed to sweat out the booze in her system. Hopefully any moisture that might try to later turn up as tears.

Despite the hour now fast approaching noon, the interior of her apartment was mostly dark. Blinds pulled. Lights off. Making a haphazard line between them, Kyla turned on as many as she could. Stopped by the coffee table and grabbed up the bottle of wine. Capped it and placed it out of sight.

Noticed the scent of it in the air. Wished there was something she could do to mask it.

A third round of knocking sounded out against the front door, the thin wooden panel rattling slightly, pulling any previous thoughts from mind.

Again feeling the dread rise within her, Kyla crossed over to the small linoleum foyer and opened the door. Expected to find the same detective she had spoken with a few times over the weekend standing before her.

At the very least, someone in a uniform.

Instead found a man she was quite certain she had never seen in her life. Appearing to be close to 50 years in age, he stood several feet back from the door. Hands clasped before him. Silver hair parted to the side. Gray two-button suit. White shirt. Diagonal striped tie. Overly wide smile.

"Uh, can I help you?" Kyla asked. Kept one shoulder pressed against the doorframe. Used her opposite hand to hold the door tight against the other.

"Hi," the man said. Voice that sounded artificially lowered so as to not sound imposing. "I'm looking for Kyla Wegman."

"I'm Kyla Wegman," Kyla offered, glancing to the driveway to see a black BMW parked behind her Honda.

Definitely not law enforcement in any way.

"Can I help you?"

"Yes," the man said. Seemed to produce a business card from nowhere and extend it toward her. "My name is Dan Harmon and I am an attorney. I was hoping we might be able to speak for a moment."

The dread within Kyla shifted. No longer was it fear that she might have to go back to jail. Now it was that she might be soon going back to court.

The girl had been awake for barely 12 hours. Already there was an attorney at her door. She wasn't entirely sure how the legal process worked, having only one botched divorce as a basis, but knew that anything moving that fast couldn't be good.

"Uh, yeah," Kyla said. "I guess."

No part of her wanted to invite the man into her home. Not with her dressed in a bathrobe. Definitely not with the place smelling of alcohol, especially given the nature of what had happened.

"Come on in."

Pushing the door open a few inches, Kyla stepped back and allowed Harmon to enter before closing the door behind him.

"If you'll give me just a couple of minutes, I'd like to go get dressed. I'm sorry, you just caught me getting out of the shower."

With his back to her, Kyla could see Harmon assessing her home. The aging couch and recliner that had come furnished with the place. Ditto for the scratched and nicked coffee table.

Underfoot, the thin blue carpet held a few stains that Kyla figured had been there since before she was born.

No pictures of any kind. No personal touches to speak of.

"Certainly," Harmon said. Whirled to face her, the same plastic smile in place. "I'm sorry to have come so early."

For a moment, Kyla considered correcting him. Pointing out she had been awake for hours, that she had just gotten back from a run.

Instead, she decided against it. Offered only a nod and retreated to her bedroom. Kicked her sweaty running gear into the corner. Grabbed her cellphone up from the nightstand and tapped out a quick message.

Attorney just showed up at my front door.

She wasn't sure if the number she had for Drake could even receive text messages, but she sent it anyway. Pulled on jeans and a Montana Tech sweatshirt. Ran her fingers through her hair before letting it fall wet around her shoulders.

Emerged less than five minutes later to find Harmon standing in front of her couch in the same position he had assumed on her porch - hands clasped before him, smile in place.

"Sorry about that," Kyla said. Motioned to the sofa. "Please, sit."

"Not a problem," Harmon said. Lowered himself to the edge of the couch. Watched as Kyla took a seat on a wooden rocking chair across from him.

"So, what is this about?" Kyla asked.

Already she knew the answer, but had to ask the question anyway, trying to give the appearance that her insides weren't squeezed into a tight ball.

That anxiety wasn't threatening to choke her from within.

Across from her, the smile faded for the first time since arrival.

"I was contacted in regards to what happened the other night," Harmon replied. "I assume you know what I'm alluding to."

Her voice catching in her throat, Kyla managed to nod once.

Said nothing.

"Right," Harmon said. "I thought you might. And I am here to let you know how serious we are taking this matter, and how much we are willing to compensate you to make it go away."

Gripped with fear, worry, it took a full moment for Kyla to realize what he had said. Another for the words to find their way in, to actually bear recognition.

Once they did, there was no stopping the confusion that flooded in right behind it.

"I'm sorry, who did you say you work for again?"

CHAPTER THIRTY-THREE

Drake was seated at his desk in the clinic office when the text came in. Responding immediately, he told Kyla to stall.

He was on his way.

All told, it took him 11 minutes to get from that chair to standing on Kyla's front porch. Despite that, there was only a single dented Honda in the driveway when he arrived, no other signs of life anywhere nearby.

The sound of his knock barely had time to fade away before Kyla pulled the door open. Stood before him in bare feet, her hair wet, wearing jeans and a hooded sweatshirt.

A look of pure confusion on her face

"Sorry," she said by way of greeting, motioning for him to enter. "I texted you and left my phone in the bedroom. Just saw your reply."

"No worries," Drake said. Knew there was plenty more for both of them to chew on without debating text message etiquette. "They're gone already?"

"Yeah," Kyla said. Extended a hand toward a threadbare sofa. "Have a seat."

Drake could detect just the slightest twinge of something in her voice. A bit of reluctance that suggested she was embarrassed by her surroundings.

He considered putting her concerns at bay. Commenting it was a nice place as he sat down. Opted against mentioning anything at all and took up a post on the sofa, extending one arm along the back of it.

"Just like that?" Drake said. "They showed up here, wanted to talk, and then vanished?"

"Yeah," Kyla repeated. Nodded. "Very strange. He was very relaxed at first, but halfway through his phone buzzed. After that, he couldn't get out of here fast enough. Basically cut the conversation off and ran."

The same look of confusion that was on Kyla's face earlier found its way to Drake. Settled as he processed what she'd said.

"Okay," he finally managed. "Walk me through it. Guy shows up..."

"Right. I was in the shower, heard somebody knocking. Scared me to death, thought for sure it was the cops coming to take me back to jail."

Drake nodded. There was no reason for her to have such a concern, but after four days in lockup, he couldn't fault her for having it.

"But when I got to the door, it was some older guy in a suit, smiling ear to ear."

Warning lights began to flash in Drake's mind. He decided to keep them at bay for a few moments more, to hear Kyla out first.

"Said he was an attorney, asked if we could talk," Kyla continued. "I figured with everything that happened, it made sense, so I told him to have a seat and went to get dressed. That's when I texted you."

"Mhmm," Drake said, a simple prompt for her to continue.

"When I came back out, I asked what it was about, and he told me it was concerning the other night."

There she paused, the perplexed look returning, now more pronounced than ever.

"Which is when he hit me with something I wasn't expecting. Started talking about a settlement."

"A settlement?" Drake said. Snapped his arm up off the back of the sofa. Leaned forward and rested his elbows on his knees. "Already? The girl just woke up last night."

"Right," Kyla said. "That's exactly what I said. Turns out the guy wasn't with the girl's family at all."

Drake could feel his brows come together as he stared at Kyla. Waited for her to continue. Said nothing.

"I guess he had heard about my claims that I couldn't see," Kyla said. "Told me he was authorized to pay me up to $25,000 to never mention it again."

Drake's mouth dropped open and his eyes bulged, three concentric circles evenly spaced across his face. For a moment he remained like that before working his jaw up and down twice. Trying to force his brain to compute what he was being told.

"Authorized by who?"

"I don't know," Kyla said. "That's about the time he jumped up and ran off. Told me the number on his card was good day or night."

"And that's it?"

"And that the offer was on the table for 48 hours."

Running a hand back over his head, Drake glanced down to the floor. Tried to make sense of the damnable information he'd just been handed.

"What happens after 48 hours?"

"I don't know," Kyla whispered. "He didn't say."

The number of things that had just been mentioned that simply didn't fit was almost too numerous to count. Where to even begin poking seemed a daunting task to say the least.

"Alright," Drake said. Pushed out a long sigh. "I admit I haven't been practicing very long, but nothing that just happened makes a lick of sense."

Across from him Kyla nodded. Remained silent.

"So I'm going to start right at the beginning," Drake said. "How did this guy know where you lived?"

A flash of horror passed over Kyla's face. It was clear she had not yet considered the notion.

"Oh, my God. I have no idea. I guess because at first I thought he was with law enforcement..."

Her voice trailed off. Wide eyes stared back at Drake.

"Okay, moving on," Drake said. Did not want to linger on that too long. Didn't want her fear to suddenly stop her from being able to tell him about the meeting.

"If he wasn't with the girl, who did he represent?" Drake asked.

This moved her past the fear just a bit.

"You know, I don't remember. He might have said it and I'm blanking, but I can't be sure."

Somehow, Drake had expected such an answer.

"Okay," Drake said. Kept moving forward. "How did he hear about your claims? I'm guessing outside of the police and me, you haven't told anybody else?"

"I haven't even talked to anybody else."

"Not your family?" Drake said.

"Would you call home and tell them you spent the weekend in jail?" Kyla countered.

For less than a second Drake couldn't help but think there was nothing more he would rather do, just to have the option to call home, to hear his parent's voices.

Pushed it aside just as fast.

Kyla didn't know, and it certainly wasn't the time to tell her.

"Good point," he conceded. "And $25,000? To never mention it again? What's that all about?"

At this point, Drake knew he was merely thinking out loud. Trying to make sense of an awkward situation. To put pieces into place.

Try as he might, nothing seemed to be coming together.

"You mentioned a card," he said.

Kyla extracted it from the front pouch of her hoodie. Held it between her index and middle finger and extended it to him.

Raising his backside from the couch, Drake accepted it. Settled back and looked down at the thick stock paper in his hand.

Plain white, with black letters.

"Dan Harmon," Drake said aloud, trying to place it. "Quincel & Harmon."

Came back with nothing.

"Address is listed as Anaconda. You ever heard of them?"

"No," Kyla said. "And believe me, in a town like Anaconda, I would have seen this guy before."

"Meaning?"

"Meaning, he was wearing a suit and drove a BMW. Anaconda isn't like Missoula or Bozeman. People like that don't just exist over there, at least not without being noticed."

"Hmm," Drake said. Accepted her reasoning. Tapped the card against his palm.

Right now, the number of questions staring at them was piling up too fast. Half a day ago, the biggest concern was waiting to see if the girl would wake up, whether or not her family would press for an assault charge.

Now there was somebody showing up unannounced and making thinly veiled threats. Offering gobs of cash to try and stifle something that was basically a non-starter anyway.

None of it made sense. If an attorney from the girl's family had shown, if somebody from the prosecutor's office had called on her, if a process server had shown up to deliver paperwork, all of that would fit. It would comport with how proceedings were handled.

This was another beast entirely.

Drake shook his head. Right now, he was just creating more questions. He needed to get somewhere he could start finding some answers.

Or at least call on some people to help find them.

"Come on," he said. Pushed himself up from the couch. "Put some shoes on."

"Where are we going?" Kyla asked. Shot straight up out of the chair across from Drake.

"To go figure out who the hell Dan Harmon is, who he really works for, and why they're willing to give you so much money not to mention something they shouldn't know about to begin with."

CHAPTER THIRTY-FOUR

Telesco had been on Drake Bell since he left the house that morning.

In place well before the sun came up, he was parked down the street as Bell emerged with a bulldog at half past 6:00. Stood in the front yard with a plume of white rising with each breath and waited for the animal to finish its business.

Was still parked there a half hour later when he and a young black male with braids climbed into his truck and drove across town. Met up with a girl and the same guy he'd been at the optometrist's office with the day before.

From there he had cut Bell loose for a while. Knew that although his truck was built to be inconspicuous, even it would be noticed after a while.

Went looking for breakfast.

Coffee.

Why they had felt he needed to be in place so early, Telesco could only guess at. Who they honestly believed Bell would be meeting with at such an ungodly hour was an even greater mystery.

If there was anything Telesco had come to know in his side venture for the company, it was that very rarely did white collar types ever venture beyond business hours.

An hour after leaving them at Blue Mountain, Telesco parked himself back at the end of the street. Armed with a bacon, egg, and cheese sandwich and a large mocha, shielded by his darkened windows, he could have waited for days.

Didn't need nearly that long.

Forty-eight minutes after he was back in position, the truck returned and both men piled out. A few minutes later was another trip around the yard with the dog.

A few more and he was headed downtown, pulling up in front of a plain office building painted white. **Missoula Legal Services** stenciled on the windows. Blinds pulled low behind it.

There he sat for more than two hours before getting a text message.

Approaching the girl's house now. Keep me posted. – Harmon.

The man's habit of using all capital letters, the text message equivalent of screaming, infuriated Telesco. The fact that he insisted on signing each one even more so.

The ultimate insult was the fact that he was fully aware of both and kept doing them anyway.

Seeing the message pop up on his screen, Telesco wagged his middle finger at it. Went ahead and started the truck. Knew that Bell would probably be emerging soon and did not want to give away his position by drawing attention to the sound of an engine turning over.

Parked on a diagonal facing the opposite direction, the nose of his truck was aimed at a branch of the Bank of the Rockies. Using his rearview mirror, he kept a watch on the office across the street. Counted seconds in his head. Made it as far 114 before the front door burst open and Bell emerged, moving fast.

"Showtime," Telesco muttered. Waited for Bell to climb in his truck and begin moving. Pulled the phone over onto his lap and tapped out a quick response.

Bell on the run. Move your ass. – Telesco.

The font and the closing were both meant to make a point.

He had a feeling neither would actually manage to pull it off.

Easing his truck out into traffic, Telesco fell in well back from Bell. He already knew where he was going, had no need to keep him in direct sight.

Circling away from the main thoroughfares, he took a dog-legged route to the home of Kyla Wegman. Arrived to find Harmon already gone, Bell standing on the front porch.

Without glancing over, Telesco drove past the house. Made a loop around the block. Took up a position as far away as possible, the front of Wegman's place just barely visible through a sliver of a sightline.

Again, the phone beside him buzzed.

You in position? – Harmon.

Telesco didn't bother to respond.

CHAPTER THIRTY-FIVE

"Hello? Everybody decent?"

Drake stood just inside the front door. Slid his shoes from his feet and waited for a response. Heard the television sound cut out.

"Depends on your definition of decent," Ajax's voice called.

A knowing smile pulled at one side of Drake's mouth, causing him to glance over to see a clearly confused Kyla beside him. A moment later, the sound of toenails prattling against hardwood floor could be heard preceding the arrival of Suzy Q, 52 pounds of jowls and affection wrapped in a bundle of white and brindle fur.

Blessed with a soundtrack that included bodily noises of every kind.

Bending at the knees, Drake squatted and greeted his girl with their usual ritual. Dug at the loose skin between her ears. Behind her neck. Around her haunches.

"Miss Kyla, this is Suzy Q, or just Q for short."

The same look that seemed to settle on most people's - especially female's - faces fell over Kyla's features. Stayed there as she folded herself in half at the waist, reached out and ran her hand along Q's back.

"Oh no," Drake said, continuing to work her over. "You've got to get in there. Really move some stuff around."

The comment drew a chuckle from Kyla. Caused her to flex her fingers and begin digging with aplomb, Q's entire body wiggling with delight.

Drake left them to it just inside the door and made his way down the hallway. Entered the living room to find Ajax back in front of the TV, a muted cityscape on the screen, a handful of printouts scattered on the floor around him.

"What's up?" Ajax said. Looked up to Drake, to Q and Kyla coming down the hallway behind him.

"Oh," he said. Eyes and mouth both formed into momentary circles. Found their original shape again just as fast. "Hello."

"Hi there," Kyla said. Waved.

"Adam Jackson, call me Ajax." Stepped forward and extended a hand across the sofa. Shook and stepped back. "My apologies for the state of the place. If I'd known we were having company..."

"Oh, please," Kyla said. Again waved a hand. "Kyla Wegman, nice to meet you."

From the looks of things, the papers on the floor were the only items out of place in the house. Most people assumed that a home for two bachelors and a dog would resemble little more than a glorified frat house.

Realized within seconds how wrong they were.

The combination of Ajax's video game design and Drake's inheritance meant both had ample funds, had been able to furnish the place in a way most people in their early 20s couldn't.

The fact that both were borderline OCD when it came to cleanliness didn't hurt either.

"I didn't know," Drake said. "Otherwise I would have before I left this morning."

Circling around the far end of the couch, Drake lowered himself down into it. Allowed the overstuffed leather cushions to conform around his legs. Motioned for Kyla to do the same.

Across from them, Ajax left the game up on screen. Dropped down into his usual spot in the chair positioned perpendicular to both the couch and television.

"Ajax designs video games," Drake said, motioning to the screen. "If you're into gaming at all, the odds are you've played at least a couple of his creations before."

"Oh," Kyla said, raising her head a few inches in understanding. "Impressive."

"Thank you," Ajax said. Bowed the top of his head just slightly and extended a finger toward the screen. "Apparently, the big thing with younger kids these days is *Minecraft*. These guys are willing to pay top dollar for it, but it is killing me."

"Tough?" Drake asked.

Never before had he seen anything his friend couldn't figure out within record time when it came to design. It was why so many people flew to their remote corner of Montana for his services.

"Boring," Ajax said. "What you see here is basically all there is. A lot of world building. Not much else."

Raising his eyebrows in concession, Drake couldn't help but agree. Most of the stuff Ajax worked on usually included zombies. MMA. Assassins.

This was a far, far cry from any of that.

Leaning back in his seat, Drake fished Harmon's business card out of his pocket. Rose and duckwalked a few feet to the side. Passed it across to Ajax.

"If you wouldn't mind taking a break then, we have something we could certainly use your help on. Be glad to match whatever rate these guys are giving you for it."

"No, you wouldn't," Ajax said. No hint of arrogance, merely a simple statement.

What the exact figure was, Drake could only guess at. Though he thought he had a ballpark idea, he must have been woefully short of the actual number.

"Dan Harmon, Quincel & Harmon, Anaconda," Ajax read aloud. "Who is he?"

"That's what we're hoping you could help us with," Drake replied. "Kyla here has lived in Anaconda her whole life, says she's never seen the guy. We did a Google search on her phone on the way over. Very basic website that told us nothing."

"What about the address?" Ajax asked.

"Given as 905 Kennedy Lane," Drake said. "Which is odd, considering the highest number on that street is 317."

"Huh," Ajax said. Pushed himself up from his chair. Walked to the workstation he had carved out from part of the dining room. "Let's take a look."

Using his chin, Drake motioned for Kyla to follow. Rose from the couch and walked over. Folded his arms and stood behind Ajax as he plopped down into his desk chair, calling the bank of monitors to life before him.

Trusting what he had already been told about a basic web search, Ajax started with the Anaconda Chamber of Commerce.

Found no mention of Quincel & Harmon.

Moved on to the Better Business Bureau.

Again, discovered nothing.

"Okay," Ajax said. Laced his fingers before him. Folded them back and extended his arms, several popping loudly. "How off-the-books are we wanting to go here?"

"Everything short of illegal," Drake said. Was not about to ask his friend to do anything that could get him in trouble or to go digging anywhere that might bring more concern down on Kyla.

"Aye aye," Ajax said. Started in the state tax records. Scrolled through several screens. Pulled up a spreadsheet and moved down through it.

"Okay, whoever they are definitely didn't pay state taxes last year, or the year before that," Ajax said.

"Meaning they are brand new?" Drake asked.

"Doubtful," Ajax said, "but theoretically possible. Did their website happen to mention how long they had been in business?"

Glancing to Kyla, Drake remained silent.

"No," Kyla said. "Not that I saw, anyway."

"Hmm," Ajax said. Paused. "That would leave us with looking for federal tax returns, but doing that would violate your everything-short-of-legal mandate."

"Right," Drake said. Raised one hand to his mouth and began to gnaw on a thumbnail. "What about the bar association?"

"Good idea," Ajax said. Went back to tapping on the keys, stopping a moment later. "Nothing for a Quincel & Harmon, or just a Dan Harmon, there either."

"Damn it," Drake muttered. Glanced over to Kyla. Could see the fearful expression from earlier returning to her face.

"Who the heck was that guy?" she whispered. "And how did he find my house? Oh God, I even let him inside."

"Easy now," Drake said. Extended a hand and rested it on her shoulder. "Maybe he really is an attorney, he's just barred somewhere else. Corporate counsel of some sort."

Pulled his hand back. Resumed the earlier stance. Thought some more.

"Ajax, can you dig around and see who might have that kind of juice in Anaconda?"

The look on his friend's face told him he was offended that the question had even been asked.

CHAPTER THIRTY-SIX

Bear McGrady could tell that Barb Rosenthal was not pleased.

Actually, based on the decibel of her breathing and the look on her face, she looked to be closer to irate.

As such, he kept his gaze averted. Stared at the surface of the small round table between them. Said nothing.

The meeting was one that had been called around mid-morning. It had come under the official designation of the public defender's office, something that was unusual, but not unheard of. Without thinking, he had accepted the invitation, only later realizing what it was most likely meant to be.

How awkward it could turn out.

Every part of him wanted to tell Rosenthal that the press conference that morning was not his idea. That he had attempted to dissuade Stiles right up until the moment she set foot in front of the cameras. Had earned himself a fierce case of stink-eye for his efforts.

He didn't, though. Instead, he sat at the table in the plain, tiny ante-room of the courthouse. Tucked away on the third floor, it was reserved exclusively for gatherings such as this.

Quick side conversations between opposing counsel or a brief moment to prep a witness.

The walls were barren, as was the table, giving McGrady nothing to focus his attention on. No sounds to mask the angry breathing of the woman beside him.

Six minutes after the agreed-to meeting time, the lone door burst open. Through it spilled Valeria Stiles, briefcase in one hand, bag looped over her opposite arm. A look on her face that said she would rather be anywhere else in the world.

As she entered and saw the two people in the room, McGrady noticed her cast a glance over her shoulder. Look to the door, as if she might bolt at any moment. Ultimately think better of it and drop into the closest chair, letting items fall to the floor beside her.

"I have 10 minutes," she said in greeting. "My son needs to be picked up at soccer practice."

"And your kids are the only ones that matter, right?" Rosenthal said.

McGrady felt his eyes grow wide. He had known since the moment he sat down that this was going to be uncomfortable. Had no idea it would be openly confrontational.

"What the hell is that supposed to mean?" Stiles said. Sat frozen in her seat. Locked her best glower in place.

As an officer of the law, McGrady had seen the best and worst of both women. Each had a distinctive style, could be nothing short of vicious in the courtroom when they needed to be. Already, though, he could tell that this was something much deeper than that. Just one exchange, and it was clear what the underlying current was.

Personal.

"Just what I said," Rosenthal replied. "You know damned well Susan Moritz told you her daughter would not be a poster child for your personal crusade.

"So what do you do? Parade everybody down there 12 hours after she wakes up and hold a damn press conference two floors down from the poor girl."

"Oh, don't *poor girl* me," Stiles retorted. Let the sour expression on her face relay exactly what she thought of the conversation. "It's not like I even used her name."

"And that makes it better?" Rosenthal fired back. "You gave so many details, anybody with half a brain knows who you're talking about."

Sitting between them, McGrady watched the interaction like a spectator sitting center court at a tennis match. Careful not to be openly staring, he moved only his eyes, taking in everything before him.

To his right was Rosenthal. It was clear she was protecting one of her own, carrying the mantle for the Moritz family.

Across from her sat Stiles, trying to do the same for hers.

There was no way things wouldn't end ugly.

"Well, I had to get my point across," Stiles said.

"And what point is that?" Rosenthal asked. "That you're still carrying a personal grudge to the point you'd exploit a 14-year-old to get what you want?"

"I didn't exploit anybody," Stiles said. Leaned forward a few inches over the table. "And even if I did, that's the only way things get done in this state and we both know it."

Across from her Rosenthal tossed both hands into the air, rocking back in her seat. "Do *not* for one second pretend this is about the state or good policy or any of your other stumping points. This is about you getting even for something that happened years ago."

"So what if it is?" Stiles fired back. "Are you trying to say that my husband is less important than some girl? That I shouldn't be concerned and wanting to fight for him?"

"No," Rosenthal said. "I'm saying your husband is a grown man and can fight for himself, but you knew that wouldn't get it done. Nobody cared about helping the rich white guy that one day a week left his Mercedes sitting at home and rode a $5,000 bike to work.

"So you had to wait until a young girl got hit so she could do your bidding."

Butterflies ran through McGrady's stomach and up into his chest. Not one word of what Barb Rosenthal had just said was wrong, wasn't something he himself hadn't thought in the preceding days.

Never, ever would have been able to say out loud.

To his left, he could see blood climb the length of Stiles's face. See her right hand ball itself up tight, her entire upper body quivering as if she might fly across the desk at any point.

"You," she hissed, pushing the word out through gritted teeth, "are nothing more than a God damn public defender and I do not have to answer to you, or the Moritz family.

"This is happening, whether you want it to or not."

Equal venom appeared in Rosenthal as she matched the stance, McGrady positioning himself in case he needed to jump in and separate the two women at any moment.

"Then you go in knowing we, *I*, will be publicly, audibly, opposing you every step of the way."

CHAPTER THIRTY-SEVEN

Zero.

Nada.

Nothing that jumped off the page. Drew a red line around itself. Garnered attention in any way.

Drake had pulled over a pair of dining room chairs and set them up behind Ajax. He was positioned over one shoulder, watching the man work. Kyla was stationed behind the other.

No one said much of anything as Ajax dug through every online directory and repository accessible to the public. More than a couple that weren't.

"I don't know what to tell you," Ajax said. Blew out a sigh and ran both hands over his face.

"Looks like your standard Montana small town. You've got the hospital as the major employer, grocery stores and banks behind that. Lot of small and private businesses filling in the gaps."

Drake drew his mouth into a tight line. Nodded grimly.

The entire time he had been watching Ajax work, he had hoped something would pop out, grabbing their attention. Giving them a clear heading to pursue.

"That sound about right?" he asked, shifting his attention to Kyla.

"Yeah," she said, shrugging with one shoulder. "I mean, my ex-husband's family owned a small construction outfit. Most of our friends either worked with it or on some other private job."

Leaning back in his chair, Drake ran a hand over his scalp. Felt the blonde hairs fold back under his palm.

"Certainly nothing that would need to keep somebody like Dan Harmon – or whoever he is – on the payroll."

"Or would be able to offer that kind of cash payout," Ajax said. "You saw the state tax returns. $25,000 is the better part of a year's income for a lot of these businesses."

Drake nodded. In Missoula, the median income was just a shade higher than that. There wouldn't be but a precious few that could even consider having that kind of money around.

And Missoula was a lot bigger than Anaconda.

For a moment he fell silent, thinking of what little experience he had with the town. Sitting right along I-90, he had driven by it at least 100 times over the years.

Trips to Yellowstone. Bozeman. Even a half dozen to Butte for a case months before.

Serving as the only major east-west thoroughfare of the state, there was no way to get across without using the interstate. No way to be on the interstate without seeing...

"The smelter," Drake said, things popping into place in his mind, drawing the attention of both Ajax and Kyla at once. "From the old copper operation."

"Didn't see anything about it in the tax records," Ajax said.

"And that hasn't been in operation for years," Kyla added. "Like, before I was born."

"That would explain the tax records," Drake said. Flicked his gaze to Ajax. "You still have to file if you have no income..."

"But not if you no longer technically exist," Ajax said. Picked up exactly where Drake was taking things.

Performing one of the most low-tech moves Drake had ever witnessed, Ajax opened a simple internet search browser and entered the Anaconda smelter. Was immediately hit with a bank of photos, all of the same dingy smokestack they had seen untold times before, each with the same cloudy gray backdrop.

Scrolling down, Ajax clicked on the first entry in the list. Gave a quick glance over the offering. Backed out and went to the second one. Sat and read in silence, Drake and Kyla both leaning in behind him.

"This is just covering the stack," Ajax said. His voice took on a detached tenor as he read. "Stands 585 feet tall, was the largest chimney in the world for almost 20 years, remained even after the rest of the smelter was demolished in 1981."

Moving to the bottom of the page, Ajax moved the cursor over a host of hyperlinks. Saw them light up under the tip of the small white arrow. Clicked on the first one.

"Here we go," he whispered.

Silence enveloped the group as Ajax spread the webpage over a pair of monitors aligned vertically. Enlarged the font so all three could read.

His gaze dancing over the page, Drake picked out the high points of the backstory.

The operation in Anaconda began in the late-1800's when outside investors tried to take advantage of the mining profits that were being enjoyed elsewhere throughout Montana.

Gold. Silver.

Struck pay dirt when they discovered major deposits of copper buried in the western part of the state.

Almost instantly, a boon pushed those investors to the status of magnates. Allowed them to buy up neighboring mines. Form a conglomerate and hire workers by the hundreds.

The largest deposit was found in Butte. Took a very small, very poor town and changed its trajectory overnight. So much so it quickly earned the moniker "The Richest Hill on Earth."

Welcomed the turn of the 20th century as the largest copper-producing mine in the world.

For a moment, Drake thought back to his previous trips to Butte. To seeing the enormous Berkeley Pit, now little more than a gaping maw, an eyesore with backfilled water so toxic it threatened the very existence of the town.

Shook his head. Went back to reading.

Through the years, the operation went through the predictable life cycles that come with the benefit of hindsight.

Purposeful stock manipulation during the Roaring '20s. A drop to coincide with the Depression in the '30s. An equally strong surge back to prominence during WWII, the need for copper bullet casings rising through the roof. Another plummet in the '50s as demand went down and mining costs continued to increase.

Skipping ahead, Drake cut to the end of the narrative. Saw that the entire operation was bought out by something called the Western Pacific Copper Company in 1977.

Operating under the name WEPCO, they had no idea what they were doing. Managed to take a mine that had produced $300 billion in copper in its lifetime and have it completely inoperable within only four years.

A low whistle slid from Ajax, Drake guessing he was reading through the same section he was.

"Scroll down some," Drake said. Watched as Ajax pushed them a bit further down the page, and continued reading.

Soon after the closing of the mine, WEPCO discovered their problems were just beginning. Decades of mining and smelting had annihilated the land and water of the Clark Fork River basin. Rendered it the largest Superfund site in the country, replete with chemical wastes that were beyond toxic.

Cadmium. Lead. Zinc. Arsenic.

The article from there became a bit thin on details. Pointed out that WEPCO had thus far spent untold sums of money on clean-up, but a great deal more remained to be done.

"We good?" Ajax asked, his voice a dead monotone that indicated his reaction was much the same as Drake's.

Just reading the backstory was enough to make a person feel dirty. Want to go take a hot shower. To never, ever set foot in Butte or Anaconda again.

Certainly never eat or drink anything caught or cooked there.

Moving back out into the search engine, Ajax moved down a bit further. Started getting into a random amalgam of newspaper stories. Clicked on one, the group quickly glancing through it.

"Black Monday," Drake read aloud. "In 1980, the smelting operation was immediately suspended due to the inability of the mine to keep up with increased demands by state and federal environmental agencies."

"In one day," Kyla whispered, "1,200 people lost their jobs. The town still hasn't recovered."

"Damn," Drake whispered. Watched as Ajax backed out before thinking better of it and closing the window entirely.

They had what they needed.

"Okay," Drake said.

Hadn't realized he and Kyla were both standing to get a better look at the screens. Settled himself back into his chair.

"So, I think we've discovered who might have that kind of money lying around."

"Right," Ajax said. "Hell, if they're dropping that kind of coin on cleanup, they wouldn't think twice about giving her $25,000 to keep quiet."

Drake nodded in agreement and thought on it for a moment.

"Maybe that's their angle. Maybe they figured Kyla's vision problems were in some way connected to the mine. Thought they were getting off cheap throwing a little cash her way."

"Yeah, because if it got out that whatever they're hiding over there is hurting the local people, they'd likely have to go in and do even more cleanup," Ajax said.

"And Lord only knows how much that would cost them," Drake added.

Returning to the computer, Ajax went back online. Entered WEPCO into a search engine. Began digging through company records and managed to ascertain that they were based in Seattle. Merely operated in Montana and managed all their finances through the west coast hub.

Obtained a company ledger.

"Son of a bitch," he said. Jabbed a finger at the screen. Waited for Drake and Kyla to lean in and see what he had found.

"I'll be damned," Drake whispered. Read through the list of board members and appointed counsel in front of him. "Dan Harmon. Plain as day."

"I mean, they don't have a photo directory or anything," Ajax said. "But what are the odds?"

"Too high to ignore," Drake said. "There's no way this isn't the guy."

Drake leaned back, folded his arms across his chest.

Across from him, Kyla and Ajax both nodded.

"Still doesn't answer the question of how they even knew, though," Drake said.

"The copper collar," Kyla whispered, her first words in several minutes, said so softly Drake and Ajax exchanged a glance before leaning in close.

"Come again," Ajax said.

"The copper collar," Kyla repeated. Raised her voice slightly. Kept her gaze aimed at the floor between them. "My grandpa used to tell me stories about it when I was a kid."

Drake and Ajax exchanged another glance, waiting for her to continue.

"I guess that was the term people in the state used to describe the hold copper had on everything," Kyla said. "They controlled the newspapers, wouldn't let them say a bad word about the mines.

"Owned many of the politicians. He even once said that when somebody new moved in they had a six-month grace period to decide if they were for or against the company.

"After that, they were branded for life."

Again, Ajax whistled.

"And you think the collar still exists?" Drake asked.

At that, Kyla raised her gaze, blinking herself back to full consciousness.

"Well, not like that, obviously. The mine hasn't run in 30-plus years."

"And there's too much media to ever keep a stranglehold on anything anymore," Ajax added.

"Right," Drake conceded. "But I mean, in town. You think maybe they have people around that tip them off when something crosses their radar?"

There was no response as Kyla and Ajax both watched him. Could tell he was leading them somewhere.

Said nothing.

"I mean," Drake said, "do you think it's coincidental that two days after Kade and I went to see Dr. Breslin, suddenly this Harmon guy is at your door offering gag money?"

CHAPTER THIRTY-EIGHT

Fifteen minutes.

A quarter hour.

That was all the time Drake had before Dr. Westerman's office closed for the day.

Waiting until the morrow wouldn't be a terrible thing. The answers he craved would be no different. There wasn't any external pressure pushing the timeframe beyond Harmon and his offer.

Still, now that he had an idea how things were connected, what it all meant, where it all could be going, he wanted to find out as quickly as possible. Could tell by the set of Kyla's jaw in the passenger seat that she did as well.

The offer had been extended for Ajax to join them. Was politely declined with a nod toward the image still frozen on the flat screen in the living room and an eye roll. A begrudging admittance that, boring or not, he still had a deadline to meet.

Left them with a thank you for the momentary distraction.

Despite the end of the workday fast approaching, traffic was mercifully thin. Six minutes after leaving the house, Drake pulled into a parking spot across the street from the doctor's office.

Found Kade's truck already waiting for them. In unison, all three climbed out and came together by Drake's tailgate.

"I see you got my text," Drake said. Spoke past Kyla to Kade on the opposite end.

"I did," Kade said. "Was in Albertson's. Got some funny looks as I piled everything back on a shelf and took off like a scared jackrabbit."

The analogy - and the mental image it evoked - both made Drake smile.

"Kyla Wegman, Kade Kuehl. Kade, Kyla."

"Hi," Kyla said. Nodded.

"Good to meet you," Kade said. Returned the gesture.

Standing three across, they ascended the front steps. Heard the wooden planks echo beneath their feet. Drake reached the door first and pulled it open. Allowed the others to enter before following them in.

The same young girl was seated behind the front desk as they entered, gave the same exact oversized grin, this one buoyed slightly by a twinge of recognition.

"Hello again," she said. "Can I help you?"

"Hi there," Drake said. "We were wondering if the doctor might have just a minute? We don't have an appointment, are glad to wait."

The smile waned a bit as the girl looked to the computer screen beside her.

"She's in with a patient now, but let me message her. If you guys want to wait, I'm sure she can see you right after."

"Thank you so much," Drake said.

Took a step back. Realized Kade and Kyla were standing right on either shoulder and decided to retreat a bit further, the three taking up seats in the corner.

The last thing they needed to do was appear imposing, standing over the daughter of the woman whose help they were seeking.

"So, what brings us back here already?" Kade asked. Glanced to Kyla. "We going to ask the doc to take a look?"

The thought had occurred to Drake on the way over, but had passed just as fast. Right now, the actions of Harmon and WEPCO were made based upon nothing more than a couple of vague questions Drake had asked of Breslin.

They didn't have a clear diagnosis. Nobody did. That wasn't the issue.

"No," Drake said. "But we've had quite the interesting afternoon. Uncovered some facts that kind of cast things in a new light."

Kade sat in silence as Drake filled him in on the events of the day. Started with the visit from Harmon. The bribe that was offered. Continued through the assistance of Ajax. The backstory of the Anaconda smelting operation and the copper collar. The notion that their fact-finding mission a few days before had drawn WEPCO right to Kyla's door.

When he was finished, Kade's face looked much the same that theirs had a short time before. Shock, mixed with just a slight bit of anger. Even a bit of information overload tossed into the mix.

"Remember when we drove over the other day," he finally said. "There wasn't a damn thing growing within miles of that tower. This is Montana. No way that just happens unless something caused it."

"Agreed," Drake said. "And if it could kill off a forest, no telling what it could do to a person's bodily functions."

On either side of him, Kade and Kyla nodded in agreement as the back door of the office opened. A woman in her 70s with glasses a half-inch thick stepped out and wrapped a sweater around her shoulders.

Smiled to the trio as she passed.

Once she was gone, Dr. Westerman appeared from the office. Looked to be on the back end of a very long day, but forced a smile into place just the same.

"Why, hello again," she said, again using the same exact words as her daughter. "To what do I owe this pleasant surprise?"

At the sight of her, Drake sprang to his feet. He wasn't sure that seeing them was anything approaching pleasant for the doctor, but was not about to miss his opening, just the same.

"Some new information came to light," Drake said. "I wonder, could we have just three minutes of your time?"

"Of course," Westerman replied. Waved them on back, not once hesitating.

Whatever Sage had said to get them in, Drake would owe her for it. In spades.

Moving fast, the three crammed into the same room Drake and Kade had been in just a day before. Remained standing.

"So, so sorry to be bothering you again," Drake said. Motioned to his left. "This is Kyla Wegman, the girl we were telling you about."

Both Kyla and Westerman nodded in greeting. Said nothing.

"The other day you mentioned that moonblink was actually a symptom, not really a malady in and of itself, correct?"

"Correct," Westerman replied, pushing her hands down into the front pockets of her white coat.

"Kyla here is a lifelong resident of Anaconda. We were wondering if there might be a correlation."

He left the question deliberately vague. Did not want to influence the answer in any way. Waited as the doctor chewed on it a moment. Saw her face pass through confusion to realization before moving on into pontification.

More than a minute passed in silence as she processed what she'd been told. Ended as she whirled around and went to one of the shelves screwed directly into the wall above her desk. Took down an enormous volume and cradled it in the crook of her left arm. Used her right hand to begin flipping through pages.

Found what she was looking for and held her right finger out as a pointer, tracing it over the page. Halfway down, she began to read aloud.

"One of the more common causes of moonblink is malnourishment, especially a deficiency in Vitamin A, which functions to strengthen the rods in the eyes."

When she was done narrating, she slammed the book shut. In the quiet office, it sounded akin to a gunshot, making Kyla flinch slightly.

Without turning back, Westerman tossed it onto the desk behind her.

"One of the more common causes of Vitamin A deficiency is arsenic poisoning," she said.

"Arsenic," Drake whispered. Connected what he was hearing with what they had read earlier. "One of the heavy metals pulled out during smelting."

"Well, that I can't speculate to," Westerman said. "That would take a lot of environmental testing and what not. What I can tell you though is if there was arsenic in the groundwater over there..."

She paused. Let her voice fade for a moment.

"It probably wouldn't be to a toxic level or she and everybody else over there would have gotten sick long ago. But trace amounts? Ingested over a lifetime? That could absolutely be the problem that moonblink is now a symptom of."

CHAPTER THIRTY-NINE

Coincidence.

Nothing more.

Lon Telesco tried to tell himself that was what he was seeing. That Harmon had gone to see the girl. Bell had shown up a moment later.

Two hours after that they, and the same Indian from yesterday, were all back visiting the doc.

Even as he tried to force the pieces into place, tried to come up with some narrative that sounded even quasi-plausible, he knew it was bunk.

They had already been sniffing things out. The visit from Harmon had just accelerated things.

For the sake of prudence, Telesco had parked his truck two streets over. Small town or not, there was only so many times the same vehicle could be spotted parked right beside where they were. Even if their entire attention was focused on the case, they would eventually have to look up and realize they were being followed.

Grabbing up an outdated newspaper from the floor of the passenger seat, Telesco went for a stroll. Sat himself on the steps of the old train station at the end of the street. Used thick sunglasses to hide his eyes as he stared down at the front of the optometrist's office.

Every so often, he'd idly flip a page of the newspaper. Pretend to be reading one of the articles from months before.

Less than 20 minutes after stepping inside, the same trio exited. Climbed into two different trucks and departed.

Internally, two emotions fought for top billing.

One part of Telesco wanted to sprint to his own truck. To keep them in sight and see where the next stop in their crusade might take them.

Just as fast, he dismissed the idea. There was no way he could follow two trucks, and even if he could, the sight of him dashing through the streets of downtown would surely draw attention.

If not from Bell, then from some other passerby. Or, worse yet, one of the many city police sprinkled heavily throughout the area.

Feeling his pulse rise, Telesco remained where he was and kept turning pages. Made a show of finishing the paper. Folding it up before standing and stretching his hands high overhead.

Only once he was certain that he would not be noticed, that whoever may have seen him had dismissed him just as fast, did he head back toward his truck. Return the paper to the passenger foot well to be used again in the future. Forego turning on the engine just yet.

Instead, he drew his cellphone over onto his thigh. Considered texting Harmon with an update. Sending another snide message with all capital letters and his name as a signature at the end.

Opted against it. Dialed the only speed dial in the device and pressed it to his ear. Waited just two rings before hearing the same husky, graveled voice he always did.

"Yeah?"

"Looks like Bell's got the whole band together," Telesco said. "The Indian is back, and Kyla Wegman is with them."

"So?" the voice snapped.

A dour look crossed Telesco's face as he shook his head. Couldn't believe he was going to have to spell it out.

"So, right after Harmon left earlier, she called her attorney. Two hours later, they were back visiting the optometrist."

An indiscernible grunt was the only response. No way of knowing if it was positive or negative.

"Where are they now?"

"They went their separate ways," Telesco said. "I couldn't follow both, and I had to proceed on foot."

He hoped the last part would be a sufficient explanation that he no longer had eyes on anybody. Knew it probably wouldn't be and even if it was, some comment would be lobbed his way just the same.

"So you let them go."

The expression deepened on Telesco's face.

"Had to. Besides, it's after 5:00. Where the hell could they be going tonight?"

The last line was out before he even realized it, the closest he had ever been to insubordinate.

The extended silence on the other end told him it had been noticed and was not appreciated.

"Orders?" Telesco asked, trying to push past it.

"Your orders were to stay on them," the man replied, a clear edge in his voice.

There was nothing Telesco could say to that, so he didn't try. Merely sat and waited. Knew the man would have to break the silence eventually.

Found that it took less than a minute for just that to happen.

"Pick them back up as soon as possible," the man said. "And keep your phone on. There might be a change of plan soon."

CHAPTER FORTY

"Well, that was interesting."

Bear McGrady tried to keep the sneer out of his voice as he made the comment. Found it quite difficult to do, especially while seated directly across from Valerie Stiles, seeing the agitation still stretched across her features six hours later.

"That...*bitch*," she snapped. "Who the hell does she think is?"

A host of responses came to McGrady's mind.

The public defender. Someone that had stood toe-to-toe with Stiles before and wasn't afraid of her or her post. The boss of Susan Moritz. A person with a vested interest in protecting her employee. A self-appointed attorney for a friend.

Or, most importantly, a decent human being.

More than anything to come from the encounter that afternoon, that was the biggest piece that had stayed with McGrady.

Rosenthal was right. Stiles was attempting to exploit a 14-year-old girl for her own selfish reasons.

Discretion being the better part of valor, McGrady said none of this. Merely sat and waited.

He wasn't entirely sure why she had asked for the meeting. Why he had been invited earlier that day or why so much trouble was being raised over one small accident.

Stiles let her original question hang in the air for two full minutes, until well past the point where it was apparent McGrady had no intentions of responding.

Eventually, she swallowed down a bit of the acrimony within her. "Anyway, I came by to see where you're at with the investigation."

It took everything McGrady had not to laugh. To keep his visage even. Impassive.

To meet her gaze with clear eyes.

"Which investigation?" He motioned to a stack of manila folders on the desk beside him. "The B&E on Reserve last night? The hit-and-run out in East Missoula? The DV incident down on Mount?"

He hoped the implication was clear. He had plenty of real cases needing real attention to work on. Neither he nor his staff had time to be dealing with something so petty.

"Don't be a smartass," Stiles said. "You know damned well what investigation I'm referring to."

Again, McGrady kept his response in check.

"Actually, I don't. I know you can't be referring to the Wegman case, because there is no case. That *investigation*, if there ever was one, has been offloaded."

"Closed and locked away."

An expression similar to what Stiles had intended for Barb Rosenthal a few moments before crossed her face.

"You can't be serious."

"Actually, I'm pretty sure you can't be serious," McGrady said, for the first time deciding to be the more proactive party in the conversation.

"We're talking about a misdemeanor here. You've admitted yourself that the maximum penalty that can be assessed is assault. Why would I bother to continue expending resources on that?"

"Um, because it's your job?" Stiles replied.

"Yes, it is," McGrady said. "And we showed up at the scene, found the driver that hit the girl and got a full confession. Held her longer than we should have, assessed her the maximum fee, and released her.

"I only wish it was always so easy to do my job."

McGrady could tell he had hit a nerve. That the earlier meeting, the personal angle, both had Stiles frazzled.

She was clinging too tight, would not be letting go any time soon.

"Drugs?" Stiles said.

"Bloodwork was clean."

"Alcohol?"

"Blew 0.0 on three different breathalyzer tests," McGrady said. Leaned back in his chair. Sighed. Wanted her to know that this was beyond ridiculous, that he was sorry he had called her in the first place.

This had started as a simple opportunity. A chance for her to maybe pick up with something she had started years before. Maybe even win him a brownie point or two with the prosecutor's office.

Now, it was becoming something much larger. Something that threatened to ruin the lives of two young girls and bring a hell of a lot more stress into his.

Across from him, Stiles continued to fume. Sounded just like Rosenthal earlier as she pushed loud breaths out through her nose.

Stared at the floor. Tried in vain to put together some other argument to bolster her position.

"What about that vision thing she mentioned? There has to be something more we can do with that."

CHAPTER FORTY-ONE

Wednesday.

Hump day.

For most people, a dead spot in the middle of the week. Something to muddle through before starting the downward slide toward the weekend.

For Drake, it was the lone standing appointment on his calendar. Something that had started years before and showed no signs of ending any time soon.

For most nurses at St. Michael's, the second shift was a torturous assignment on par with Hell itself. The first shift had the burden of boss supervision, but allowed people to have a normal life. Keep 7:00 to 3:00 hours. Be around to pick up their kids after school. Have dinner with their spouses in the evening.

The night shift wreaked havoc on a person's body clock, but it at least came with the upside of no badgering from the higher ups. Very few nervous family members second guessing every step.

The second shift had neither comfort. The first half of the shift, supervisors were still on hand and families were packed in tight. On the backend things slowed down, but ensured that there was no way employees ever enjoyed anything resembling a social life.

For most, it was a rite of passage. Something to be gotten through while they were the low man on the totem pole before requesting a transition at the first available opportunity.

To Sage, it was just something she did with no intentions of changing. Had never admitted that it was in no small part so she could run with the Crew in the mornings.

Didn't have to.

In an effort to acknowledge the sacrifice, Drake had started meeting her for dinner every Wednesday. More often when he could.

Sometimes he brought the rest of the Crew. Sometimes he brought food from the outside.

Never did he miss.

On this particular evening, he arrived with Kade and Kyla both still in tow. Found Sage seated at their table in the back waiting for them.

Allowed the other two to peel off and go directly into the service area. Walked back to the corner as Sage stood and greeted her with a hug.

"I see you brought a friend," Sage said. Released the hug. Leaned past him to see into the kitchen area.

"Two of them, in fact," Drake said. Looped an arm over her shoulder. Felt her pretend to put up a fight for a moment before sliding a hand around his waist.

"You know what I mean."

"I'll explain in a minute," Drake said. "At least wait until you hear everything before getting huffy."

"Mhmm," Sage replied. Pursed her lips. Tried to give an exasperated expression.

Ended up cracking into a smile.

Matching it, Drake peeled off. Loaded a plate with chicken tenders and French fries. Filled a saucer with ranch dressing.

Knew he would probably regret it later. Could not possibly care less.

Met Sage by the cash registers and paid for both of them. Noticed that Kade and Kyla had already departed. Followed their lead back to the table that they had been using since the Wednesday night dinners started years before.

"Sage, Kyla. Kyla, Sage," Drake said as he sat down. Watched the two ladies nod to one another, Sage taking a seat beside him. Didn't even attempt to begin eating. Instead leaned back in his chair and launched straight into a recap of the day for her.

His third such rendition of the story, he had it down to a science. Hit all the high points in short order. Talked uninterrupted for a full five minutes, the others eating while he spoke.

Salads for the two girls. Burger and potato wedges for Kade.

By the time he was done, he felt out of breath. Finally was able to look down at his food. Tear a tender in half and dunk it in ranch before cramming it home.

"Wow," Sage said, the first to comment. "That was quite a day. What's the next step?"

"Great question," Drake said. Swallowed the chicken and wiped his greasy fingers on a napkin.

"I'm not terribly familiar with environmental law, so first thing tomorrow, I'll do some digging. See what jumps out, where to take it from here."

"You thinking about bringing a lawsuit?" Sage asked. Idly twirled her fork through the greens on her plate.

"Don't know," Drake said. "My initial guess is, this is something a little above our pay grade."

"Meaning?" Kade asked.

"Meaning, if what Westerman told us is true, this probably falls under some sort of federal environmental standards thing. Something for a prosecutor to be bringing or the EPA to be checking into."

"Yeah, but they tried to bribe her," Sage said. "That must mean she has a case, too."

"For sure," Drake said, "but I don't think we're there yet. We'd have to do a lot of digging first. Make sure to nail down ironclad causation."

"And I don't want to file suit," Kyla said, her first words since sitting down.

Through the course of the conversation, Drake had not noticed that she had stopped eating. Was sitting with her hands in her lap, attention aimed down at the table.

"You don't?" he asked.

"No," she replied. "I'd be happy just taking the $25,000, giving it to that girl and being done with it."

Drake's jaw dropped open. Things had been moving so fast over the course of the day, he had forgotten to have a conversation with Kyla. Completely let it slip that all this was done for the express purpose of getting her off of whatever the police department and the prosecutor might try to hit her with.

"You're right," Drake said. "I'm sorry. We're getting ahead of ourselves."

He glanced to Kade and Sage. Saw them staring intently at their food.

Kyla doing the same.

"Let's just have dinner right now," he said. "Tomorrow morning, you can come into the office and we'll discuss it start to finish."

A few feet away, Kyla nodded. Drew her mouth into a tight line. Picked up her fork, but made no attempt to use it. "Do you think there's a chance we can go see her?"

With a fry halfway to his mouth, Drake stopped. Pulled his brow in tight. Stared at her.

"Hmm?"

"The girl," Kyla said. "She's being treated here, right? Do you think there's any way we can go see her?"

CHAPTER FORTY-TWO

Tough.

Extremely difficult, even.

It was not easy running an organization that technically did not exist. Even less so in a town such as Anaconda, where everybody recognized one another, noticed faces on the street. Far less still when the defining characteristic of the company that wasn't supposed to be there was a tower looming over everything at all times.

As a result, the preceding decades were beginning to take their toll on Michael Pittman and Darren Welker. Each wore the telltale signs of their careers on their faces as they sat in silence and sipped at the high-ball drinks positioned in front of them.

Occasionally glanced at the typed notes sent over from Lon Telesco just a couple of hours before.

They were in unusual territory. Instances such as Kyla Wegman had not arisen in quite some time. Rarely had there been the involvement of legal counsel. Never had they occurred so far from home.

The confluence of everything left them in a precarious position. Had them both sitting in silence for the better part of a half hour, each deep in thought, trying to consider how to best play things.

Keeping the EPA at bay, the various government watchdogs they employed, off their asses was enough of a chore.

The presence of such agencies was needed as a cover, not as an actuality.

They did not need something like this compounding things, causing them to stay long after hours. Forcing their other partners to start asking questions.

Having to make decisions that their age and post dictated just didn't suit them any longer.

"So, two optometrists and now a trip to the hospital," Welker finally muttered, opening the conversation.

"Yep," Pittman said. Let the same weariness Welker had employed permeate his voice.

"Any clue what it all means?"

"No more than you," Pittman replied, his gaze averted, his voice detached.

If left to his own devices, he would call Telesco now. Have him end it. Put a finish to their concerns.

On the flip side, he also wouldn't mind getting up from the table and walking away. Disappearing into the cold night air, never to be heard from again. His financial future was secure, his real estate holdings varied. It wouldn't take much for him to be gone, to never lose a second of sleep to anything that happened in Anaconda again.

As much as he knew Welker could do the same thing, may even be entertaining the exact thoughts just a few feet away, he knew just as surely that he could and would not make good on it.

The Western Pacific Copper Company long predated them both, but for the last 20 years, it had been their baby. They had come on board as nothing more than kids, had taken it over when there was little reason to do so, had managed to simultaneously stop pulling ore from the mine and turn the largest profit the company had ever seen.

For a company that technically didn't exist, it continued to act as a conduit for washing dirty funds from all over the country. Was known as a haven far and near for anybody needing to scrub money clean and have it return in a reputable manner.

Purportedly dropping untold sums on *environmental cleanup* had a nice ring to it. The kind of thing the government and the media accepted without ever looking too closely.

Not only was what they were doing too important, they were strapped to too many nefarious individuals for them to ever just walk away. It was the reason they continued monitoring everything as closely as they did, the same reason they dealt with situations such as this one.

The very same as to why both knew they weren't going anywhere.

"Have we heard back from Harmon?" Welker asked.

Pittman paused a moment, flicking his gaze to Welker before responding, "No, which means he hasn't heard from the girl, either."

"Right," Welker intoned. "And Telesco?"

"Just what we have here."

Again, Welker nodded, processing the information in silence.

They both knew how things would progress. It was the reason there had been no need to call on Larkin, the outcome of their discussion already assured.

Not that this was the kind of meeting that would ever make it onto the books.

"Call Dan," Welker finally said, his voice rolling out with a sigh. "Have him double the offer."

A reflexive snort was Pittman's initial response as he rolled his attention toward Welker.

"Harmon flew back to Seattle the first chance he got. We want it done now, it has to be on Telesco."

The statement floated in the air for a moment before Welker again fixed his gaze on Pittman. Just the slightest flicker of a smile caught at the corner of his mouth.

"Then have him do it. And maybe put a little bit of a scare into her, too."

CHAPTER FORTY-THREE

Drake went in with two clear goals in mind.

First, to get a feel for the tenor of the room. See how Susan Moritz was holding up. Introduce himself. Extend his apologies for what happened to her daughter.

Determine what kind of condition everybody was in.

If that went reasonably well, he would move on to step two. See if it would be alright if Kyla stepped inside and had a brief conversation with them.

Drake was still not certain it was a good idea. Knew that it was all Kyla had thought about for days. That it would continue to eat at her until at least some effort was made to reach out.

It was the second major mistake he had made on the afternoon. With all the excitement, the movement, of the day, he hadn't been thinking when he failed to ask Kyla what she might want. Even less so when he brought her to the hospital.

Of all the places in Missoula, bringing her to the cafeteria was quite possibly the very worst. Had to almost seem like a slap in the face to her, so much so that he felt the need to apologize as Sage led them through the semi-darkened corridors of the critical care unit and stopped at the tiny waiting area.

Left Kyla settled in one of four burgundy waiting room chairs as he and Sage headed toward the end of the hallway.

"You sure about this?" Sage whispered. Brought her body so close her shoulder was just a few millimeters from his as they walked.

"Not at all," Drake admitted. "You sure it's okay that we're even back here?"

"You're not," Sage said. Pulled up next to the last door in the hallway. Raised her eyebrows so Drake got the insinuation.

"Roger that," Drake whispered. Extended a hand and grabbed hers. Squeezed twice.

Sage matched the squeeze. Offered a faint smile before departing back down the hallway.

So far in his burgeoning legal career, Drake had done a lot. Much of it was things he'd never even dreamed possible, others the very definition of monotony.

This, though, was a first.

Taking a deep breath, Drake allowed the air to expand his lungs. Raise his shoulders a few inches. Reached out and tapped on the door with the back of one knuckle, making a sound that was just barely audible.

A moment later, the door cracked open a few inches. A woman's face appeared in the opening.

Middle-aged. Dark hair. Worry lines etched around her mouth and eyes.

"Susan Moritz?" Drake asked.

"Yes," she replied. Narrowed her gaze, showing obvious suspicion.

"My name is Drake Bell. Can I have just a couple minutes?"

A flash of dark hair was visible as the woman twisted to stare back into the room. Just as fast, her face returned as the door parted a bit. Turning sideways, she stepped through and closed the door behind her, folding her arms across her chest.

Under the lights of the hallway, Drake could see she was a bit younger than he'd first suspected. Dressed in jeans and a sweater.

Every bit as worried as his first assumption.

"What can I do for you, Mr. Bell?"

It was an interesting opening volley, one Drake hadn't quite expected.

For a moment his thoughts spun before he drew in a breath. Slowed his thinking, putting things into a logical order.

He had a simple request to make. An apology to deliver. Nothing more.

"Ms. Moritz, I am the attorney for Kyla Wegman, the young woman who..."

"Yeah, I know who she is," Moritz said. Clipped words. Obvious bitterness.

"I understand you work for the public defender's office," Drake said. "So when your office was unable to help, they called me at Missoula Legal Services."

His hope was that the explanation might soften her stance a bit. Make her realize he had been handed a client much the way her office often was.

Felt relief to see it worked. Barely.

"I know this is an unusual request, but we saw on the news that your daughter was awake-"

"And so you showed up here to ask that we not press charges?" Moritz hissed. Leaned toward him so he could see the fierce look in her eyes, the way her body quivered with anger.

"What? No," Drake replied. Was as stunned by her posture as the question.

Had never once considered the notion.

"I came here to say how sorry I am, and that whenever you and your daughter are up for it, Kyla would like to apologize as well."

It was clear that the statement was the very last thing Moritz expected to hear. Some of the animosity visibly fled her body.

Drake could tell there was no chance Kyla was getting to see them this evening. Now his best chance was to allay some concerns, hopefully lay some groundwork for a future encounter.

"I know this is terribly unorthodox," Drake said. "I just happened to be here this evening for an unrelated matter."

He motioned down to the jeans and running shoes he was wearing.

"As you can tell, this isn't an official visit at all. I just wanted to introduce myself and to tell you how very sorry I am that this all happened."

Again, Moritz's mouth parted. A puff of air passed her lips, but no sound came out.

Having delivered his message, Drake took a step back.

Had one final thought come to him.

"Oh, and to assure you that I have no idea what Valerie Stiles is up to, but I find it just as appalling as I'm sure you must."

CHAPTER FORTY-FOUR

Early.

Not to Drake, who was used to being up with sun - in many cases, before it even - but to Wyatt Teague and Greg Mooney, he could tell 8:00 a.m. felt like the crack of dawn.

To help with that he had a box of Bernice's Bakery caramel rolls waiting as they shuffled in. Two of the largest coffees the shop served.

The smell permeated the small office as the front door rang open with a jangle of the bell wrapped around the handle. Seemed to instantly perk them up.

The call to bring them in had gone out the night before, right after Drake left the hospital. The best way to approach the situation was still something of a gray area, trying to navigate his old role as friend and his new one as boss.

Given the situation he was in though, and the potentially truncated timetable he was on, he didn't see where he had much of a choice.

Called them both and asked them to be in by 8:00 and to plan on staying as long as they could. He would write them excuses for any classes missed. Sign off on time-and-a-half clinic hours.

Whatever it took. He was in dire need of assistance, even if these two were the best he could do.

Times like this he really wished his old partner Ava Zargoza hadn't returned to LSU for her final semester.

"Is that what I think it is?" Teague asked, the first to seize on what was balanced in the middle of his desk.

"Yes," Drake said. Sat on the edge of the desk with one foot on the floor, the other raised and swinging in front of it. "A bribe."

The crack brought smiles to both men's faces.

"At least the man's honest," Mooney said.

"And he did bring breakfast," Teague agreed.

It was clear neither had been awake more than a few minutes. Wrinkled clothes and hair askew. Crust in the corners of eyes.

Given how late in the week it was, Drake was just glad not to smell any lingering alcohol on them. The rest would be easy enough to overcome.

Each fell into their respective chairs and dove into the food stuffs waiting for them. Threw down caramel rolls with aplomb. Washed it back with coffee.

For his part, Drake laid back. Gave them a full 10 minutes to do their worst with what he had brought. Sat and sipped sweet tea, trying to formulate a plan for the day ahead.

Wednesday had been a good day, all things considered. Dan Harmon showing up at Kyla's was a bit disturbing, and clearly had rattled her somewhat. The fact that she wasn't able to speak to the Moritz's was also unfortunate.

Beyond that though, things were falling into place.

By trying to get out in front of things, Harmon had tipped his hand. Exposed himself in a way that Drake might never have uncovered otherwise. He was a front for a very powerful company, one with exquisitely deep pockets and an enormous secret they were willing to pay to keep quiet.

There was also a clear trail between that secret and Kyla. On past her to the Moritz's.

Now it was time to start connecting dots. To figure out how everything strung together and what they could do about it.

Mentioning to Susan Moritz that he despised Valerie Stiles had turned out to be a stroke of genius. Instantly it had removed her armor, unveiling the real person lurking beneath.

She wasn't a hardened employee of the legal system. Didn't despise him for doing his job any more than she had ever despised herself for doing hers.

More than anything, she was a mother. One that was scared. Worried. Had come within an eyelash of losing her firstborn and was now being harassed by someone with a personal vendetta and a love for the spotlight.

If put in her situation, Drake had to concede he would probably react much the same way.

Glancing to the clock on the wall, Drake noted the time. Emerged from his office to find Mooney and Teague finishing the last of their meals. Decided they could listen while polishing off what remained.

"Okay," he said. Walked up through the narrow alley splitting their desks. Pulled the visitor chair over from in front of Mooney's desk and put it directly between them. Settled into it, his legs extended before him.

"Thank you guys for coming in so early this morning. I know anything before noon isn't exactly your default setting."

On one side, Teague smirked. To the other, Mooney simply nodded in agreement.

"But I appreciate you doing it, and promise I wouldn't have asked unless it was important."

In quick order, he laid out everything he had. Started with the message Mooney had left for him less than a week before. Took it right up through his talk with Susan Moritz 12 hours earlier.

Watched as their faces expressed all the proper responses, ranging from shock to disgust.

When he was done, both had finished eating and shoved the packaging into the trash. Sat with eyes open wide, coffee cups in hand.

"Alright," Mooney said, "so you asked us here today to do what exactly?"

"Research," Drake replied. "We need to know everything about what's going on here, and we need to know it fast. The fact that Dan

Harmon has already shown up, offer in hand, means he is way out in front of us."

"Probably has a whole team of people squirreled away doing this kind of thing," Teague said.

Drake nodded, having thought of the same thing. Imagined a bunch of recent graduates in suits tucked away in a high rise somewhere in Seattle.

If not for the enormity of the moment, he would almost be compelled to laugh at the juxtaposition between that and the three of them in jeans in Missoula.

"And I'm guessing this is far from the first time this has happened," Drake added. "Best assumption is this is a spit polished process from start to finish. They know who to hit and how to hit them."

Mooney nodded. "Calculate their offer accordingly."

"More than that," Drake said. "They knew Kyla lived alone. Knew that sending a guy unannounced to her door would frighten her."

It was clear neither of the others had gotten far enough yet to consider that.

Both looked surprised. Nodded in agreement.

"So, what are we looking for?" Teague asked.

"Everything," Drake said. "Wyatt, I want you to start on CERCLA. The Comprehensive Environmental Response, Compensation, and Liability Act. Find out anything you can about what it says and what it requires. Any existing case law on it."

"Greg, hit Anaconda specifically. I don't care who the named parties are, I just want to know of any case that has come out of there that might be relevant."

"State or federal?"

"Yes," Drake replied. "I don't even know if they have city, but if they do, feel free to dig there too."

There was no doubt what he was handing them was a tall order. The kind of thing a regular employer would give them a week or more to push through.

He was asking for it in a number of hours.

"Informal is fine," Drake said. "I don't need a brief, damned sure don't want anything in IRAC format. We're not going before a judge on this. We're just trying to put together enough evidence to have some conversations. See where things go from there."

A sense of foreboding seemed to have settled on the group, making it clear that everybody understood the severity of the situation. That today was not going to be fun, but was very, very necessary.

"What about you?" Mooney asked.

At that, Drake stood, moving the chair back into its original position. "I'm going to find everything there is to know about WEPCO."

CHAPTER FORTY-FIVE

Faint.

Indistinct.

Just barely penetrating his senses.

Drake was so immersed in his research that the sound of the front bell barely resonated with him. Flashed by on the periphery of his consciousness, there and gone in an instant.

Not until Mooney knocked on the frame of his door and leaned in did Drake even look up from his computer screen.

"Hey, you've got a visitor."

The statement jerked Drake from his trance, causing him to snap his attention toward the door. Feel just the slightest palpitation in his chest.

"A visitor?"

"Yeah. It's Kyla."

Drake's eyes grew a bit larger as he stood from behind his desk. Saw Mooney disappear. Followed him out through the doorway to see Kyla standing in the exact spot he had been sitting two hours before.

"Kyla."

"Hey," she said. Wore jeans and a sweater, her arms straight down by her sides. Seemed to be swaying slightly from side to side with nervousness.

"Sorry to come by like this, but I stopped by your house and Ajax said this is where you would be."

Small bursts of light went off like warning bells in Drake's mind, causing his heart rate to increase a bit higher.

"Yeah, absolutely. No problem. We're all here working on your case today anyway."

He smiled so she knew the last line was a joke.

Received only a flicker of one in response.

"This is Greg and Wyatt, my friends and partners here. Guys, this is Kyla."

All three mumbled greetings and half-nods. Nothing more.

"Come on back," Drake said. Extended a hand and motioned toward himself. Waited for Kyla to pass through the desks and into his office. An extra second to see if either of his friends would turn to watch her go.

To their credit, neither did.

"Have a seat," Drake said. Pointed to one of two cracked black leather chairs across the desk from him. Circled around and took one himself.

Together with the desk, the two of them managed to fill almost the entirety of the tiny space.

"So, what's up?"

As if by magic trick, Kyla produced a business card from the palm of her hand. Gripped it between her index and middle finger and extended it over the desk to Drake.

Bending forward, he accepted it from her before retreating to examine it.

Before him was an exact copy of the business card Dan Harmon had left the day before. The only differences were a small black smudge streaked through the middle of the front of it and the words *$50K. Last chance.* written in black ink on the back.

"That was wedged under the windshield wiper on my car this morning," Kyla said. Voice, tone, letting it be known the entire ordeal had her spooked.

Again, a response Drake could not even pretend to argue with.

"You're kidding me," Drake said. Felt his insides clenching, his disdain for WEPCO, Dan Harmon, and everybody associated with them growing by the minute.

"No," Kyla said. "And it definitely wasn't there last night. After you dropped me off, I ran back out to my car for something."

"What time did you find this?" Drake asked.

"About an hour ago."

Drake flicked his eyes to the corner of his computer screen. Found that it was just minutes after 10:00.

"So at some point before 9:00 a.m., he was at your house."

Kyla's eyes slid shut as she nodded. Maintained the pose. Said nothing.

Whatever was going on here was spiraling fast. Clearly had WEPCO spooked. A day ago, Harmon had said she had 48 hours to consider his offer. Less than half of that was expired and already they were doubling it.

They were getting desperate, and in Drake's limited experience, bad things tended to happen when people were desperate.

Especially people that worked for organizations such as WEPCO.

Already he and Mooney and Teague were working on a time crunch. This couldn't help but accelerate that.

Drawing in a deep breath, Drake forced himself to slow down. To assess things one at a time, to not make the mistake he had the night before.

"Okay," he said, "first things first, do you want to accept this offer?"

Kyla's eyes popped open. Tendrils of red crisscrossed over the whites, though there were no tears. "What?"

"No, seriously. Like you said last night, you don't have any desire to be in a lawsuit. Do you want to just accept this offer and have everything else go away?"

It was clear the question was something Kyla had not anticipated. Her jaw dropped open and twice she attempted to formulate a response.

Nothing more than, "I...I..." crossed her lips.

"I know it's been a rough morning," Drake said. "The last few days would have shaken up anybody."

"I honestly just want to apologize and move on," Kyla whispered. "I don't want people showing up at my house anymore, really just want to forget any of this ever happened.

"There's a reason I moved away from Anaconda, after all."

Again, Drake couldn't help but nod in agreement, which made what he was about to say next that much worse.

"I can't even imagine what you must be going through right now, but unfortunately, I need you to give me some kind of bearing. If you want to accept, we can do that. If you want to just sign a gag order and not take a nickel, we can do that too."

He paused, making sure she was with him. Understood what he was outlining.

"Of course, if you just want to take a little time and sort through things, that's okay. We don't have much, but there is still a little."

It was clear what her preference was. At mention of the third option, she looked up, eyes a bit wider.

"How much time?" she whispered.

The right side of Drake's face scrunched slightly as he considered it.

"Early afternoon?"

"I could do early afternoon," Kyla said.

"Also," Drake said, "for the time being, I don't think it's a very good idea for you to be going home. Not with them knowing where you live, not with this offer on the table."

"You think they'd try to force it on me?" Kyla asked.

Every part of Drake wanted to reply with an emphatic yes, but he knew just as surely that it would only frighten her further.

"I don't know," Drake said, "but we probably shouldn't leave anything to chance right now, don't you think?"

Kyla paused a moment. Considered it.

"Probably not, but I know you're busy. I can't ask you to do that."

"You're right," Drake said, "but I'm not talking about me."

A look of confusion passed over Kyla's face. Departed just as quickly.

"Ajax was working when I stopped by earlier. I can't bother him either."

"Relax," Drake said. Pulled his cellphone from his bag. "I'm not talking about him, either."

CHAPTER FORTY-SIX

The handwriting was Harmon's.

It had to be for the sake of continuity.

He had written his cellphone number on the back of the first card he gave her. Added a few more words of nonsense that didn't really concern Telesco.

In keeping up appearances, he had also drafted out a handful more as well. Each done in ascending $25,000 increments up to $150,000.

After that, things went one of two ways fast. Either the person they were leaning on sat down and negotiated some other figure, or they were handed over to Telesco, at which point they usually ended up accepting the original $25,000 offer.

If they even could.

Harmon had scrawled out each of the cards the day before. Handed them over to Telesco with as much disdain as he could muster. Muttered a few comments about hating Missoula, Anaconda, and the whole state of Montana before boarding a plane back to Seattle.

Throughout, Telesco had remained silent. Merely accepted the stack that was now tucked away in the glove compartment of his truck.

Arched an eyebrow as Harmon spoke.

Waved a middle finger as he departed.

That morning, Telesco had gotten the go-ahead from corporate. Been told to make the next offer. To have it in a visible place, but not to be seen himself.

As if that were so simple in a town like Missoula, especially in a neighborhood as dense as the one Kyla Wegman lived in.

His first thought had been to use the mailbox. It was a trick he had used before, finding it quite effective.

Of course, that was in Anaconda, where people lived in single-family homes and checked their mail every day. Didn't spend an inordinate amount of time with a lawyer and his friends.

The fallback option then became the front windshield.

Even in the pre-dawn morning, the white smudge stood out against the mud brown exterior of the car. Made it impossible to miss upon approach, blatantly obvious to whoever might be sitting inside.

With his delivery made, Telesco had retreated back into the morning. Took a long, looping route back to his truck. Risked the few minutes of losing surveillance for the benefit of not being seen making a direct path.

In the slim event she did come out, see it, and depart, it wasn't like he didn't know exactly where she would go anyway.

The day before had more than proven that.

Once he reached his truck, he had moved it into position and gotten comfortable. Worked his way through a box of chocolate glazed donuts as he sat and watched.

From start to finish, his wait was more than two hours, long enough that he twice had to move the truck to avoid suspicion. When finally she did emerge, he could see the effect it had on her. The stiffened stance. The hand rising to cover her mouth. The fervent glances in either direction.

As if he would be foolish enough to still be in her line of sight.

Her first action after getting it surprised him a bit. Wheeling on the ball of her foot, she turned and ran back inside. Was gone only a few minutes before returning, a bag over her shoulder.

The second thing she did fell much closer in line with what he expected.

With no regard at all for counter-surveillance, she went straight back to Bell's and practically sprinted from her car to the front door.

Parked at the end of the street, Telesco couldn't see who was inside. Knew it couldn't be Bell, as his truck wasn't in the drive. Figured it to be the black guy with braids he had spotted a few times before.

This time too she was only inside a few minutes before returning to her car and heading downtown.

Easily enough to piece together, Telesco veered from her tail. Worked his way through the backstreets. Came up on the opposite side of the street from Missoula Legal Services just as she was parking directly in front of it.

Spotting Bell's truck parked a few spaces down, Telesco again settled in and allowed his eyelids to drift closed. Put his body into a low power state so he could sit and watch.

The respite was short lived.

Twenty minutes after the girl went inside, another truck pulled to the curb. Even larger than Bell's, Telesco recognized it instantly, was not surprised as the Indian kid with long hair stepped out and strode to the front door.

Remained inside just a few minutes before exiting, Kyla pressed tight against his arm.

Unable to resist, Telesco allowed a small chuckle. All he had done was place a single business card on a windshield. In response, these guys had turned things into a scene from a bad James Bond movie.

Just as fast, any mirth he felt died away. There would be time for that later.

Instead, he eased the gear shift down on the side of his steering wheel and waited for the enormous rig to pull away from the curb.

Made his way out into traffic behind it.

CHAPTER FORTY-SEVEN

Fear.

Concern.

Dread.

All three emotions were firmly entrenched in the pit of Susan Moritz's stomach. Seemed to be an equal head of the same beast, her own personal Cerberus nested deep within.

Walking alongside the orderly pushing her daughter toward the front door, she cringed to think of what she might find waiting for them. At what Valerie Stiles's little circus stunt had created the day before.

"Now, you have all your prescriptions and instructions from the doctor, right?" the orderly asked.

The kindly black woman with thick hips and a bun of graying hair was nice enough. Had spent an inordinate amount of time popping by the last week, more than earning the role of being the one to escort them out.

Still, she had been prattling on since the moment they left the room. Seemed oblivious to the trepidations of Susan, the exhaustion of Mandy.

"Yes," Susan replied. Wasn't sure if the question was aimed at her or her daughter, but decided to answer it anyway.

Like most things that had occurred in the past week, this wasn't fair. Going home should be a joyous event, something to be celebrated.

Ben should be the one pushing the wheelchair. She should already be out in the parking lot, pulling the car up to the end of the sidewalk. Mandy should be alert and smiling.

Together they would all three pile in and make a direct line for MacKenzie River Pizza, Mandy's favorite restaurant. Sit in their usual corner booth, order their usual large pie and fence posts.

Talk and laugh like they hadn't a care in the world.

Instead, she had sent Ben home that morning to get things ready. To make up a bed on the couch so Mandy didn't have to navigate the stairs in her condition.

On the drive back, she intended to hit Wendy's, knowing there wasn't a scrap of food in the house that wasn't either frozen or expired.

Even more important, there was not one iota of joy.

Mandy had survived a terrible ordeal. Had suffered a fractured skull and broken leg. Spent five days in a deep sleep.

And she had made it.

She was still lethargic - would be for a while longer - but her body would heal. Her bones would mend. There would be no lasting damage.

None of that sat at the forefront of Susan's mind, though, as they made their way forward. Ignored a handful of sideways glances as they went. Passed through the occasional sunspot streaming through the windows lining the outer wall of the hospital.

Instead, all she could think about was Valerie Stiles. About that damn bill she seemed so intent on trying to get passed and the number of reporters that might be waiting to ambush them the moment they stepped outside as a result.

Ahead, the front door loomed. Through it could be seen more of the same mid-day sun, a sight that at any other time would be welcomed, especially at this time of year.

Now, it only raised the wariness within Susan. Made her reach down and clamp a hand on her daughter's shoulder. Extend an unspoken message that she was there, that things would be okay.

The nurse stopped the procession just short of the large red carpet on the floor. She set the brake on the back of the wheelchair and walked around to the front. Bent at the waist and hugged Mandy, her prodigious backside extended behind her.

There she stayed for a moment. Whispered something in Mandy's ear. Pulled back to reveal a veneer of tears covering her eyes. Looked to Susan and mouthed the words, "Good luck."

Seeing her, it took everything Susan had not to break down herself. To take a moment and draw in a deep breath.

Steady her quivering lip.

"Thank you," she replied. "For everything."

The nurse raised a hand to the underside of her nose and nodded once. Disappeared back in the direction they'd just come from, walking fast, before both sides broke down completely.

Taking a step forward, Susan waited for her daughter to slide on a pair of thick sunglasses. Not to keep out the press, but to ease the tension of sunlight on her aching head.

Once she was ready, Susan grasped her hand. Helped her to her feet and led them both out through the front door.

Stopped just a few feet beyond it, her heart in her throat, and scanned the parking lot in both directions.

Thanked every deity she could think of that not a single person was within sight.

"Come on, Sweetie. Let's go home."

CHAPTER FORTY-EIGHT

Similar.

Somewhat.

Drake knew that the Public Defender's Office and Missoula Legal Services served something of the same purposes. Both were meant to provide aid to the less fortunate in the community, those that had neither the resources nor the inclination to look out for themselves. Existed to make sure they received their constitutionally afforded rights not to have to tackle issues on their own.

Whereas Legal Services was mainly aimed at things in the civil arena, the Public Defender's Office was reserved for criminal offenses.

Because of that, Drake knew that the clientele each served was a bit different.

Had no idea the two offices would appear to be from entirely separate stratospheres.

His office was small. Functional. Rarely had more than a client or two in at once. Was never at a shortage of work but nothing he, Greg, and Wyatt couldn't handle.

Never was it on the border of getting out of control.

Stepping foot into the public defender's space, the single word that came to mind was *chaos*.

The place appeared to be more what Drake would imagine a campaign office to be than a legal center. Standing just inside the door, every available waiting area chair was filled. The people seated in them ranged in age and appearance. Went from the most derelict of teenagers to an older gentleman in starched Wrangler's and a snow-white Stetson.

A few of them glanced over as he entered, all with the same curious expression. Seemed to be sizing him up, seeing what he had done to be in need of help.

The waiting area was separated from the rest of the building by a waist-high counter that acted more like a partition. Behind it sat a single woman with thick glasses. Hair pulled back in a bun. Heavy cardigan sweater.

On past her, a small army of people in business casual attire bustled about. Carried armloads of papers and case files.

Around the outer edge of the room was a series of offices. Some with doors standing open. Many more with doors closed, client meetings most likely underway within.

"Help you?" the woman behind the counter asked. Voice huskier than anticipated.

Drake took a step forward. Stopped just short of the counter, careful not to touch it.

"Drake Bell here to see Barb Rosenthal."

The woman nodded once. Made a few keystrokes on her computer and read from the screen before her.

"Oh, yeah. The attorney. I'll let her know you're here."

Bowing his head in thanks, Drake took a step back. Could feel the stares of several of the people on his back. Didn't dare turn around. Stood with his hands clasped before him, hoping that Rosenthal would be quick.

To his surprise, it took just three minutes for her to appear.

The outer appearance seemed to fit with what Drake had imagined a *Barb Rosenthal* to look like. Short dark hair arranged in curls around her head. A double-breasted jacket last seen in the early '90s.

She walked out of the rear corner office and came straight for him. Stopped halfway and called his name, motioning for him to come on back.

The woman behind the desk pressed a buzzer, the gate on the far end of the counter unlatching with an audible click.

Passing through it, Drake cut a path through the mass of people moving about. Went straight to Rosenthal, his hand outstretched.

"Drake Bell. Thank you so much for meeting with me."

"Barb Rosenthal."

She said nothing more while leading him back to the office she had emerged from. Not until the door was closed behind her did she add, "I must admit, I was a little intrigued to get your request earlier."

As she spoke, she circled around behind her desk and motioned for Drake to sit.

Despite the extra space of the outer area, the office was only nominally larger than Drake's. Like his, it was dominated by a desk and chairs, case folders seeming to take up the bulk of the remaining area.

"Please excuse the mess," Rosenthal added. "As you can imagine, I'm very rarely actually in here."

Drake nodded. He could imagine.

"Appreciate you making the time."

At that, Rosenthal nodded. "Susan told me you stopped by last night."

She left it there for a moment and stared at Drake. Seemed to be waiting for a response that didn't come.

"That was a very classy gesture. Even more so keeping your client away and asking permission. You'd be amazed how many people seem to lack such basic humanity during tough times."

"Like Valerie Stiles?" Drake asked. Realized the words were out before he'd even said them. Felt his face tighten into a wince, wishing he hadn't been quite so quick to play that card.

"Yes, very much like Valerie Stiles," Rosenthal responded, letting the amount of distaste she had for the woman hang from the words.

Drake had gotten the impression the night before that whatever hatred Susan Moritz had for the situation was not exclusive to her.

It was with that in the back of his mind that he had called on Rosenthal.

Starting there wasn't how he would have planned things. Ideally, he would have laid out what he had and eventually worked around to it.

Since that didn't seem to be the way things were playing out though, he decided to roll with it.

"I didn't catch her press conference in real time yesterday," Drake said. "But after speaking with Susan, I found it online."

There he paused, recalling the footage he had seen. "The woman does have a flair for the dramatic, I will give her that."

A derisive snort was the only response, it clear that Rosenthal was biting back a host of retorts.

"Let me back up, though," Drake said. Took a breath and tried to formulate a clear order of things in his mind, especially given this new starting point. "Last night, Susan mentioned that for all intents and purposes, you are her attorney."

"That's correct," Rosenthal responded. "But, you should know, Susan Moritz has been a paralegal here almost as long as I've been the PD. She doesn't need an attorney."

Drake had also gotten that impression the night before, but knew better than to say as much.

"And as such," Drake said, "I wanted to talk to you about some things that have come to light in the last couple of days."

Rosenthal waited, keeping her face impassive, giving away nothing. The exact characteristics of someone that had spent a lifetime in front of a jury, more often than not playing a hand they knew to be a losing one.

"Let me start right up front and say, this has nothing to do with the accident last week," Drake said. "At least, not directly. Kyla Wegman has admitted guilt, will continue to do so."

Both knew that even if she didn't, the charges would be minor. That it went a long way as a sign of good faith that she so clearly accepted her culpability anyway.

"I see," Rosenthal said. Nothing more.

"She has, however, asked me to look into something else in the time since, and that's the reason I've come to see you."

He took a breath. Felt his insides clench, warmth forming along the small of his back. Never before had he attempted something like this, or even heard of it being tried.

Could only hope it wouldn't end badly.

"To run a proposition by you, and if possible, to ask for your advice on something."

CHAPTER FORTY-NINE

The feeling of resignation was gone, replaced by a feeling that had grown well past annoyance and was moving into open hostility.

Based on the reports of Lon Telesco, there was no way to know definitively what was going on. Just that a lot was happening, none of it good.

Thus far, two offers of a settlement had both been rebuffed.

Check that. Not rebuffed, *ignored.*

Not one iota of a response had been made to either one, the latter being nearly twice what the average Anaconda resident made in a given year. Only a handful of times had it ever gotten higher than that figure, and even then only after some negotiating.

For there to have been no response at all was unusual to say the least.

Coupled with the fact that the girl ran straight to her attorney, that together they then went to see the public defender, pushed things into a different arena. Threatened to bring about the kind of messy public spectacle they had worked so diligently to avoid over the years.

Pacing at the head of the same conference table that always served as their designated meeting place, Michael Pittman kept his focus aimed at the ground. Watched as the faded black WEPCO emblem passed under his feet, easily distinguishable against the red carpet of the room.

Seated in his usual spot to the right was Cam Larkin. As was his standard position, he held both hands folded in his lap. Stared down at them, the beginning of a bald spot peeking out as Pittman glared over at him.

The decision to include him tonight wasn't his. There was only one way the impromptu meeting could end, a fact that he and Welker both knew. There would be no deadlocked vote, no need for a third party to bear witness to what was about to take place.

In fact, the fewer people that knew about it in general, the better.

The thought sat at the forefront of his mind, pulling a dour expression to his face. Twice he glanced to the clock on the wall as he continued walking. Waited for the third member of their trio to show so they could execute the orders to do what needed to be done.

Thirteen minutes after the hour, Darren Welker entered. Walked straight to the thin table lining the side wall and poured himself three fingers of whiskey. Downed them, loosened his tie from his neck, and poured another three fingers.

Only then did he turn back, taking in the scene before him.

"I assume we already know why you asked us here?"

Stopping his pacing, Pittman turned to stare at Welker. Felt a stab of something deep in his stomach resembling animosity, one of the few times his partner had ever evoked such a response.

"Well, it's why I asked *you* here."

He left the statement at that, not even bothering to flash his gaze over to Larkin, letting the insinuation fill in the blanks for him.

Judging by the look on Welker's face, the color flushing Larkin's cheeks, it managed to do just that.

"The news from Telesco wasn't good," Welker said. Pushed right by the comment. Phrased the sentence as a statement, certainly not a question.

Pittman paused a moment, making sure his point was made, before letting a tiny bit of the vitriol within bleed out.

A simple twist of his head was the only response.

"How bad?" Welker asked.

"She went straight to the lawyer."

"No response to Harmon at all?"

"Who then went straight to the public defender's office," Pittman finished, bypassing the question entirely.

It was clear the statement brought about just as much confusion for Welker as it had him, the man's face contorting itself slightly.

"The public defender...why?"

"No clue," Pittman said, raising his eyebrows slightly. "Maybe it's unrelated, she can't be his only client, but still..."

"Right," Welker said. "We have too much at stake, too many people starting to get curious. We can't take that chance."

Pittman felt his eyebrows rise a little higher. Looked over to see Larkin raise his gaze just slightly, the last sentence having resonated with him as well.

"Does that mean we are in agreement?"

CHAPTER FIFTY

The meeting was scheduled for later than usual. Certainly later than anything Drake would have called himself.

Coming from Barb Rosenthal though, being held at the Public Defender's Office, there was no way every one of the invitees wasn't going to show.

Each of them had their various reasons for doing so, ranging from rampant self-interest to abject curiosity. Enough to bring them all out on a Thursday night under short notice.

Drake stepped back into the building just minutes before 7:00, Kyla by his side. After managing to avoid the place for his first seven years in Missoula, it was his second stop in as many hours, the place looking markedly different than his first pass through.

Gone were any of the clients, the chairs sitting empty along the front wall. Missing also was the gatekeeper behind the desk, the entry on the far end standing open.

A couple of paralegals and interns still dotted the space. Gone was any of the manic energy, though, many appearing to be dozing as they worked, half-empty food containers beside them.

The smells of various offerings - going from fried chicken to Chinese food - hung in the air.

Given the design of the office, Drake couldn't help but wonder how long the scents would linger as he tried to motion Kyla through. Saw her nervousness and decided to lead the way himself.

Walking one behind the other, Drake wove his way through the room. Past Rosenthal's office standing open along the side wall, lights still on, toward the conference room in the back.

Stepped inside to find a white oblong table stretched 10 feet in length. Made from four smaller tables fitted together, thick seams were obvious. A handful of mismatched chairs sat around the outside.

On the end in front of them stood half a dozen bottles of water, condensation dripping down the sides of the plastic. Beside them sat a wicker basket, apples and oranges inside.

Seated at the opposite end was Barb Rosenthal, Bear McGrady across from her. Neither had chosen to use the seat at the head of the table, instead choosing to sit facing one another.

Both sat and stared in silence as Drake entered, McGrady appearing more than a little surprised to see Kyla come in behind him.

The notion of bringing her along was something done at the suggestion of Rosenthal that afternoon. At the time, Drake was adamantly against it. Knew how fragile Kyla still was, given the events of the past week. Wanted to keep her tucked away with Kade and Ajax until everything was resolved.

Rosenthal had other thoughts. Reasoned that there needed to be someone in the room to keep Valerie Stiles from getting too far off script.

Since Susan or Mandy Moritz was clearly not possible, that left Kyla.

She hadn't explained any more than that, though Drake got the distinct impression there was a lot more to the story than he was being told.

Decided to let it go.

Barb Rosenthal was going out on a limb to aid them both. She also had 20 years of experience dealing with Stiles and others like her. If she believed this was the best way to handle things, he would believe her.

Would even hope to garner a few bonus points in doing so.

"Detective, Ms. Rosenthal," Drake said. Nodded to both. Pulled out the chair next to Rosenthal.

"Drake."

"Mr. Bell," they replied in order.

"And you both know my client, Kyla Wegman," he said. Knew that Rosenthal had not yet met her, but did not want to give that impression in front of McGrady.

Another tip from earlier in the afternoon.

Once more, both nodded and murmured greetings.

Kyla did the same as she took up a spot next to Drake, the division at the table becoming apparent. Sitting three in a row, they all stared across at McGrady, the detective appearing increasingly uncomfortable with each passing moment.

A full 10 minutes after the hour, the final person to be invited passed through the doorway. Armed with her ever-present briefcase and shoulder bag, she strode directly to the head of the table and fell into her seat. Made a show of dropping both items to the floor by her feet and blowing out a lungful of air in a huff.

"Who in the world calls a meeting for 7:00 p.m. on a weeknight?"

No salutations. No greeting of any kind.

In his periphery, Drake could see Rosenthal clinch up beside him. McGrady's forehead grow a shade darker.

It was exactly the way Rosenthal had forewarned him things would go. The kind of thing that was a known secret in the legal community.

Valerie Stiles, she had shared with him, had a very distinct style. Something akin to a bull in a China shop, mixed with a healthy dollop of self-absorption and none of the accompanying self-awareness.

Despite whatever else the meeting was pretending to accomplish, the biggest thing was to get past Valerie Stiles.

"I did," Rosenthal said, "after meeting with Mr. Bell here this afternoon."

"Who?" Stiles snapped, pretending she didn't see Drake and Kyla sitting at the end of the table.

In spite of his every thought being to keep his temper down, to not let her get to him, Drake could feel his ire starting to climb. His body temperature began to rise.

"Drake Bell," Rosenthal said. "Counsel for Kyla Wegman."

She motioned to the two of them sitting nearby.

"You know, the other person you're trying to railroad with this personal crusade of yours."

The words found their mark.

Drake drew in a tiny bit of pleasure at seeing the reaction on Stiles's face. The way her mouth dropped open and her jaw quivered just slightly.

Already he could tell he was going to like Barb Rosenthal just fine.

"And so you thought you would all ambush me here this evening?" Stiles finally managed to push out. Turned her attention over to McGrady and leveled an accusatory glare on him. "You'd all get me in a room and gang up on me. Well, I can tell you right now..."

"Stop," Rosenthal said. Held a hand up in front of her. Extended the palm toward Stiles. "Just stop right there, before you get too carried away on this self-righteous freight train of yours."

This time, Drake was unable to stop the flicker of a smile that crossed his lips. Seeing the indignation that stretched across Stiles's face simply wouldn't allow it.

"Why...I..." she huffed, again trying to find her words.

The more she sputtered, the more Drake couldn't help but begin to wonder about her abilities in front of a jury. To question how she must react in a courtroom whenever a curveball presented itself.

What kind of impression she no doubt left on observers.

All of those, he kept locked away. Watched as Rosenthal continued to work her over, going through the things they had discussed that afternoon.

Once Drake had opened the floor to her earlier, the public defender had laid out an extensive plan. Had made it clear she had been thinking on it for some time.

She did not appreciate Stiles attacking her friend and colleague Susan Moritz. Would not stand for the woman to use Moritz's 14-year-old daughter as a stumping point, no matter how important the reason.

After that was on the table, Drake laid out everything he had discovered. Watched as Rosenthal was a bit dubious before becoming openly curious.

Finished by reaching the same conclusions he had.

More than an hour had passed as inch by inch they mapped out a plan for the evening. For the coming days.

One that would effectively get at WEPCO. At Valerie Stiles. Perhaps even Bear McGrady.

Would in the end extend just enough of an olive branch so that everybody went home at least quasi-happy. Or at least got to save face, which might be the best they could hope for.

Rocking her weight from side to side, Stiles reached toward the floor. Took up the handle of her briefcase. Snatched at the straps on her bag.

"I do not, and I will not, sit here and listen to this," she snapped. "I am a prosecutor for the State of Montana. This is an outrage."

"That's right," Rosenthal said, "you are a prosecutor. You're not an activist, you're not a lobbyist, and you're damn sure not a legislator."

The comment managed to do two things simultaneously.

First, it heightened the indignation already plastered across Stiles's face. Forced her to huff even more, to look as if she might explode at any moment.

To Drake's surprise though, it also managed to pique a tiny bit of a question within her.

He saw it the moment it flickered behind her eyes. The way she slowed just a second in grabbing up her things.

"Meaning?" she asked.

Rosenthal paused a moment before responding. Made sure the point was made that she had struck a chord.

"Meaning you're going to put aside this malarkey about a cyclist's Bill of Rights. And in return, we're going to hand you something much, much bigger."

CHAPTER FIFTY-ONE

Things were definitely picking up.

That much had been obvious for a day or two. Ever since the girl was released from jail, there had been a lot of activity.

The attorney meeting with optometrists. He and the girl coming together quite often.

Since the insertion of Harmon into the mix though, Lon Telesco had noticed things reaching a fevered pitch. Not only were things happening, but there was a palpable sense of urgency to them.

The girl was perpetually looking over her shoulder. Was moving quickly. Kept the lights off in her home, even when she was there.

Leaving the business card that morning had sent things to another level yet again. Since that moment, she had not spent a single minute alone, bouncing between Bell's house, his office, and his friends.

Where they were or what they were doing all afternoon Telesco couldn't be certain, there being only one of him to try and track multiple people.

What he did know was that Bell had spent that time at the public defender's office.

Why or how he could be there, Telesco could only guess at. While he was a man with tremendous skills, he freely admitted that the legal arena was well beyond his normal circle. As far as he knew, there was no cause for the public defender to be involved.

And perhaps they weren't. Maybe the meeting was about a different matter entirely.

Either way, Telesco had thought it odd at the time.

Even more so when Bell returned seven hours later, Kyla Wegman in tow.

Parked in front of a no-name bar across the street, Telesco had arrived a couple minutes after them. Just long enough to allow them to exit the truck and pass through the front door.

Easing himself into a diagonal spot, he glanced at the neon signs on the establishment mere feet from his front bumper. Read over the various alcoholic offerings on display.

Felt the pang of longing deep within.

Pushed it aside just as fast.

There would be a time and place for that. The money this assignment alone brought with it could keep him more than sated for the foreseeable future.

Until then, he needed to see this through.

Settled low behind the wheel, he knew nobody could see him. Anyone paying a great deal of attention might have thought it odd that no one exited after parking, may even stare for a few minutes, but would eventually give it up.

If they were out and about on a Thursday evening, they had better things to be doing than worry about the dilapidated truck parked on the street.

For the third time on the day, Telesco pulled his cellphone over onto his lap. Opened the recent call log and saw the number he was looking for, the only one in the list, repeated several times in a row.

Pressed send.

The first ring was barely complete before it was snatched up. The sound of heavy breathing could be heard on the other end. Whether it was from anger or running to pick up, Telesco could only guess at.

Found himself not especially caring.

"Yeah?"

"Bell is back down at the public defender's office," Telesco reported.

Just like the man on the other end, he didn't bother with a greeting. Didn't pretend to put even the slightest bit of joviality in his tone.

They were not friends. No point in fronting otherwise.

"Shit," the other side muttered.

Telesco nodded in agreement. Did not bother to respond. Instead kept his attention aimed at the rearview mirror. Fought the urge to turn around and openly stare through the back window.

"And it just got worse," he added.

There was a long pause, enough that it was clear the opposite end was waiting for him to continue before eventually getting tired and prompting him.

"How so?"

"The state prosecutor, what's her name..."

"Stiles," the man inserted quickly.

"Yeah," Telesco said. Felt the name click into place in the back of his mind. "Her. She just walked in, too. Something's going down."

"Shit," the man repeated, adding an extra amount of vitriol that was unmistakable.

Again, Telesco nodded. Said nothing.

It was obvious what was coming next. It wasn't the first time he had been in the position. He knew what their default setting was. How they preferred to handle similar situations to this in the past.

The only question was when they would decide to move on it.

"You know what you have to do."

Telesco nodded.

"The $100K offer?"

He knew what the answer was before asking, but had to push it out there for assurance anyway.

"No. The other," the man said. "Just be sure to make it look like an accident."

CHAPTER FIFTY-TWO

Gladness.

Relief.

The two emotions rolled off Drake in a ratio of about two-to-one. Poured out of Kyla in the same proportion, with each side flipped.

Together it formed a mixture that was of equal amounts, filling the interior of the truck. Working something like a narcotic, it sent them both floating high above the bench seat they sat on.

"Well now, that was something," Drake said. Reached out and squeezed the steering wheel, using it to ground him. To hold him in place until he convinced himself that what he thought just occurred had actually done so.

"Yes, it was," Kyla replied. Ran her fingers up through the hair on either side of her head and squeezed. Shook the entire tangled mess from side to side.

The meeting was one that Drake wasn't that sold on when Rosenthal first mentioned it. Definitely had to be persuaded to take part in, to bring Kyla along for the ride.

Both had known every last reason before walking in why it could be a disaster. The ways in which Stiles could derail things.

The fact that Rosenthal may have just wanted to get Kyla in a room so she, McGrady, and Stiles could tee off on her.

That feeling of uncertainty, of dread, had filled them on the way over. Had caused neither to say much of anything as they drove. Pulled them both into a tight clench as they walked inside.

Never could they have imagined things playing out the way they did.

"Did you see how fast Stiles's tune changed once Rosenthal told her it could be something much bigger?" Drake asked, allowing no small amount of marvel to creep into voice.

"Right?" Kyla replied. "Just dropped both bags and folded her hands in her lap."

On the opposite end of the seat, Kyla mimicked the action. Pulled her face into a snooty grimace. "I'm listening."

Drake couldn't help but laugh as she delivered the line.

If not for the obvious joking overtones, it was surprisingly close to what Stiles had actually sounded like.

"And then once we started explaining things-" Drake said.

"And she just jumped!" Kyla said. "Like the whole damn thing was her idea!"

"Did you see her light up when we talked about it being WEPCO? And that there could be huge state and federal implications?"

Reaching out, Kyla slapped at the front dashboard. Pulled back and clapped her hands in front of her.

"I don't know the first damn thing about any of this, and even I could see how ridiculous it was."

"I know!" Drake said. "She was all Sally Cyclist up until the moment something bigger came along, then poof! No more caring about her husband getting sideswiped by a truck."

Again Kyla laughed, pointing her face toward the ceiling and guffawing with everything she had.

From his perch behind the steering wheel, Drake couldn't help but do the same. If not for what had happened in the conference room, then for the display going on beside him.

Valerie Stiles was a wench. There was no denying that. But it was also clear that the reaction of Kyla went a lot deeper than seeing one uppity woman have her personal crusade handed back to her on a platter.

This was about release, letting go of a tension that had plagued her for a week solid. The first bit of good news the poor girl had experienced in quite some time.

Once the initial burst of laughter passed, Kyla wiped at her eyes. Ran both hands back over her head, straightening her hair. Turned to Drake, the smile still in place. "So, what happens now?"

Feeling the smile on his own face lessen a bit, Drake looked back at the front door of the office they had just exited. At the plain brick exterior and the straggly row of juniper bushes lining the front walk.

The entire design that just screamed 1975.

"Well, you heard the conversation," Drake said. "It's kind of on us. The sooner we lean on the front end, get that taken care of, the faster they can start moving on their side."

Beside him, Kyla followed his gaze. Processed what he'd just told her.

"Huh," she said. "Again, complete newbie to all this, but that's kind of what I thought they said."

Nodding once, Drake arched an eyebrow and glanced in her direction.

"So what do you say? Wait for a new day, or try to ride this wave of good fortune as far as it'll take us?"

The smile fell from Kyla's face, replaced by confusion.

"Meaning?"

Reaching into the side pocket of his bag, Drake extracted the first business card Dan Harmon had left and held it up for Kyla to see.

"Shall we give Mr. Harmon a call? I guarantee he's awake. The man probably hasn't slept a wink since he first came to see you."

CHAPTER FIFTY-THREE

Loud.

Intrusive.

The sound erupted from the cellphone perched on the nightstand by Michael Pittman's bed. As he had not yet fallen asleep, or even attempted to, it didn't wake him. Certainly performed its intended purpose of grabbing his attention.

A low groan erupted from deep in his chest as he rolled over onto a shoulder. Extended a hand and snatched up the phone, depressing the button on the side to stop the ringer mid-tone.

Knowing there were only a handful of people in the world that had that particular number – all of them in some way connected to what had been going on over the previous week – Pittman didn't bother checking the caller ID.

Instead smashed it straight to his cheek and answered using the same low graveled tone he saved for the phone.

"Yeah."

No other greeting of any kind. Just a single brusque word meant to relay that whatever came next had better be important, and, if the caller knew what was best, good news.

"Michael? Dan Harmon here."

Pittman pushed a long breath out through his nose and rotated up onto a hip. Used his body's momentum to swing his feet to the floor and sat with his elbows resting on his knees.

"Yeah," he repeated. Nothing more.

"Just calling to let you know that Drake Bell contacted me a few minutes ago and asked for a meeting in the morning. I'll be flying over on the 7:10 to meet with him and Kyla Wegman."

It wasn't until Harmon mentioned the girl's name that Pittman was able to place the name Drake Bell. Only once or twice had Telesco used it in his reports, most of the time referring to him simply as *the attorney*.

As he worked his way through things, he remained silent, waiting for Harmon to get to the point of his call.

"Just thought you should know, this thing will hopefully be all wrapped up in the morning."

Pittman chose not to respond. Instead worked at the thin layer of soft flesh lining his forehead. Felt it moving back and forth beneath the rough pads of his fingertips.

When at last he spoke, his tone was so low he could barely hear it in his own ears.

"Actually, it'll be over long before that."

There was no verbal response of any kind on the other end of the line. A simple inhalation just loud enough to be heard and nothing more.

"The call's been made," Pittman said. "Probably be best if you were still on that flight anyway, but I wouldn't plan on doing much negotiating."

On the other end, Harmon could be heard breathing loudly, almost panting. Pittman knew the man was a consummate attorney, was probably preparing another of his long-winded tirades about being bound to report any impending crimes that may take place.

Also knew the man wasn't foolish enough to voice them. That doing so would not end any better than the last time he had tried to do so.

"Just thought you should know."

CHAPTER FIFTY-FOUR

Fourteen hours.

That was all Kyla had to wait.

At that time, she, Drake, and Dan Harmon would sit down in the Montana Legal Services office. Together they would hash out whatever the settlement was going to be.

Finally, he would leave her alone.

No more showing up unannounced as she climbed from the shower. No more notes stuck under the windshield wipers on her car.

Hopefully, just enough money to finally turn a corner and begin anew. Make things right.

Drake had put the call on speaker so she could hear as well. It was clear within an instant that Harmon had not expected to hear from them. That he wasn't a fan at all of hearing Drake's voice on the other end of the line.

To his credit, he had tried everything he could to turn the power dynamic back in his favor. Had insisted they wait until Monday to meet. Said he needed the weekend to go over things.

When that was shot down, he tried anything he could think of to get them to come to Anaconda for the meeting. Again, Drake had been unwavering.

Tomorrow morning, in his office.

After that, any talk of a settlement would have to be done in front of a judge.

Covering her mouth to keep from emitting a peep, Kyla had listened as Harmon eventually capitulated. Let it be known he did not appreciate the way things played out.

Agreed to be in Missoula at 10:00 a.m. the next morning just the same.

Not until the call was complete did Drake start the truck. Pull away and circle back through town, stopping outside her house at a quarter after 9:00, a full 12 hours after she had left for the day.

"Thank you for the ride, again," Kyla said as they eased to a stop. "My car is still parked outside your office downtown..."

"Right," Drake replied. "So I'll need to pick you up in the morning. Not a problem."

"Last one," Kyla said. "I swear."

"Not a problem," Drake repeated. Looked past her to the darkened apartment sitting just up off the street, the sloped yard rising almost level with the hood of the truck.

"You sure you don't want to stay with us tonight? We have a spare bedroom you're welcome to."

"Oh," Kyla said. Had figured he might offer. Didn't want to have to explain that after so many nights in a jail cell, followed by another one hugging her pillow and fearing Dan Harmon might show up again, she just wanted a peaceful sleep in her own bed.

"I appreciate the offer, but I'm okay. Kind of looking forward to going in, taking a shower, and crawling into bed."

"You sure?" Drake said. "We even have a vicious guard dog there to protect you, in case you need it."

The mental image of Suzy Q being anything resembling a *vicious guard dog* caused Kyla to smile. She held the pose a moment, thinking of the little wiggling ball of brown and white, before opening the passenger door.

Felt the cold night air swirl in around her legs.

"Thank you," she said. "But you guys have already done more than enough for me. One more day, then I promise, I'm out of your hair."

"Naw, don't do that," Drake said. "Hasn't been that way at all, and you know it."

"Still," Kyla said. Extended a hand to Drake, wrapping it around his wrist. "It's meant a lot."

Just as fast, she released her grip. Stepped down out of the truck and walked up the front lane to her door. Unlocked the door and pushed it open.

Stopped and turned to wave, letting Drake know she was in safe.

Made it two steps over the threshold, just far enough to close the door behind her.

Heard the slightest moan of a floorboard before the world cut to black.

CHAPTER FIFTY-FIVE

The wave.

That was the signal Drake was waiting for prior to pulling away from the curb. The sign from Kyla that she was through the front door.

Once he saw that, he dropped the truck into gear and pulled a U-turn in front of her place. Went back in the same direction he had just come from.

It had been a good day. An excellent one, in fact.

What had started rough, asking Greg and Wyatt to do some digging, had gotten a bit uglier. Included Kyla coming by the office. His first meeting with Barb Rosenthal.

From there though, the trajectory was decidedly upward.

The meeting with Rosenthal, McGrady, and Stiles was much better than he ever could have hoped for. He had concerns walking in there, but trusted that the public defender knew what she was talking about, would not hang him out to dry.

Soon found out just how right she was.

Valerie Stiles had made it seem to the world like her one driving force was to look out for cyclists. To make sure what her husband, her family, had been through never happened to somebody else.

In truth, she just wanted a soapbox to stand on. Something to trumpet to the masses.

Rosenthal had said that afternoon she suspected Stiles had her eyes set on running for a major political office. After seeing the way she lit up at the mention of going after WEPCO, Drake could see that might have been an understatement.

All in all, things were on the upswing. He still had the face-to-face with Dan Harmon in the morning, but the phone call had made it clear how that would probably play out.

It was time for a cautious celebration.

Which of course meant the Firetower.

The thought of going for pizza hadn't occurred to Drake until Kyla was halfway to her door. Otherwise, he would have invited her over to join them. Even then, the thought of calling out to her occurred to him.

Just as fast it had faded though, her making it clear upon her exit that she wanted to be done for the night. And he couldn't blame her. He wanted to be done, and he hadn't been through half of what she had in the past week.

Easing to the stop sign at the end of her street, Drake reached out. Turned on the radio and found a local classic rock station.

Could not help but smirk at the irony of AC/DC's "Moneytalks" streaming through the speakers.

Resting his hands high on the steering wheel, he used his thumbs to play along to the beat. Was all set to belt out the final stanza when something caught his eye.

Rolling halfway through the intersection, he smashed his foot on the brake. Felt the truck lurch, thrusting his upper body forward before rocking back into place, setting him flush against the bench seat.

With the music still blaring around him, Drake turned his full attention down the side street feeding in from his left. Stared past the first couple of houses, their fronts lit up by security lights.

There was no earthly reason for the truck to catch his attention. In a town like Missoula, every street was dotted with them. Big or small, every color imaginable, they were one of the preferred means of transportation in a place that saw seven or more months of winter each year.

Still, this one in particular caught in the back of his mind. Resonated deep within, begging his psyche to catch up, to seize on where he had spotted it before.

Tucked away in the shadows, Drake could just see the front half of it. Dark and ominous, it was tucked beneath the overhanging branches of an Aspen tree, clearly meant to be hidden from view.

Still, there was no mistaking the distinct rust pattern stretched over the front hood. The streak of yellow tape that covered part of the front caution lights.

Taken singularly, none of it was enough to make the truck memorable. As a whole, though, it was too much, as if the owner was *trying* to be inconspicuous.

"The optometrist," Drake whispered. Pictured it sitting just two spots down a couple days before. Felt something else click into place, his mind working forward again. "And my office. Sonuva-"

Feeling a roil pass through his stomach, Drake reached out and snapped off the radio. Pulled his cellphone from his bag and with one hand he called it to life.

With the other hand, he pulled another U-turn and headed back in the opposite direction. Ignored the sound of squealing tires as he did so, thankful no other cars were in the intersection.

With his attention fixed on the road, he didn't have time to dig out Bear McGrady's number. Instead he pressed the second speed dial and put the phone on speaker. Depressed the accelerator down hard and felt the big engine rumble as it surged ahead.

Heard a familiar voice pick after the third ring.

"Yo," Kade answered.

"Call the police, then get to Kyla's as fast as you can. We've got trouble."

CHAPTER FIFTY-SIX

An accident.

Make it look like an accident.

Given the location of the girl's apartment, Lon Telesco opted to subdue her the moment she walked in.

Living on a busy street, all it would have taken was one errant scream for a neighbor to get antsy. To put in a call to the police. Bring a very abrupt end to his presence and, by extension, everything WEPCO was trying to do as well.

Compounding the issue was Drake Bell.

Hoping that the girl would come home was a shot in the dark, a stab that he had to take. Based on nothing more than pure hope that whatever fears she had that morning about the business card had abated.

Given that she had spent the evening meeting with half the attorneys in town, it made sense that she would be calmed at least somewhat. That whatever fears she had would be allayed, thinking there was no chance Dan Harmon would be paying her a visit any time soon.

As if it had been Harmon that visited her that morning.

The other worry where Bell was concerned was if he followed her in. As such, he'd had no choice but to be lying in wait. To prepare a sneak attack to subdue him the moment he entered.

It hadn't taken more than a quick Google search to see that Bell was a former Montana football player. Having watched him for the last week, Telesco could certainly believe it. He wasn't nearly as large as he once was, but still carried himself with the easy grace of an athlete.

Had at least an inch or two and several pounds on Telesco.

Hence the need for the element of surprise.

And the length of iron pipe Telesco kept in the truck for just such occasions.

Tucked away behind the front door, he had hidden for more than an hour. Was prepared to wait at least twice that much longer. There was no way to know how long the meeting would last. If they would go for dinner afterwards. If she would even come home that night.

All he knew was she would have to come back at some point.

Pinning his shoulders into the corner behind the door, Telesco had let his weight rest against the drywall. He leaned the pipe against his calf and allowed his eyes to drift partially closed, his body again entering a relaxed state.

The moment the low rumble of a pickup engine found his ears, his entire form reenergized. His eyes popped open wide. He bent at the waist and picked up the pipe.

Squeezing the rusted metal in his right hand, he felt his heart rate rise. Sweat droplets dotted his forehead, his breaths coming in short bursts.

In through his nose. Out through his mouth.

Seconds ticked by as footsteps approached. The sound of keys jangling could be heard. Metal teeth ground against the lock mechanism.

All breathing stopped as the door opened. Weather stripping wheezed. A puff of cold air entered.

A single silhouette passed in front of him.

Just as fast, the door swung closed.

The girl was alone. And for the next second or two, she was in the dark.

In one quick movement, Telesco stepped forward. Cocked the pipe to his ear as if about to throw a baseball. Brought the bludgeon forward, connecting right at the base of her skull.

Just as he had expected, the blow did its job, her body seemingly melting before him. Fell straight to the floor as if liquid.

Taking another quick step forward, he managed to just get his hands beneath her armpits before she landed. To catch the bulk of her weight prior to hitting the floor and making an audible thud that could be heard from the outside.

Leaving her in a heap, he walked over to the front windows. Watched as the truck reversed course and headed in the opposite direction. Waited until the taillights faded from sight before pulling the curtains shut and turning on a single lamp alongside the window.

No part of him wanted to do so. A pang of animosity even passed through him as the bulb ruined his night vision. Seared through his brain.

He knew he had to, though. That anybody watching from the outside would expect it.

That Bell would notice if he happened to drive back past.

Once his vision returned to normal, Telesco took a look around the apartment. Assessed what little there was on hand. Remembered his directive to make it look like an accident.

The place as a whole wasn't a dump. It was neat and clean, the kind of thing one would expect a single young woman to live in.

At the same time, it was a shit box. Everything in it – from the carpet to the furnishings – was badly outdated, in dire need of updating.

Reminded Telesco of the first apartment he had lived in years before.

A quick pass through the place confirmed what he had been thinking since getting his orders hours before.

The girl had been wacked at the base of her skull with an iron pipe. Any medical examiner worth their salt would see it right off. Maybe even be able to collect some flakes of rust from her head.

To combat all of that, Telesco had to stage things so it looked like a fall. Something severe enough to knock her out, to cause some damage.

And he still needed a method of both dispatching her and cleaning up the ensuing mess.

That left only a single option.

Leaving the pipe where it lay, Telesco again grabbed her beneath the armpits and hefted her limp body from the floor.

Headed toward the bathroom.

CHAPTER FIFTY-SEVEN

Options.

Too damn many options.

As Drake raced back to Kyla's place, the possibilities of how to play the next few minutes were simply too many.

He could wait for Kade, though what that extra time might mean for Kyla he had no way of knowing.

He could slow down and try calling her, though if she was in danger, doing so would only tip off whoever was there.

He could take the extra time to stop and call Bear McGrady, tell him he'd spotted a truck that he'd noticed at many of the same places they'd been the last couple of days. Knew he would probably get laughed at and told not to call again.

Or he could simply burst in through the front door. Run the risk of tearing the thing off the hinges and earning Kyla's wrath. Just hope that explaining it to her after the fact would be enough to assuage any damage his hasty actions might cause.

Running them one time after another in his head, Drake opted for the latter. Tried to tell himself he wasn't just being jumpy, that the anxiousness of Kyla wasn't now rubbing off on him.

The thought of stopping a few houses short of Kyla's occurred to him. Brought with it the brief notion that he could approach unseen.
Was pushed aside just as fast.

If somebody was in there, wherever he parked wouldn't matter. They were there for the express purpose of hurting his client. His friend.

There was no point in given them any extra time to do so.

"Come on, Kade. Move your ass," Drake whispered. Felt his heart rate pick up, beginning to pound through his temples.

For one of the few times since hanging up his cleats years ago, the familiar rush of adrenaline flooded into his system. Drake let his chin rock back a few inches, the warm feeling flowing through his body.

Returning to him like an old friend.

Veins throbbed on the backside of his hands as he put the truck in park. Killed the engine. Spun out from behind the wheel and popped the top on the metal toolbox running the width of his truck bed.

Without glancing in, Drake grabbed the first thing his fingers wrapped around and sprinted toward the house. Looked down just long enough to see the jagged teeth of a pipe wrench in his hand.

Heart pounding, sweat streaming into the small of his back, Drake didn't bother knocking. He checked the door handle and found, to his surprise, it turned easily in his grasp.

Lowering himself into a crouch, he stepped inside. Heard the sound of water running. Turned his attention toward it.

Felt a whiff of air pass within inches of the top of his head.

CHAPTER FIFTY-EIGHT

Too high.

It was obvious the attacker lying in wait had not expected Drake to enter in a crouch.

The blow that swung past his head was delivered in a vicious arc. Was designed to at the very least incapacitate, if not outright kill.

A grunt of exertion was released from the man as Drake planted his right foot. Drove himself back into the corner without seeing who was behind him.

Prayed there was only one.

Less than a second later, his shoulder found the soft flesh of a stomach. Heard the air escape from the man's lungs as Drake drove him into the wall. Backed up a few inches and repeated the measure.

Gripped the wrench tight in his hand and brought it in for a uppercut, aiming at the soft tissue between the man's legs.

Halfway into his movement, an elbow crashed down onto the top of his shoulder. Pitched his body to the side. Sent the wrench careening off at an angle, glancing the man's leg and nothing more.

Needing to regroup, Drake pushed himself out of the corner. Turned to face his attacker for the first time.

There was something vaguely familiar about the man, though

nothing that jumped out at Drake as having seen him before. A little smaller than he was, he was dressed in jeans and a Henley. A flannel shirt over it. Light brown hair cropped close. Facial growth of the same length.

A look that said he was trying entirely too hard to look tough, just as his truck was trying entirely too hard to blend in.

Like Drake, he was carrying a single blunt weapon in his right hand, the man opting for a short length of pipe. His left was free, extended out away from him.

Neither one said a word as the man rushed forward, starting with a left-handed punch designed to do nothing but get Drake to react.

Sensing as much, Drake charged straight. Stabbed the end of the wrench out before him. Felt it connect solidly with the man's chest, driving him back a few inches.

Using the backward momentum, the man pivoted on the ball of his foot. Swung the pipe in a backhanded swipe. Again just missed the top of Drake's head as he dropped beneath it and rolled through.

Came up on his feet on the opposite side of the room.

There they both paused, the intruder holding a hand to his chest where Drake had hit him. Rotated his arm a couple of times. Let a glower show Drake he did not appreciate what had happened.

Drake gave no outward reaction. Switched the wrench into his left hand and back again.

Somewhere in the rear of the apartment, he could hear the water continuing to run. Could only guess at what the man had done with Kyla.

Knew he had no more than a few minutes to find out.

Armed with that knowledge, this time he took the initiative. Charged straight ahead and tried the man's own tactic, leading with a looping left hook.

The hope was to try and get the man to feign right. To create an opening that would enable him to smash the wrench into the man's face.

Instead, the man side stepped toward it. Used his free hand to block the wrench. Brought the pipe up in a jabbing motion that caught Drake just above the eye.

Opened a cut as it glanced off his forehead.

Warmth crept over Drake's face as blood streamed down along the side of his cheek. Spotted the carpet beneath him as it dripped off his chin.

Brought a smile to the other man's face.

"You bleed just like the girl."

At once, the full weight of the moment flooded in around Drake. Seeing the grin on the man's face. Feeling his own blood drip from his jaw. Hearing the water continue to run.

Together they all mixed with the adrenaline bolting through his system. Fed into the acrimony roiling within.

Pushed him to do something he would never have thought to otherwise.

Relaxing his grip on the wrench, he let the head of it fall toward the floor. Grasped the handle just before it left his hand, wrapping his fingers around the very bottom of it.

Didn't hesitate as he snapped it forward alongside his leg, aiming it directly at the man's throat.

Threw the misshapen object as hard as he could in an underhanded swing.

For a moment, the smile remained on the man's face. Evaporated as he saw the wrench flying straight for him.

Driving his body forward, Drake followed the wrench as it flew. Saw the man flail with both arms to try and knock it away, spinning out to the side just in time to avoid it.

The moment he did so, Drake buried his shoulder into the man's spine. Felt vertebrae pop beneath his weight. Heard the man grunt as they pitched straight forward.

The flimsy coffee table was no match for their combined weights as they landed flat atop it. Toppled to the floor in a mass of limbs and shattered particle board.

The smell of sawdust instantly filled the air.

On contact, the man's body went limp for a split second. Just long enough for the pipe to fall from his grasp. To land on the floor beside them.

Springing forward, Drake buried his left knee into the man's back. Forced his head down to the ground. Picked up the length of pipe and aimed it at the base of the man's skull.

Heard the satisfying crunch of steel connecting with the occipital bone.

Felt the man go completely limp beneath him. The urge to raise his arm again. To aim for the center of the man's skull.

To smash it down as hard as he could.

Fortunately, he also felt an arm snake around his waist and pull him backwards.

Heard the voice of Kade in his ear, keeping him from doing anything he would come to regret.

"I got this. Go get Kyla."

CHAPTER FIFTY-NINE

Tired.

Groggy.

Stiff.

Every step reminded Drake of exactly what he'd been through the night before. Of the battle with a man he now knew to be named Lon Telesco. Of finding Kyla weighted down in the bathtub, unconscious, the water level just inches below her nose.

The long hours spent with Bear McGrady and his team. Sitting soaking wet on Kyla's couch. Watching them take Telesco away. Ask him the same set of questions in triplicate as medics stitched his forehead together.

Arriving home and helping Kyla into the spare bedroom.

Emerging just in time to find Sage waiting on him, having finished a shift only minutes before. A sour look on her face from checking her phone on the way home to find a message from Kade telling her what happened.

Spending most of the night awake, Sage acting as his own personal wet nurse, insisting he stay awake to fend off the mild concussion he'd been diagnosed with. Both of them eventually falling asleep on the couch together anyway.

Waking less than 45 minutes before he had to be into the office. His head swaying as he sprinted into the shower, forcing him to press his hands into either side of the stall to stay upright. Wanting so badly to sit and let the hot water beat down on his head, but forcing himself to lean away and keep his stitches dry.

The weight of all of it was obvious as Drake acted in slow, disjointed movements. Pulled out a charcoal Brooks Brothers suit he had not worn regularly since the summer before and selected a pale blue shirt and a patterned tie to go with it.

Knew that Dan Harmon would show up looking to impress, trying to use his image to establish some sort of upper hand.

Was not about to give him the satisfaction.

As he dressed, he fought to clear his head. To remember everything that had been discussed at the meeting with Rosenthal, Stiles, and McGrady the night before.

Despite just 14 hours having passed, it felt like days or even longer. The exact particulars of the plan seemed like a distant memory, no longer quite as important, brushed to the side by what transpired at Kyla's.

Leaving Kyla and Sage both asleep at the house, Drake nodded to Ajax, an unspoken request to watch over them that was understood and agreed to. Climbed into his truck. Watched his mirrors the entire time he drove to the office.

Saw nothing.

Scanned the length of the street before climbing out after parking. Again, saw nothing. Entered the office to find Teague and Mooney back at their desks.

Both looked up as he entered. Saw the crescent moon of stitches above his left eye. The accompanying robin's egg rising around it and the bruising that promised to get worse in the coming days.

"Later," he said. Raised a hand to stop whatever questions he knew was coming. Did not particularly feel like answering them at the moment. Knew that doing so would only make him angry.

For the time being, he needed to keep his head clear. To be able to meet Dan Harmon head on. To best the other half of the team WEPCO had sent out to defeat him.

"Also, you guys can let up on the research for the time being. I'll explain that later as well."

Drake left it at that and ducked into his office. Had barely touched down into his seat when the bell on the front door rang out. The sound of wingtip shoes could be heard walking across the floor and a voice full of bravado and bluster echoed through the office.

A moment later, Mooney appeared in the doorway. "Your, um, appointment is here."

"Send him in, please."

A low groan escaped Drake as he stood so he was positioned behind his desk as Harmon entered. Saw the suit Drake was wearing and looked a bit surprised. Glanced around at the tiny workspace and immediately wore the expression Drake had expected him to show up with.

"Good morning," Harmon offered. Extended a hand across the desk. "I don't know that we've actually been introduced. Dan Harmon."

The man was exactly as Kyla described him. Had the look of someone that would be hired to be a television spokesperson attorney, practically a caricature unto himself.

"Drake Bell, counsel for Kyla Wegman."

The shake was a little longer than necessary. A little more forceful as well.

Drake made no effort to back down from it. To turn his head so Harmon couldn't see the battle wound stitched together on his face.

"Will Ms. Wegman be joining us?" Harmon asked. Opened his shoulder bag and took out a sheaf of papers. Placed them on the desk before settling down into his chair.

"No," Drake said. Made sure his tone was clear. "She doesn't need to be here for this, especially after what you guys tried last night."

The statement seemed to give Harmon pause. His movements slowed as he positioned the documents just so before looking up at Drake.

"I'm sorry?"

"You should be," Drake said. "For what you did to her."

"For this," he added, motioning to his forehead. "For everything you've done in the last week."

A bit of color flushed Harmon's cheeks. It was obvious the words had hit home, that the older man knew exactly what Drake was referring to. Was not about to admit as much.

"I'm not sure what you think you know, Mr. Bell, but I assure you, I came here under good faith this morning."

"Bullshit," Drake said. Realized how unprofessional he was being. Did not much care. "You weren't expecting to come here at all this morning. It wasn't until you got a call late last night saying Telesco failed that you even had any intention of showing up."

This time, in a stark contrast to just a moment before, the color bled from Harmon's face.

"Let me guess," Drake said, "caught the 7:10 over from Seattle?"

Watched as Harmon shrank back into his chair.

"Yeah, I know all about your office over there," Drake said. Fueled by venom and adrenaline, he could feel his pulse rise. Tell as each heartbeat pushed more blood through the knot on his forehead.

"Turns out, you don't need a fancy high-rise or the backing of a seedy mining operation to gain access to information."

Long past the point of responding, Harmon leaned back in his seat. Tried his best to make a dubious face. Crossed his right leg over his left and laced his fingers over his knee.

"You don't even need those," Drake said, gesturing to the stack of case law printed out between them.

Any sense of legal decorum was out the window. Dan Harmon, WEPCO, everybody associated with the case had lost that privilege long ago, back when they had put in place an agreement with Alex Breslin to have him spy on people in his own community.

Clear back even to Lord knew when, to a time that they first began employing such actions.

The mere thought of how many Kyla Wegman's they had done this to over the years made Drake's stomach clench.

How many people they had bought off. Had sent Lon Telesco or someone like him to dispatch when that didn't work.

How many people like Susan and Mandy Moritz had been affected tangentially because of it.

"Well then, why exactly am I here?" Harmon said, attempting to sound bored and indifferent. Unable to hide the fact that he knew he was a man that was beaten.

Drake let the question hang for a moment. Knew he was going to relish answering it.

"To write a check. A great big fat check worth a hell of a lot more than that pittance you started with a few days ago."

CHAPTER SIXTY

The jacket was gone.

Drake wanted so badly to have shed the tie as well. To have cast it aside and rolled up the sleeves on his dress shirt.

Knew that he needed to play the part a little longer.

Not that Barb Rosenthal would care. They worked with a similar client base. Saw past the surface. Knew what really mattered.

Valerie Stiles was a different case altogether, though. To her, the sizzle was just as important as the steak.

Both women knew that he had met with Dan Harmon that morning. Step one of several that were laid out the evening before.

Arguably the most important, left to the most junior man in the room by quite a considerable margin.

Given everything that had happened, both before and after their previous meeting, it could also be argued that he had the easiest as well.

Just before noon, Drake stepped into the public defender's office for the third time in the past 24 hours. Nodded to the woman at the front desk and was buzzed right through.

Ignored the sideways glances from several of the employees in the office. The open stares of others.

Entered to find Rosenthal seated at the head of the table. A not-so-subtle statement that this was her office. The time of trying to play nice and give the illusion of equal footing was past. To her right was Valerie Stiles, for once having arrived a few minutes early.

Both women looked up as he entered.

Rosenthal was the first to react. Raised a hand to her mouth and appeared aghast. Had the social grace to say nothing. To wait for him to explain.

Valerie Stiles had no such compunction.

"What the hell happened to you?"

"Well, good afternoon to you as well," Drake said. Took up the seat McGrady had used the night before and put his bag on the table beside him. Stared directly across at Stiles.

Whatever deference he might have shown her as recently as the night before had vanished. Perhaps it was having gotten a glimpse behind the curtain, having seen what she was really made of. Maybe it was the events of the previous night, the fresh stitches and lingering adrenaline keeping his manners at bay.

More likely, it was the feeling of elation that was still roiling through him after taking Dan Harmon to the cleaners.

Turning his attention to Rosenthal, Drake said, "WEPCO happened to me. And to Kyla."

He paused there, watching as color drained from Rosenthal's face.

"One of their goons was in her house when I dropped her off last night." Another pause. A glance to Stiles to see if her reaction betrayed even a shred of humanity.

There was none.

"And he did that?" Rosenthal asked.

"Mhmm," Drake said. "Much worse to Kyla. Bashed her head with a pipe, tried to drown her in the bathtub."

Silence fell as both women stared. Said nothing.

"Of course, Dan Harmon denied everything this morning, but come on," Drake said. "It wasn't hard to figure out, especially given how much he ended up settling up for just to get us to go away."

"Oh, my God," Rosenthal whispered.

"Yeah," Drake said. Nodded in agreement. "I'm going to meet with

Detective McGrady later this afternoon, see how much they've gotten out of the guy, if we can tie a direct line between him and WEPCO..."

Again, he glanced to each of them in turn.

"If so, then your jobs just got a heck of a lot easier."

A faint flicker of a smile appeared on Stiles's face. In a surprising move though, she said nothing.

"They have the man in custody?" Rosenthal said.

"Yeah," Drake said. "He got in one good shot with a pipe, but I still won. He was face down on the living room floor by the time McGrady arrived."

Rosenthal's eyebrows rose high up her forehead. It was obvious several questions rested right on the tip of her tongue.

She remained silent.

"So, armed with all that, I sat down with Dan Harmon this morning," Drake said. Almost laughed as he thought of the man walking into his office, full of swagger and the usual tricks.

The way it was short lived, at best.

"Came in with a big stack of case law. Tried to pretend we were actually going to be debating the merits of the matter."

This time, he allowed a crack of a smile to form.

"Didn't take long for that to change."

The entire agenda for this meeting was so he could brief them on what had transpired that morning. To prep them so he could hand things off, allow them to take the lead from that point forward.

The floor was his. Neither one of them would be saying much of anything.

"Two million," Drake said. Jumped right to the punch line, angling for shock value.

Saw that the single statement achieved that and then some.

"Come again," Stiles said, her first words since commenting on his face.

"Two million," Drake repeated. "He came in and acted like he was in charge. I quickly let him know that wasn't going to fly.

"Opening value was half a million. I countered back at five, knowing there was no way it would fly. We met at two."

The smile grew a bit larger as he glanced to Rosenthal.

"I could tell he was in way over his head on that one, would end up getting his ass chewed for it, but that's not our problem."

"No, it is not," Rosenthal agreed. Rotated her head slowly from side to side. "And what did you agree to with that?"

"Just as we suspected. Kyla will not file suit, will not go to the press, will not even utter the word WEPCO."

"Anything else?" Rosenthal asked.

"Like what?" Drake countered. "He can't stop the prosecutor's office from going after them. Can't keep the people in Anaconda they haven't already bought off from bringing a class action."

All of these were things every person in the room knew. Things that had been discussed the night before.

In the grand scheme, Kyla settling might not bring about the enormous social justice that was required, but it did at least allow for her to officially move on. To put things behind her.

To ease the enormous guilt that had been gnawing on her.

It also gave Valerie Stiles something to do. Allowed her to have a new stumping ground. Ensured that even if she did take up the issue of cyclist rights again, she would be doing so without exploiting Kyla or Mandy Moritz.

For Drake, that was a victory.

For him, and his client.

A moment passed without response. Drake met Rosenthal's gaze, the two eventually sharing a nod of understanding before turning their attention to Stiles.

"Well, Prosecutor," Rosenthal said, "I believe the floor is now yours."

CHAPTER SIXTY-ONE

"How's the head?"

Drake smiled at the question. Glanced over from the driver's seat to look at Kyla seated across from him.

"How's yours?"

Subconsciously, Kyla raised a hand and patted lightly at the back of her skull.

"Almost seems fitting, given what I did to that poor girl," she said. Once more, she ran her hand back over her blonde hair before dropping it into place on her lap.

"Besides, at least I can cover mine. Yours is right out there in the open for everybody to see."

Unable to argue with her, Drake remained silent. Wound through the streets on the south end of town. Pulled up in front of a modest one-story ranch home, the exterior constructed from brick. Hedge squared even beneath the front windows. An SUV and a 10-speed bike both parked in the driveway.

"You're sure you want to do this?" Drake asked. Eased to a stop. Heard a slight squeal roll from the brakes as he did so.

Took his focus from the house to Kyla sitting beside him. Saw her attention aimed at the home before them.

"Yes," she said. Sighed heavily, letting it raise her shoulders on either side of her neck. "I have to."

Drake had known that before even asking the question. Felt the need to put it out there anyway.

Nodded as he shoved the gear shift into park and turned off the engine.

The day was a bit warmer as they stepped outside. Bright sunlight hit them at an angle as they walked up the front path.

The symbolism of the moment was not lost on Drake.

Arriving at the front door, Kyla stayed back. Remained on the ground level, allowing Drake to ascend the front step.

Somewhere inside he could hear a television playing as he walked up. Knocked twice, the outer storm door rattling slightly in its frame.

Movement could be heard in the house as he took a half step back and waited. A moment later, the front door pulled back to reveal Susan Moritz. Dressed in much the same way as she was a few nights before, she seemed different, even at a glance.

No longer did heavy bags underscore her eyes. Gone was the veneer of exhaustion and desperation that had clung to her on their first meeting.

To be sure, she still bore the effects of the last week, but much like he and Kyla, Drake could tell she was on an upward trajectory.

Sometimes, that's the best that could be hoped for.

"Good afternoon, Ms. Moritz. Thank you for letting us stop by like this."

"Thanks for coming," Susan replied. Tone betrayed just the slightest hint of uncertainty.

Stepping to the side, she pushed the door out away from her. Allowed a whiff of something apple-cinnamon to waft out at them.

"Please, come in."

Stopping to wipe his shoes on the rug, Drake stepped inside. Waited for Kyla to follow him. Could sense her palpable uncertainty.

"Also, allow me to introduce you to Kyla Wegman."

Drake left any introduction at that. Stepped to the side as the two women looked at each other. Saw the tears that formed in Kyla's eyes.

Watched as they stood apart from one another for a moment before embracing.

Neither harboring any ill will about the previous week, both ready to move on. Needing to put things to rest. To cleanse whatever bitterness might linger from their lives.

The hug lasted the better part of a minute before Susan released it. Kept one hand on Kyla's forearm. Used it to steer her into the living room.

Remaining rooted in place, Drake allowed them to go. Could hear Susan introduce Kyla to her daughter.

Hear Kyla say hello, voice still thick with tears.

A moment later Susan returned, eyes wet and red. Using the top of her head, she motioned Drake back out through the front door.

Side by side, the two walked in silence. Moved away from the house, making it almost to the curb. Made sure they were out of earshot before turning to face each other.

"Thank you so much again for doing this," Drake said. "I know it was an unusual request."

Pulling her mouth into a tight line, Susan nodded.

"It was actually Mandy's idea. She said she was just as much at fault as Kyla was. Said it didn't do any good to be angry about it."

Drake nodded. If in Mandy's position, he would like to think he'd react the same way.

Kyla had meant no harm. Had freely admitted her guilt. Was here now in an attempt to make things right.

In the end, that's all anybody could ever do. Accept their mistakes. Hope to make amends, to learn something.

Move on.

"Dare I ask what happened to your face?" Susan asked.

"WEPCO," Drake replied, leaving it at that. Knew by the way her eyes slid shut that she understood.

"Kyla got it worse than I did, you just can't see it underneath all that hair."

At that, Susan's eyes opened wide. Her jaw dropped open.

"But you're both..."

"Yeah," Drake said. "We're okay."

There was so much left to say, so many places that he could begin, it was almost impossible to pick just one. So much had happened in the preceding day. So many things that would need to be addressed in due course.

They didn't all have to be discussed now, though.

"I met with Valerie Stiles earlier this afternoon," Drake said. "You should be glad to know she won't be pursuing the cyclist Bill of Rights, or whatever catchy title she'd given it. Or, at least if she does, she won't have her name on it, won't be going anywhere near a camera."

"Meaning, my daughter won't be anywhere near it either?"

"Right," Drake said. "You guys can rest easy on that."

"Thank God," Susan whispered.

"No, thank Barb Rosenthal," Drake corrected. "That woman really went above and beyond for you this week. Will continue to do so moving forward, I'm sure."

Drake saw as renewed moisture came to Susan's eyes.

He didn't bother explaining the full breadth of what his last comment meant. Like a great many things, it would no doubt be explained in the coming weeks.

This trip wasn't about all that, though. It was about setting things right. Letting Kyla make her apologies.

Sharing the one final big piece of information Drake had with Susan.

"Also, I met this morning with a man named Dan Harmon, attorney for WEPCO," Drake said. "After everything that happened, they offered a settlement to Kyla."

"Oh," Susan replied.

"It was clearly a move to cover their rear, and will do nothing to insulate them from the criminal charges or environmental lawsuit fast coming their way, but..."

He paused there, uncertain how to approach the last part.

It wasn't exactly the kind of thing you just dropped on a person, especially someone that had been through as much as Susan Moritz in the past week.

"We hope you don't mind, but Kyla had them split the total right down the middle. One half payable to her, the other to Mandy."

CHAPTER SIXTY-TWO

Red.

Puffy.

Blotchy.

Drake hadn't asked how the meeting between Kyla and Mandy went. There was no need. She wore the effects of it plainly enough across her face.

It being the same exact look that Susan Moritz now wore, finding out she was the new recipient of $1,000,000, courtesy of WEPCO.

Despite the inordinate number of tears, Drake couldn't help but smile seeing so many people in a much better place now than they had been a few days before.

Having things to look forward to.

Winding away from the Moritz home, Drake pushed the truck up Russell Avenue. Turned east toward the Hellgate Canyon. Followed the Clark Fork River back into town.

Somehow, another week had slid past. His every thought had been so consumed with the case, he had missed the awakening of spring around him.

The first signs of buds on the trees. The sun that was getting steadily warmer. The increased level of activity from local residents.

This, too, managed to raise his mood. Buoy him to the cusp of happiness as he parked outside the Missoula Police Department. Stepped out of the truck and joined Kyla for what was hopefully the last official meeting they had to make on the week.

If either of them had their way, the last they would have to make about the case, period.

Stepping inside, Drake recognized the young officer working behind the desk. Nodded and asked to see Detective Bear McGrady. Was shown to his office just a moment later.

Caught the way the young man's jaw opened as he buzzed them through. The way his gaze lingered just a bit too long on Drake's brow.

Ignored it just the same.

Stepping back to the same office he had first encountered a week before, Drake knocked on the door frame. Saw McGrady look up from his computer screen, rise to a half-standing position behind the desk.

"Hey, come on in," he said. Motioned with a hand toward himself.

Rocking back a few inches, Drake allowed Kyla to enter before following her in. Didn't bother closing the door behind him as he settled into the one remaining free chair across from McGrady.

"Thanks for stopping by," McGrady said. "Just wanted to give you guys an update."

"Sure thing," Drake said.

Heard Kyla mumble something similar beside him.

A moment of silence passed as McGrady studied each of them. Made no attempt to hide the fact that he was checking out Drake's stitches. Running his gaze over Kyla.

"How you guys doing?" he asked. "Everything okay? Working like it should?"

Drake glanced over to his right. Ceded the floor to Kyla. Allowed her to nod. Explain that she had a headache from the sun. That a time or two her balance had been off.

That, all in all, she was okay. Would make it just fine.

"And you?" McGrady asked.

Like Kyla, Drake had a splitting headache. Had a handful of fresh stitches. Would likely having a visible scar for the rest of his days.

Like her as well, he was okay. Would make it just fine.

"All set," Drake said.

Once more, McGrady looked over each of them. Seemed to sense that they were underplaying things tremendously.

Opted not to press it.

"Okay," he said. Pulled over a dark brown folder and flipped it open, a sheet of paper affixed at the top by metal clips flapping as he did so.

"The man you subdued last night is one Lon Telesco. In the system from about 15 years ago for some low-level stuff in Silver Bow County. Nothing since then."

Drake nodded. Figured that was about the time he had gone to work for WEPCO, right about the time that environmental cleanup requirements had become even more stringent.

Since then, they had most likely been running interference for him.

"There wasn't anything on his person," McGrady said, "but his truck was a gold mine. Thank you very much for pointing us in that direction."

Drake nodded. Said nothing.

"Whole stack of business cards from Dan Harmon," McGrady said. "All made out in various settlement amounts. Cellphone showing direct communications between the two."

Heat rose within Drake. Seemed to be in direct correlation with the smile he was fighting to keep off his face.

"We picked up Harmon this afternoon at the airport about to catch a plane back to Seattle," McGrady added. "In true lawyer fashion, you can imagine how he took it."

This time, Drake made no attempt to hide the smile.

"No offense," McGrady added, extending a hand toward Drake.

"I've met him," Drake said. "None taken."

"Right now, they're both being held here," McGrady said. "Harmon will probably be out soon. We don't have a lot on him, and he's already had an army of attorneys calling and threatening us with everything under the sun.

"Telesco we have no intention of letting see sunlight for quite a while. Attempted murder, criminal trespass, assault. The list is lengthy and we're guessing once we start working with Anaconda PD, we'll find a whole bunch of other stuff to charge him with too."

Shifting his attention, Drake looked over to Kyla. Saw her turn to meet his gaze.

Both nodded.

After meeting Mandy Moritz, ensuring she would not have to look over her shoulder for Lon Telesco was easily her biggest concern.

Now, it sounded as if that would never be a worry again.

"Thank you, Detective," Drake said.

"Thank you," McGrady echoed. "At some point we'll need depositions from you, maybe even testimony if it gets that far, but for the time being, your statements should suffice."

Sensing that the reason for the meeting was finished, Drake stood. Extended his hand across the desk. Opposite him, McGrady did the same.

"As a detective, I'm not supposed to say this, and will deny it to the end once you leave here..."

Already Drake knew where it was going. Would probably say the same thing if in McGrady's position.

"But damn fine job last night. It must have been satisfying as hell to lay that bastard out."

For a moment, Drake paused. Thought back to the night before.

To smelling his own blood. Having it drip down his face. Hearing the water running in the bathroom. Feeling adrenaline light up his senses in a way he hadn't experienced in years.

Felt the smile return to his face.

"Yeah, it really was."

CHAPTER SIXTY-THREE

The thought of running had occurred to Michael Pittman.

Much like he had several days before, he considered his accumulated finances, the various real estate holdings he had stashed in random locales. The extra passport he had printed up years before with an alias known only to himself and God.

Just as fast though, the notion was dismissed. Approaching 50 years of age, he had no desire to begin a life on the lam. Knew that Darren Welker felt the exact same way.

Was the reason the man was seated in his customary seat to the left of Pittman.

Gone was his usual shirt and tie. Even the slacks and wingtips he normally accompanied them with.

Instead he donned jeans and boots, neither having the slightest smudge or scuff on them, clearly an attempt to survive what they both knew was coming.

For his part, Pittman had made no such concessions. The truth was, he had known such a moment was coming for the better part of 20 years. To try and hide from it, or at the very least deflect any of what they both had coming, would be disgraceful.

He was better than that.

The room was silent, the television off, no phones in sight. In it sat just the two men, each with a highball glass before them, enjoying the last quality libations they would likely see for quite a while.

"Larkin?" Welker asked, his voice punctuating the silence, his gaze not once looking toward Pittman.

"Home," Pittman said. "Started crying when I broke the news. Said he'd rather spend the last few hours he had with his wife than sitting around this damn table with us."

A tiny flicker of mirth passed over Welker's face as he snorted.

"Funny, I don't recall him ever referring to this as a damn table when he was showing up and rubberstamping things."

The same thought had occurred to Pittman more than once. "Getting paid quite handsomely for it too, I might add."

Another nod of the head was Welker's only response to the comment.

"Telesco?"

"Pinched," Pittman said. "And in true caveman fashion, used his one call to phone me."

"Jesus," Welker replied, drawing the word out several times the normal length. "Will he talk?"

"Most likely. He knows they'll be here soon enough, probably won't see any point in trying to cover for us."

"So he'll say whatever he has to to cover his own ass."

This time, it was Pittman's turn to simply nod in silence.

It didn't do either man any good to sit and analyze where things had gone wrong. There were simply too many instances dotting the past decades to ever truly pin it down. They had known when they first took the reins of a sinking ship that it would probably end in disaster.

Had that very same conversation when they shifted their focus from trying to oversee a Superfund mining site into creating an ironclad money laundering system.

Now that their time had come, they would do as they always accepted they must. They would accept their punishment, keep their mouths shut, and pray that the authorities didn't look too far into their books.

If they did, prison would be the least of their concerns.

The clock on the wall read exactly 5:00 pm as the first knock sounded at the door. A moment later the second one came, this one much harsher than the previous, a trio of bangs made by a heavy fist, followed a moment later by a deep baritone voice.

"Michael Pittman and Darren Welker, this is Agent William Stanson, FBI."

Neither man said a word. Made any effort to stand and answer the door.

Instead, they both reached for their glasses, draining what remained of the dark russet liquid as the door before them exploded open.

CHAPTER SIXTY-FOUR

One final stop.

Drake eased up in front of Kyla's house at just after 5:00. A little over one week to the minute since Bear McGrady first called him. Since he'd first heard the name Kyla Wegman.

So much had transpired in the preceding days, it was almost impossible to fathom that it had been only a week.

So much, for so many people.

So many things that were irrevocably reversed. Would be carried by all forever moving forward.

Sitting on the front curb, both stared up at the shabby one-bedroom apartment. Saw that even under the late afternoon sun, it was dilapidated, in dire need of repair. Same for the car sitting in the drive.

"What a day," Drake whispered. Packed everything he was referring to into three simple words.

Harmon. Rosenthal. Stiles. Moritz. McGrady.

All checked off one after another. Even Telesco, if he really wanted to think about it.

For seven days, all of these people had managed to rotate in and out of their orbit. In one fell swoop, they had managed to finalize things with every last one of them. From this point forward, any interaction would be by choice, not circumstance.

"Yeah," Kyla murmured. Continued to stare at the house. Eventually snapped her attention over to Drake. Sent her blonde hair twirling behind her.

"Do you realize a week ago I was sitting in jail?" Fresh tears appeared beneath her eyes. "And now I'm sitting outside a place I could buy right now if I wanted to?"

Not once had Drake thought to put things in those terms.

Realized they weren't in the least bit wrong.

"Congratulations," Drake said. Smiled.

"No," Kyla said. Shook her head. "What I meant was, *thank you*."

Added emphasis on the last two words. A soulful pressure meant to relay just how much they meant.

"There's no way I can ever thank you for what you've done."

Drake met her gaze. Let the corners of his mouth curl up just slightly.

"You just did."

"Can I please give you half the money?" Kyla asked.

"You already gave half to Mandy."

"Half of what's left," Kyla said. Voice on the verge of pleading.

Drake paused again. Wanted her to think he was considering it. Wasn't dismissing the notion out of hand, no matter if that was exactly what he was doing.

"I can't. Even if I wanted to, my job won't allow it."

The answer sounded plausible enough, though Drake had no idea if it was true, had never bothered to even check.

That was her money. A way to start anew.

"Besides," he said, "after I talked to Harmon this morning, I put in a quick call to Dr. Westerman. She said that while moonblink can be reversible, there is no way of knowing for sure how a body will rebound.

"You might need that money to take care of yourself. I wouldn't dream of interfering with that."

It was clear Kyla had never considered that, and everything it might mean. Having to deal with potentially never driving after dark again. Potentially losing her sight again.

Drake hoped none of that ever came to pass. That her time away from Anaconda allowed her to heal, in more ways than one.

There was just no way to be certain yet. The only thing that could answer any of that was time.

"If there is anything I can ever do…" Kyla said. Let her voice trail away.

Drake nodded. Appreciated what she was trying to do. The fact that she acknowledged everything that he had done in the previous week.

Many clients weren't nearly so inclined.

"What do you think is next?" Drake asked. "As the newest millionaire in Missoula, the options are virtually unlimited."

Kyla coughed out a laugh. Raised a hand to her face and dabbed at the end of her nose.

"Just to be clear, I don't have to share any of that with my ex-husband, do I?"

This time it was Drake's turn to laugh, a short burst that echoed through the cab.

"No," he said. Full smile on display. "They might try to come after it, but that money is yours. Enjoy it."

"Good," Kyla said. Moved her hand from her nose to the back of her head. Lightly patted it. "I'm not supposed to get on an airplane for a while, until my head heels, but after that, maybe get away? Never really been outside of Montana."

"I think that's a great idea," Drake said. "If you need any suggestions, feel free to stop by the house. The Crew is pretty well traveled, can tell you some damn good stories from the road."

"Yeah, I'm sure they can," Kyla said. "And if it's alright, I might pop by from time to time, just to say hi anyway."

"You better."

The same wistful smile fell over her face as she turned back to look at the house.

Drake could only imagine what she was thinking. The possibilities for the next months, years, of her life were almost limitless.

She could travel, for sure. She could also go back to school, as she'd mentioned. Move on from Montana altogether.

Again, only time would tell.

"How you feeling?" Drake asked.

It was the third time on the day he had posed the question. Realized each time he did so that it was a direct result of Sage imprinting her propensity to hover on him.

"I'll live," Kyla said. Voice far away. Mind clearly elsewhere. "You?"

"Same," Drake said. Flicked his gaze from the house to the rearview mirror.

Saw that the bruising had gotten worse. The swelling a little more so as well, his stitches pushed to capacity on his forehead.

"Besides, I'm told chicks dig scars."

The crack brought Kyla's attention back around to him. Her gaze lingered a moment before her lips came together, pressing themselves into a line, as she averted her focus, avoiding his eye.

"True, but I think in your case you should just say *chick*. Singular."

EPILOGUE

Drake was tired.

Exhausted, even.

The events of the day had left him drained, especially considering the way most of the previous night was spent.

Whatever residual bump he had gotten from the meeting with Dan Harmon had slowly faded over the course of the day. His spirits were high. His mood was good.

But he was tired.

His mind held a very simple goal as he headed for home. To find some ibuprofen to help ease the throbbing in his head. To order an unhealthy amount of food, most of it fried. To prop his feet up and watch mindless television with his dog.

If said television happened to include Maggie Grace, all the better.

Two automobiles parked in the front driveway told him it most likely wouldn't be so simple. That while not close to what he endured the last few nights, it wouldn't be quite as low-key as he was hoping for.

Stopping along the front curb, Drake climbed out and lumbered up the driveway. Past Kade's truck. On by Sage's car, despite it supposed to have been sitting at St. Michael's for another six hours.

Passed through the front door to find every light in the place on, the smell of something wonderful in the air.

Pausing on the front foyer, Drake kicked his shoes off. Bent down and straightened them into position along the wall. Maintained the pose as the sound of toenails came toward him.

Hitting a knee, Drake patted his thigh. Beckoned Suzy Q near. Waited as she bounded up to him, a compact ball of wiggling happiness wrapped in fur.

"Hey, gorgeous," he said. Used both hands to scratch at her ribs. Buried his face into the folds of wrinkled skin behind her neck. "How's my girl? Huh? How's my girl?"

"She's not the only one here, you know!" Kade called from the living room.

Brought an instantaneous smile to Drake's face. Caused him to give Q one last scratch before rising to full height.

"No, but she's the only one that came to greet me," Drake called back. Descended the hallway and stepped out into the living room to see the rest of the Crew in their usual positions.

Ajax in his armchair. Kade in the loveseat opposite him. Sage on one end of the couch.

All three were turned to face him, the television off, no music playing in the background.

"Poor dog didn't know any better," Ajax said. "She thought it was somebody else bringing more food."

"*More* food?" Drake asked. Again noticed the smell in the air. "Is that Firetower I detect?"

"For starters," Kade said. Motioned toward the kitchen table, to the pile of foodstuffs spread across the top of it. "We've also got some wings and potato skins from Despo's."

"Chips and guac from Cinqo de Mayo," Sage added.

"And my personal touch, more than a gallon of sweet tea from the Dino," Ajax said.

Letting his jaw drop open, Drake looked from his friends to the kitchen. Aligned the menu they had amassed with what he'd been fantasizing about just a few minutes before.

Found that they had nailed it. To the letter.

"What is all this?" Drake asked. Circled around to the front of the couch and dropped himself unceremoniously down onto it beside Sage. "And how are you here right now?"

Raising her palms toward the ceiling, Sage shrugged. "Ajax called and said it was important."

"What was?" Drake asked. Looked past Sage to his roommate.

"Well," Ajax said. Became aware he had the floor. Raised his voice a bit, adding dramatic effect. "Since no self-respecting person could call what happened last Wednesday a proper celebration..."

"And now you really have something to celebrate..." Kade added.

"And just maybe we feel a little bad about your face resembling Frankenstein's..." Ajax said.

Drew smiles from Drake and Kade. A frown from Sage.

"We put together a Drake Bell celebration," Ajax finished.

"No fancy restaurant, no big expensive outing, just a whole bunch of crap in front of the TV," Kade said.

"Speaking of which, we also rented *Lockout* and *She's Out of My League*. One, because it features the illustrious Miss Grace, the other because, well, it's actually a movie the rest of us like, too," Ajax finished.

"Ha!" Drake spat. Felt the smile grow across his face. Looked at each of his friends in turn.

The Zoo Crew. The only people in the world that, if forced to celebrate, he would have any desire to do so with.

"Thank you. Seriously, all of you, for everything this past week, and even long before that."

"You're welcome," Ajax said. Snapped to his feet. Clapped his hands together before him. "And before we let this get any further down the rabbit hole to awkwardness, let's eat!"

A similar roar of approval went up from Kade as he too stood. Joined Ajax as they headed for the impromptu buffet line.

Drake could feel the bemused expression linger on his face as he watched them go. Heard them planning the best way to attack the bounty before them.

"Better get in there," Sage said. Drew his attention in her direction. "You know how those two can be when they get going. Might not be much left."

"Meh," Drake replied. Glanced over in their direction. "That's quite a spread you guys put together. Think I'll be okay."

"Yeah?" Sage asked. "And you feeling okay? Kade gave me the full rundown today on what happened last night. Sounded pretty grisly."

For a moment, Drake paused. Thought back to everything that had transpired. To what Kade must have thought bursting in.

"Oh, did he?" Drake said. Arched an eyebrow toward his friend.

"Told me he walked in to find you a bloody mess, sitting on the bathroom floor cradling Kyla in your arms."

Again, a reactive smile formed on Drake's face.

It was not quite the scene that Kade had walked in on. Might not have even been a scene that occurred at all.

For whatever reason though, that was what Sage had taken from things. Her true passive-aggressive nature in full display, stating something she knew to be at least partially false so he could correct her.

"Actually, kind of surprised she's not here now," Sage added. "Word is you two have been pretty inseparable this week."

Again, Drake paused. Thought back to the conversation he'd had with Kyla just a short time before. To the comment she had made before climbing out.

Perhaps it was the moment. The joy of what he'd accomplished. The gratitude at what his friends had put together for him. The relief that he had escaped with only a bump on the head.

Maybe it was more than that. The realization that there was a truth to what Kyla had said. Something far beyond what he had ever bothered to stop and acknowledge.

Whatever it was, Drake reached out and took Sage's hand. Slid his fingers through hers and squeezed tight.

"Maybe, but what's a week compared to three years and counting?"

———

Turn the page for a sneak peek of *The Shuffle*, A Zoo Crew Novel book 6.

SNEAK PEEK

The Shuffle, A Zoo Crew Novel Book 6

Rigid.

Unflinching.

Drake Bell stared straight ahead at the two men across from him. Both in their early-to-mid thirties, they looked to epitomize all of the stereotypes that had popped up in recent years regarding men in their profession.

Wearing sneakers and zip-up hoodies to a business meeting. Insistence on using bro speak. Turning down the provided pastries and coffees with an offer of marijuana-infused edibles.

Seated shoulder to shoulder, the two practically beamed. Kept their hands laced atop the table before them. Tried their best to pretend that nothing was amiss.

That they were nothing more than a couple of rubes. Guys running a start-up, doing their best to get a toehold in the big leagues.

Two neophytes that thought they were smarter than everybody else. That all they needed was to hire the right designer. Use their superior backgrounds to hoodwink everybody. Put on the requisite outfit to keep anybody from noticing.

Drake was having none of it.

Just sitting and staring at them, he could feel his anger rising. His right leg began to move up and down slightly.

Not out of nerves, but from agitation at the pair sitting a few feet away.

"So," the one on the right asked. A guy that had introduced himself upon first entering, but whose name Drake had immediately forgotten. Replaced it in his mind with the abbreviation DZ.

Douchebag Zuckerberg.

"Do we have an agreement?"

Beside him, his lackey attorney shifted his attention from DZ to the far side of the table. Resembling a dog begging for approval, it was all he could do to keep his head from bobbing in place.

Or his tongue from wagging out of his mouth.

Forcing himself to look away, to not give up his position, Drake shifted his focus to the right. Looked at the man that was one of his three closest friends in the world. For the last seven years, his roommate.

And for the purposes of this meeting, his client.

Meeting his gaze, Adam Jackson – or to those that really knew him, Ajax – asked, "Drake?"

The terms of the contract that the two across from him had sent over a week before were already bad enough. Not quite unconscionable, but clearly drafted by someone that thought they could squeeze a few things by.

Which made the bait-and-switch they'd tried to pull today that much worse.

Forcing aside the roiling angst within him, Drake drew in a sharp breath. Flicked his gaze back over to the pair across from him.

Made no effort to match the smiles on their faces.

"Let me answer your question with one of my one," he began. "Do you two have any idea who this is by my side?"

DZ's smile waned just slightly. Beside him, the lackey's remained at a luminescence just below megawatt, clearly not connecting what was just asked.

Or having any clue what was about to be levied.

"Of course," DZ replied. "This is Adam Jackson. The man behind

Ajax, Ltd., and one of the most sought-after video game designers in the country."

A handful of responses drifted across Drake's mind. Ranged in intensity from merely wanting to shame these two all the way to yearning to destroy them.

In every way possible.

"That's correct," Drake replied. "Now, I know you two are new to this whole thing, but let me offer some advice. The next time you're lucky enough to so much as get a meeting with someone of his caliber, you might want to take it seriously."

The smile on DZ's face faded completely. His mouth settled into a circle, his eyes the same.

A weak effort to feign misunderstanding. Perhaps even a bit of shock.

An expression that only strengthened the resolve flooding through Drake.

"And you definitely might want to consider the fact that he didn't get to where he is by being an idiot."

Extending a hand before him, Drake motioned to the pair of contracts before him. Resting the pads of all five fingers on the stack to the right, he said, "Now, take the document you sent over a couple of days ago. You seriously expect the game's *designer* to sign off any claim to licensing? Merchandising? Future projects?"

Lifting his hand, he shifted it six inches to the side. Dropped it on the second document before him.

"Or that you could walk in here today with a new payment structure that was four percent lower across the board and expect him not to notice?"

Pulling his hand back, he paused. Gave the pair of gaping men across from him the chance to respond.

Wasn't the least bit surprised when it was Ajax that jumped in instead.

"Needless to say, we won't be signing anything here today," Ajax said. Reaching to the table beside him, he took up his cellphone. Wagged it at them. "And if I might make a suggestion, you two may want to start looking for a new career path."

Taking a moment, he made a show of pressing a button. Turned the volume on his phone up loud enough for everybody to hear the familiar birdcall of a tweet being sent into the ether.

"Because as of this moment, every single competitor, contractor, designer, and influencer in the video game community was just made aware of the stunt you tried to pull here."

Scads of additional replies came to Drake's mind. One at a time, he pushed them aside.

Took a moment to sit and relish the expressions on the faces across from him.

East coast bluebloods that thought they could come to the mountains. Wave around some big smiles. Dress the part and offer edgy snacks. Walk away without the poor unsuspecting kids from Montana being any the wiser.

From one second to the next, Drake watched as their expressions shifted from confusion to shock.

Shock to anguish.

Dropping a hand to his side, Drake drew up his bag from the floor beside him. Stuffed both of the contracts inside it.

Rose and followed Ajax to the door.

Left the two men behind him gaping in silence.

———

Continue reading *The Shuffle*, A Zoo Crew Novel Book 6:
dustinstevens.com/Shwb

THANK YOU

Dear Reader,

As always, first and foremost, thank you for taking the time to read my work. Given the amount of virtual entertainment available today, in all different forms, please know how much I appreciate your support.

This novel marks my fifth return to the Zoo Crew, something I hope will continue well into the future. Many readers have commented that what they like best about the stories is the camaraderie between the characters, which is the reason I enjoy writing them so much. Originally they were designed as loose composites of the wonderful people I knew while living in Montana, but over the last couple of years, they have really become unique individuals that I always enjoy spending time with.

Per usual, if you would be so inclined, I would greatly appreciate a review letting me know your thoughts on the work. As promised, I do follow reviews, and try very hard to incorporate feedback, something I hope is reflected with each new release.

THANK YOU

In addition, as a token of my appreciation, please enjoy a free download of my novel *21 Hours*, available **HERE.**

Best,

FREE BOOK

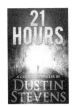

Join my newsletter list, and receive a copy of 21 Hours—my original best-seller and still one of my personal favorites—as a welcome gift!

dustinstevens.com/free-book

DUSTIN'S BOOKS

Works Written by Dustin Stevens:

Reed & Billie Novels:
The Boat Man
The Good Son
The Kid
The Partnership
Justice
The Scorekeeper
The Bear
The Driver

Hawk Tate Novels:
Cold Fire
Cover Fire
Fire and Ice
Hellfire
Home Fire
Wild Fire

Zoo Crew Novels:
The Zoo Crew
Dead Peasants
Tracer
The Glue Guy
Moonblink
The Shuffle
Smoked
(Coming 2021)

Ham Novels:
HAM
EVEN
RULES
(Coming 2020)

My Mira Saga
Spare Change
Office Visit
Fair Trade
Ships Passing
Warning Shot
Battle Cry
(Coming 2020)
Steel Trap
(Coming 2021)

Standalone Thrillers:
Four
Ohana
Liberation Day
Twelve
21 Hours
Catastrophic
Scars and Stars
Motive

DUSTIN'S BOOKS

Going Viral
The Debt
One Last Day
The Subway
The Exchange
Shoot to Wound
Peeping Thoms
The Ring
Decisions

Standalone Dramas:
Just A Game
Be My Eyes
Quarterback

Children's Books w/ Maddie Stevens:
Danny the Daydreamer...Goes to the Grammy's
Danny the Daydreamer...Visits the Old West
Danny the Daydreamer...Goes to the Moon
(Coming Soon)

Works Written by T.R. Kohler:
The Hunter

ABOUT THE AUTHOR

Dustin Stevens is the author of more than 50 novels, the vast majority having become #1 Amazon bestsellers, including the Reed & Billie and Hawk Tate series. *The Boat Man*, the first release in the best-selling Reed & Billie series, was named the 2016 Indie Award winner for E-Book fiction. The freestanding work *The Debt* was named an Independent Author Network action/adventure novel of the year for 2017 and *The Exchange* was recognized for independent E-Book fiction in 2018.

He also writes thrillers and assorted other stories under the pseudonym T.R. Kohler.

A member of the Mystery Writers of America and Thriller Writers International, he resides in Honolulu, Hawaii.

Let's Keep in Touch:
Website: dustinstevens.com
Facebook: dustinstevens.com/fcbk
Twitter: dustinstevens.com/tw
Instagram: dustinstevens.com/DSinsta
Facebook Group: dustinstevens.com/RideAlong

CPSIA information can be obtained
at www.ICGtesting.com
Printed in the USA
FSHW021952111020
74726FS

9 781536 896657